Big Charlene's

WEIGHT-LOSS SUPPER CLUB & TAXI DANCING

a twisting creek mystery by

RJ HUDDY

A PEACE CORPS WRITERS BOOK

Acknowledgments

A thousand thanks go to James Burgett, Tom Sumner, Cubby Keathley, Darcy Meijer and Kathy Houslander, all of whom tried to make me look good in spite of myself.

Cover design by James Burgett
Interior by Tom Sumner

ISBN: 978-1-935925-40-8
Library of Congress Control Number: 2013952019

A Peace Corps Writers Book.
An imprint of Peace Corps Worldwide.

First Peace Corps Writers Edition, November 2013.

Big Charlene's Weight-Loss Supper Club and Taxi Dancing.

"Revenge is sweet—and not fattening."

—*Alfred Hitchcock*

1

HOW DID I wind up in a Kentucky jail cell? I can't put all the blame on Angela Van Landingham. She had her own brand of wickedness—and I'm not talking here about frilly pink handcuffs or tantric love collars—but she's not the one who made me fat. I did that to myself. And how did being fat land me in jail? Because I didn't go to Mexico, as I'd planned. That's where I was headed when I fled from New York, only I made a little detour. If I'd stayed on course and made it to the border, everything would be different now. But I was fat, and I didn't go to Mexico. And now look where I am.

This whole thing started almost three years ago. Angela Van Laningham was both my boss and my lover. A booby-trap of an arrangement if there ever was one. In that kind of set-up, you get dumped, you also get fired. Two of the most traumatic events in contemporary American life, and Angela slammed me with both in the space of one goodbye.

Not that she cared. She took me for the ultimate sap. But little did she know. Nobody plots revenge like the ultimate sap.

A pink Dodge Neon piece of shit was the cheapest thing on the lot. Perfect.

An hour before dawn on a Monday morning I backed it up against the little loading station at the rear of our restaurant. Excuse me—*her* restaurant. I took a quick look around at the apartment complex surrounding our back lot, but saw no faces peering through curtains. So far, my luck was holding.

I got out of the car and didn't make a sound when I

closed the door. The morning breeze was soft and fresh, but that didn't matter. I needed to wear a jacket with the hood up, screw the weather. I checked on my collie, Jezebel, in the back seat. She wanted out for a romp, but I told her to lie down flat back there and remain absolutely silent. I circled to unlock the trunk of my car.

The Neon was so unfamiliar to me that I nearly had to abandon the whole enterprise simply because the trunk lock decided to stick. I had to fish around under the dash for an interior trunk release. It's funny to think that my entire future existence hinged—so to speak—on one little plastic knob that my fingers bumbled into. If it had controlled the steering wheel position or opened the gas cap or something, I don't know where I would be now. Certainly not in a jail cell in Kentucky. But I pulled the lever and heard a clunk. Through the rear view mirror I saw the trunk lid lift obligingly, and my future course was set.

I removed the empty cartons one by one. I tried to make each one look heavy by showing strain in my arms and back, as though the boxes were full of produce. Then, when once inside the restaurant I filled them with kitchen equipment and carried them back outside to the car, they needed to appear empty, as light as air. This wasn't as easy as it sounds, for while cheap aluminum cookware is lightweight, professional grade copperware has real heft.

After I eased the trunk lid closed, I glanced around one final time at the surrounding apartments. All appeared serene. A few strips of light showed between gaps in curtains, but during my brief survey I saw no prying eyes peeking through. The lit apartments probably belonged to early risers. Every place has a few people who check email at four-thirty and walk the dog at five, right?

I went back inside to wipe down fingerprints. Not to hide my own, of course. The police would expect to find my prints on every square inch of that kitchen. No, I wiped areas clean because that's what a real thief would do. Am I right? It only makes sense.

I allowed myself a quick farewell to the kitchen that had been my real home in the city for almost a decade. I tried not to make an event of it. Just looked all around, locked up, got in my car and drove away.

I left New York with neither destination nor plan. I suppose I was looking for a sign. I had but one vague strategy: hit the Holland Tunnel and follow the sun until it set in the Pacific Ocean. I had in mind a vague vision of a Mexican beach resort, mainly because I once saw a movie about an open-air restaurant there, where a barefoot chef stood directly on the sand, grilling shrimp and red snapper over charcoal in half an oil drum, while guests got up to various hijinks and fell in love. If I was about to suffer a long, lonely winter, I would suffer it with sun on my back and an ocean before me.

So, with my little car packed solid with French copper cookware, German ceramic knives, a few clothes, and Jezebel, I exited the tunnel into a still dark New Jersey. With no sun to guide me, I began to obsess about the collapse of my relationship with Angela. Face it, Bradley, I told myself. You were naïve and gullible. A born patsy waiting for the take-down. This is what happens to people who trust.

I can freely admit that now. I trusted Angela in every way. I trusted her financially and I trusted her in love. I didn't question the way she set up the company any more than I did the way she came up behind me and kissed the top of my head when she told me she and Delia had a book club meeting. Or that she needed to meet with Eric to work out something in the loan structure; or with Ryan about the new print ads. I believed her when she said marriage was the institutionalized enslavement of women, and children were the chains they used to tie you down. (Funny—this from a woman who owned velvet wrist and ankle straps in varying shades of pastel.)

I'll admit all that. If that had been the end of it, I'd never have considered retaliation. What irritated me, though, was that she assumed I was both naïve *and* stupid. They're not the same thing—as she was about to find out. I suppose once she'd labeled me a complete idiot, she had no incentive to look for gradations, or compartments; little pockets of clear sight that could function even in my half-light image of her. She didn't credit me with the ability to learn. It didn't occur to her that I might connect her book club meeting with the novel on her nightstand and its bookmark stuck for a month at page thirty-two. She didn't think I'd ever notice that, after her meeting with "Ryan," our Village Voice ads remained unchanged.

Not that I was completely innocent. There were a couple of alcohol-fueled dalliances with waitresses, but these came after Angela had turned stone cold toward me (though apparently not toward everyone). What's more, I don't think she even knew about that bewitching Jamaican named Fiona something-or-other, or the Austrian woman who tried to blow marijuana smoke up Jezebel's nose. And by the time I had a brief fling with Jezebel's vet, Angela wasn't interested enough in me to care. Looking back on it, I realize that in her mind I was already gone from her life, even if I was in her kitchen every evening and in her bed every night.

I was so thoroughly deleted from her consciousness that she couldn't imagine me taking my revenge. She wouldn't have dreamed that the week before I left New York I had slipped away alone to buy an old car. The night I left, she wasn't curious enough to ask where she could reach me. It would never occur to her that I chose to leave on a Sunday because the restaurant was closed on Mondays, and an extra day of cold trail would only work in my favor. She didn't think to change the security code or the locks to the kitchen. She didn't credit me with smarts enough to make myself an extra set of keys.

gut their fast-food franchises, and their creditors come calling. I can't say I exactly weep for them, though. Let them serve better food. Simple as that. Charlene and I didn't steal their customers. Our members walked in on their own. Waddled in, more like it. And now they're dancing and falling in love. These are the people who *Yo! Jake!* me on the street, people who now race their kids past McDonald's on their way to the park. And these are the people I can't bear to disappoint. What will they say after they learn I'm in jail? In a small town like this, will a whiff of scandal mean the end of all that?

Never mind the town—what will Charlene say? If my scandal bankrupts our beloved Big's, can she possibly continue to love me? Can I survive this with my life and love intact? Or have I seen the last joy I'll ever know?

They shut me in here at about two o'clock this morning. I tried not to go to sleep so I wouldn't wake up bewildered—as, in fact, I did—but one of those funny things about life that I suppose makes it more interesting is how if you try to fall asleep you can lie there for hours with your eyes glued to the ceiling, while if you try to stay awake, you're out like a light.

It's just another one of those oddities that happen to people like us. Like one grim Manhattan morning you're on the Upper West Side, walking through Riverside Park, mulling over menus and maybe attempting to walk off a mild case of the blues. You pause to watch a mother and her young son playing with a litter of collie puppies. One pup breaks away, runs right up to your feet, sits down sideways in its puppy fashion, and starts singing its heart out.

Or you might be driving from New York down to Mexico and not even know what state you're in, but just as it's getting dark you reach the top of a hill and look way down to the valley floor, where stands a woman weighing in at, at least, two-fifty, and claiming to have once been over three hundred. Way more woman than you'll ever need. Yet need her you surely will.

Freaky, semi-creepy shit like that. That's how I woke up in jail.

By the way, did you know that obesity in women is an obstacle to fertility? It somehow interferes with ovulation. Yet look at you, growing away in there.

Anyway, I only slept about two hours and woke up in the dark, in jail. Whether I'd slept or not, I would still be in jail, but by staying awake I could have avoided that horrible sick feeling you get when you wake up, still under the spell of a nice dream, then *wham* you remember some recent tragedy: a dog that won't be there this morning to lick your face, a lover not by your side. Bars covering the single square of window way up on the wall, too high for you to see out.

I guess you're going to want to know the whole story, and I'll be happy to tell you exactly how it unfolds, but before you start reading this, go and make yourself a cup of coffee. As things stand right now—right now as you read this—it's possible you and I know very little of each other. And of course right now as I write this I have no way of knowing your current BMI, but if you're not watching the carbs and cals, cut yourself a piece of pie to go with your coffee. Or if you do happen to have a weight problem, get only the coffee, and then settle in while I describe for you how this whole ordeal develops. I'll tell you everything I know just as soon as I know it. And, if my worst fears turn out to be justified, I'll have more than enough time to make a thorough job of it. That's why you're going to need that coffee.

Even into Pennsylvania I kept checking my rear view mirror for arrest lights. In my head I rehearsed, "Look, officer, I didn't steal nearly as much from her as she did from me. The only difference is that she arranged for her theft to be legal, while I simply loaded my trunk."

Of course it wouldn't work. And of course she would try to track me down, out of sheer pique, if nothing else. How dare I outsmart her even a wee bit?

A very wee bit, you're thinking. She must be laughing her ass off. In return for my life's savings and a decade's labor, I get a few kitchen utensils? You'd be right to think that—if you haven't checked the price of professional cookware lately. If you buy your kitchen knives at Walmart, you can't imagine what a set of diamond-sharpened German ceramics costs. And prestige copper pots? Talk about sticker shock! I was probably the only man on the road that day transporting a fish poacher worth more than the car he transported it in. You'll be pleased to know I was well up the felony scale.

Remarkably soon, however, I managed to forget all that. I stopped looking for cops on my tail. The miles meant nothing to me; the minutes meant even less. In my head I wasn't even driving a car. I was mentally clicking through a slide show of Mexican beach moments. One had me flinging a Frisbee across the sand while Jez made her balletic grab. In another, I was caramelizing pepper shrimp and sipping some sort of fruity drink. In no scene did I have a thirty pound roll of blubber around my waist. In no scene did prospective employers ask for references.

Come to think of it, avoiding reality was probably my best choice of tactics. At times like that, it's healthier to allow your mind to remain disengaged. Otherwise you will come to understand that you're almost forty years old and your entire life fits comfortably into a pink eight-year-old Dodge Neon, with room for more in the passenger seat. I guess the good news was that if I felt like it I could pick up a hitchhiker.

After a rest area near Harrisburg, everything became a blur. Pennsylvania went by like an autumn travelogue playing in my peripheral vision. The road went through dips and rises for a while, then we seemed to be surfing some mountain ranges. I vaguely recall passing a sign that said something about West Virginia, entering it, or maybe leaving it. I gradually became aware that I was hungry and my shoulders were aching, and Jezebel, with her uncanny ability to put my thoughts into living motion, released an insistent whine and nuzzled her wet nose into the side of my head. Only then did I notice that dusk was already descending on the eastern valley.

"Me too," I told her. "Hang on till the next exit."

When we crested a rolling summit I saw that streetlights were already shining in a small town below. Not far ahead there loomed giant neon signs for a motel, a gas station and a fried chicken joint. I didn't know exactly where we were. To be honest, I wasn't even sure what state we were in. But I knew it was time to call it a day.

Across from the gas pumps, Jezebel found a grassy strip to her liking. I didn't have the heart to put her straight back in the car, so I looped her leash around a signpost while I checked out the motel. I didn't exactly announce to the desk clerk that I had a dog with me, but Jez was clearly visible out his back window, if he'd bothered looking. Maybe he was a collie lover himself. Anyway, I checked in without incident, carried my stuff into the room, and fed her. I hadn't packed her food dish, so that evening Jez ate from a four hundred dollar *au gratin* oval and drank from a six hundred dollar *bain marie*.

She needed a walk. That was really my only purpose—let her get some exercise on our way to that chicken place. I could see they had a patio with some playground equipment. The evening, though cool, was pleasant enough for a quick picnic. If some kids spotted Jez, no doubt they would want to come outside to pet her. She would like that. Probably she missed Angela too.

On the way there, she spotted a flatbed truck in the parking lot, and made a grand leap. Jez loves flatbed trucks. In fact, she loves any sort of elevated platform. She leapt onto the empty bed of the truck, struck a heroic pose, and laughed. If you don't think collies can laugh, that means you've never had a collie. Jez stood there, stock still except for her breathy little laugh, with her eyes and mouth pinned back in a grin, her tail stuck straight out in one direction and her nose in the other, looking for all the world like a monument to canine virtue. She does this every time she finds a suitable pedestal. She's like some guy you meet in a bar who tells the same joke over and over and laughs before he gets to the punch line. You should see her at old-fashioned graveyards, hopping from tomb to tomb and adopting that cinematic stance. It's embarrassing.

"Get down from there," I said.

She complied readily, bouncing down to my side, but with a sidelong glance that said, "You know you love it. You're just playing the hard guy."

I bent to fasten the leash on her, and as I rose I noticed that the truck bed wasn't completely empty after all. Flexible cables toward the cab secured in place a flat cardboard box and the metal frame of a big neon sign, a sort of marquee. There were sockets for standard light bulbs all around the perimeter, and tracks for tube lighting. The neon strip was missing—maybe that was safely tucked inside the cardboard box—but with some difficulty you could decipher the message by following the embedded metal clasps that would eventually support the lights. I stepped back to get a clearer view of it, and read:

Big Charlene's Weight-Loss Supper Club and Taxi Dancing

At least that's what it looked like. My eyes retraced the

path of metal hooks. The phrase didn't make a lot of sense, and what limited meaning you could squeeze out of it seemed—let's just call it surprising.

A tug on the leash caused me to turn to my left, where a man was approaching. He had a clipboard in one hand and a canister of coffee in the other. He jammed the clipboard under his arm to free up a hand. Jez was straining to decide whether this man was to be trusted. When he put his free hand into his jacket pocket, Jez released a couple of uncertain warning yips. A true New Yorker, she braced herself for the worst, but then went into her wavering full-body-arc greeting, because the hand emerged, not with a can of pepper spray, but with a doggie treat. He tossed it to her and she deftly reared to snare it.

"You've made a friend for life," I told him. She was struggling to slip her leash and to rub her long nose across his knee.

"I always carry treats. Beats the hell out of gittin' bit."

I realized he must be some kind of delivery man, perhaps the driver of the truck with the cryptic cargo, so I said, "I was just trying to figure out what that sign says. Can you read it?"

He stared at it, tilting his head this way and that, exactly as Jez listens to unusual sounds. Finally he shrugged affably and said, "Nope." Then his face lit up. "Maybe 'iss hyur paper says." He read from his clipboard. "Big Charlene's Weight-Loss Supper Club and Taxi Dancing."

"That's what I thought. Taxi dancing is when you buy a ticket and a girl will dance with you, right?"

Again he confessed his ignorance, in an assured tone implying that the people who knew the answer to that question were the odd ones, not the ones who didn't, and added, "I'm a truck driver, myself."

The mystery drew me forward much as Jez did in her quest for a second treat. And then occurred a moment of true mystery. I can't possibly explain the timing, but it was exactly then that I began to feel the squeeze of my trousers around my waist. Even my new Dockers expanders pinched. I reached to adjust my belt and realized I wasn't wearing one. I looked down at myself, only to see another's belly there. I noticed an unexpected tension on the lower button of my shirt. I mean, I knew I'd put on a couple of pounds. But this much? Whoever it was that had been me for thirty-some active and nutritious years, that wasn't the person I had transported down here from New York. Indeed it seemed I had picked up a hitchhiker after all: myself. A dinner of extra-crispy fried chicken didn't sound so appealing anymore.

Even as I was looking at my new blob of fat cells, a cancer seemed to spread in several directions at the same time. Before my very eyes did the former Bradley Michaels, so recently secure in romance, in finance, in figure, and in moral standing, metastasize into a lonely, broke, pot-bellied thief.

This had gone far enough. I had to plant my battle flag and make a stand. A light, nutritious dinner seemed a good place to start. Maybe find a pretty girl to dance with. There once was a time when I could turn heads with my graceful dips and twirls. Could I still? I wondered what sort of dancers might be for rent down here in these mountains. Down-and-out welfare queens? Oxycontin addicts? Or more likely, in a weight-control club, big bruisers trying to earn an honest dollar while they danced off a pound or two.

It didn't really matter to me. In a couple of hours I'd be back at the motel, and by morning I'd be gone. By this time tomorrow I could be somewhere in Texas, and the next day— *Bienvenidos a Mexico!*

The trucker was in his cab. He started his engine and then looked down to wave goodbye to me. To Jezebel, really. But I managed to catch his eye. I made that cyclical motion with my hand that even today causes car windows to be lowered. He complied, and I asked, "Where are you taking it?"

He looked again at his clipboard. "110 West Liberty Road. Know whur 'at is?"

"No, but I've got a GPS."

"Me too," he said. "Take 'er easy. Bye Lassie."

Jezebel looked up at me with that gritty-eyed threat she always issues when somebody calls her Lassie. I used to tell her that until she saves a family from a burning barn, or indeed gets a Hollywood film contract, she has no right to complain, but this time I didn't say a word. By now she knows the deal.

I called to the truck driver, "Where am I, anyway?"

"Just off I-64."

"I mean, what's the name of the town?"

"Twisting Creek."

"Twisting Creek?"

"Yessir, Twisting Creek. And not fur up yon way is Big Bone Lick."

"Fur up yon way?" I repeated.

"Couple mile."

"Big Bone Lick?"

"Yessir. But 'iss hyur is Twisting Creek. And if you keep on attaway you'll hit Beaver Lick."

"Beaver . . . ? Oh, I get it. You're messing with the city slicker. That's what you're supposed to do, right?"

"I ain't shittin' ye, buddy. I wusht I wuz."

Honestly, I didn't know what he was saying, but his face was sincere, so I asked, "Twisting Creek . . . um . . . West Virginia?"

"Damn," he said. 'At's a good-ern. Maybe you in West Virginia, ol' son, but 'at dog a'yorn's in Kentucky." He revved his engine but I could still hear him laughing as he pulled onto the entrance ramp.

I fished out my GPS. West Liberty Road turned out to be less than four minutes away, so back into the car we went.

The GPS lady probably said "Turn right next exit" but what I heard was "Gun this mother!" I whizzed by our flatbed friend at such speed that when I put my arm out the window to wave goodbye, the wind nearly dislocated my shoulder.

An old song about a taxi dancer came to mind, so I belted it out, Ethel Merman style: *"Ten cents a dance, it's a queer romance, I'm here till closing time, dance and be merry, it's only a dime."*

I told Jezebel, "This is our new beginning, babe! We're going to rescue our lives from the scrap yard! I just know we are! I can feel it in my bones! You know how I know?"

She was paying no attention to me whatsoever. She was busy scrutinizing every person we passed. She liked these southern people. Good things happened down here.

I let her ignore me. What did I care? I was ten feet high and rising. I said, "There I was on my knees, crawling around in life's filthy gutter! But I raised my face to the heavens and called out ... " Here I put on my worst southern accent. "I said, Sweet Lard Jay-zus! Gimme a sign! An' lo! A sign I did behold!"

Disassembled and enigmatic though it was, there's no denying it was a sign. A marquee, even. Way bigger than a stone tablet. And more colorful, once it's hooked up.

Four minutes later, we crested the summit of one of the hillocks that underlie the western outskirts of Twisting Creek, and there, down in the valley floor, I saw something that caused me to pull the car to the curb, kill the engine, and switch off the headlights.

Without headlights it was even more striking. The autumn evening had achieved that shade of dusk that in the mountains is less like the approach of night than a layer of coal dust settling across the landscape, thickening to a deep lignite brown, bringing with it the smell of fallen leaves, humid and peaty, a fine whisky smell. At the foot of the hill I saw an unlit parking lot, empty now but for one pick-up truck. Beside the parking lot was a long, low building with gunmetal gray aluminum siding and a flat red roof. It looked more like a warehouse than a nightclub. A wide-striped awning lit by a bare bulb marked the main entrance.

Jezebel didn't know why we'd stopped. She put her nose to the door handle, but I said, "No. Look."

Under the single light of that awning, someone—identifiable even at that distance as a magnificently obese woman—was dumping debris from a container of some kind into a barrel. She tapped the bottom of the container a couple of times, set it down beside her, pushed the sleeves of her sweatshirt up her forearms, rested her hands on her hips, and turned to look up the hill, straight at us.

She didn't move from that position when our headlights came on. We started moving in her direction. I could feel the pull of her. She hadn't budged from that position even after we'd crossed over into her parking lot and I got a leash on Jez and then we walked toward her in the lit area under the awning. Her first movement was to put out a hand.

I shook it, and she said, "I'm Big Charlene. Big Charlene Farley. As you can verify right here." She jutted an enormous breast in my direction. I wasted a couple of seconds trying not to stare, then realized I was supposed to stare, at least long enough to read a name badge pinned there. Underneath *Big Charlene Farley* it said *Mind Reader*.

Her bright round face gave off a glow, in burnished, Cherokee-like tones. Her brown eyes were slightly pinched, and she had a bounty of dark hair that feathered down over her shoulders.

"Pleased to meet you. I'm . . . " I hesitated. It occurred to me that I might not want to use my real name for a while. "I'm Jason." My middle name is Jason. Hopefully you already knew that.

"I know what you're thinking, Jake," she said, instantly giving me a nickname that everybody in Twisting Creek uses to this day.

"Because you can read my mind?"

"That's it exactly. Allow me a two-minute conversation and I'll prove it to you."

"Okay . . . "

"Like for instance right now you're thinking, 'I've run across a big fat hillbilly woman who says she can read minds, but she's full of shit.' Am I right?"

I shuffled nervously and answered, "I wouldn't say that."

"Of course you wouldn't say it. That's my job. And who's this you're keeping on such a tight leash?"

Jez was trying to run her nose up Big Charlene's thigh. "That's Jezebel."

Big Charlene ran a meaty hand across Jez's back. "And what brings you two down here all the way from New York?"

My first thought was to run straight for the car and head for the nearest Mexican border crossing, but I assured myself it was my accent or my license plate that gave me away. "I was on my way to eat some fried chicken, but when I saw your sign I changed my mind."

"My sign?" She walked to the edge of the entrance area to where she could see metal scaffolding erected above the awning. "I don't have a sign yet. I won't even be open for business for another couple months. Are you one too?"

"One what?"

"A seer. A clairvoyant. Somebody who can decipher signs nobody else can even see."

"No, no. Nothing like that. I'm just a regular guy with a weight problem."

She laughed. "Is that what New Yorkers call a weight problem? Look at me, Jake. I've lost fifty-five pounds, and counting."

I did her the courtesy of a once-over. "That's amazing."

"As one seer to another, let me read your thoughts. You're thinking , 'If this big fat woman is fifty-five pounds lighter than she once was, she must have been a real whale.' Now, am I right?"

"Not at all!" I protested. In fact I was thinking *blimp*.

She laughed and slapped me on the shoulder, making her neck fat jiggle. "You're a terrible liar, Jake, you know that?" She seemed willing to let it go at that, but then her face went more serious and she added, "Whale. Battleship. Blimp. Whatever."

Just then Jezebel heard something, whirled around, and fixed her stare on the summit of the hill. Charlene asked, "What's up with her?"

I looked behind me and saw the flatbed truck starting down the hill.

Jez's eyes confirmed the data from her ears. That feathered collie tail started whipping against my leg. I said, "Oh, she's had a premonition that the driver of that truck will pull into your parking lot and give her a treat."

Big Charlene's mouth dropped open and got wider and wider as the truck slowed, crossed the bump into the parking lot, and the driver called out, "Hey there, Lassie." I unclipped the leash just when a dog biscuit came sailing from the truck window. Jezebel jumped to snag it, and sauntered back toward us, holding the treat between her teeth, gently laughing.

"Shoot far!" Charlene said. "Can you believe that? That makes all three of us!"

2

WHY DID I, of all people, look for comfort in fast food? When your life is junk, why not fill your body with junk? I suppose that was my rationale. This was four or five years ago. I continued to go to work every day and prepare what our tongue-twisting slogan called *Delicious Nutritious Dishes*, but I stopped eating them. Over my whole life, my spiritual leanings had extended only to what I might call the purity of healthy habits: keeping fit with regular exercise, choosing organic food where possible, a daily yoga session, weekly tennis with Angie. I may have my emotional cycles, but I have an engrained reverence for nature, which I consider myself to be part of. It's as close as I come to a religious dogma: your body is a temple.

For more than thirty years, this was my defining principle. It's why I became a certified nutritionist in the state of New York. It's why I became a chef. In my religion, being a chef is like being in the priesthood. Yet as I moved into my mid-thirties, I turned away from plates of my own salmon capellini with bergamot-dill yogurt sauce (234 calories), only to scarf down a bag of sliders at White Castle (1430 calories) or a large chili cheese fries in the East Village (910 calories) topped off with a double pistachio gelato (500 calories) on the way home. I would walk two blocks for a McDonald's deluxe breakfast (1,220 calories) and feel self-righteous about walking.

I unconsciously rejected my own beliefs. I became an apostate to my own cult. It didn't make any sense then and I certainly can't explain it now. Maybe I saw the future coming and wanted to escape it. Or maybe I just had a bad case of the blues. But I can tell you this: those blues and those extra thirty pounds are gone now. Long gone. As gone as Angela Van Landingham.

Will Charlene think I'm capable of murder? She says I'm crazy enough to make life interesting, but surely she knows I'm not insane enough to murder a kinked-up ex-girlfriend. Then again, Charlene doesn't know about my burglary, and I'm sure not going to tell her now. I mean, that was three years ago. I was certain I'd made a clean job of it. To be honest, until now, I'd almost forgotten about it. And anyway, how can I be implicated in the disappearance of an Angela Van Landingham who can't possibly be *my* Angela Van Landingham? My Angie would be the last person in the world to rent a lakeside cabin in backwoods Kentucky. Yet look what happened last night, and where I woke up this morning.

Even at your age you may know this feeling. You wake up in a dark room and don't know where you are or how you got there. You emerge from deep inside some silly dream and for a short time afterwards you can't make sense of anything. It's unclear where the dream gives way to reality. All you can think is: *Where am I?* And when finally it all falls into place, the reality is so chilling you wish you could reverse the process and return to your dream.

Now comes a more threatening question: *Why am I here?*

I was all twisted up in my bedclothes. The air pushed hard against my lungs, and when I exhaled, the sheet tightened around me like a boa constrictor. I struggled to sit up, and saw a small square of dawn outlining a window high up the facing wall, higher than possible, high where no window could be. Yet there it was, a patch of illumination that did not relieve the darkness.

I managed to extricate a hand. I reached down to where

normally I would sink my fingers into Jezebel's thick collie mane, but instead my fingertips met a pock-marked stone floor. Next I felt behind me for Charlene, but my hand slammed into a wall. A wall where no wall could be. That's when I knew, beyond any doubt. I'm in a locked room. I'm a prisoner. I've been caught.

Delicious irony for the real Angie, who sometimes handcuffed herself if I was slow out of the gate.

Why did they lock me in here? Somehow they've connected me with this disappearing woman who apparently signed herself in as Angela Van Landingham. They believe a rigorous investigation will lay the case wide open. They imply I'm a flight risk.

But weapons? Did they really need to cock their side arms and hide behind trees? I take that personally. My running was over long before the deputies turned up.

Do they know I robbed Angie's restaurant in New York? I don't know the answer to this one either, but I sure would like to. In a way, this is the burning question. It vexes me more than the question of the missing tourist. It would make for an interesting discussion in some law school setting: should a prisoner be more worried about a potential murder in Kentucky that he knew he didn't commit, (maximum sentence: death) or a third degree grand larceny in New York that he knew he did? (maximum sentence: seven years) Even worst case in New York I'd be free by age forty-four, while in Kentucky I could turn forty-four in a casket. That makes it a no-brainer, right?

No, not with me. I'm aching to know what they know about New York. For three years I've quietly congratulated myself on my one go as a cat burglar. I planned my heist thoroughly, pulled it off deftly, fled New York clean, and landed on my feet here in these graceful, concealing mountains. NYPD has no clue.

Or have they? That's the one question I want an answer to.

I suppose every criminal is delirious to find out what was the one little mistake that destroyed his perfect crime. However, I can hardly be expected to call out through the bars of my cell, "Hey, Sheriff! Put my mind at ease here. You guys don't know about that New York gig, do you?"

And if they do know about the robbery—a revenge robbery at that—surely they'll see my hand in Angela's disappearance. Or—good god—in her murder.

That leaves me with a dilemma. No, it's worse than a dilemma. In a dilemma you have a choice between two bad outcomes. I have only one outcome, and it's brutal. Sweat everything. Sweat whatever they have on me and the missing tourist; sweat the seven years at Rikers Island. Sweat something will happen to Charlene. Or to you. Or to both of you.

Even that doesn't tell the whole story. Whether I get out clean or not, this little episode right now might be enough to destroy me. What will this do to my local reputation? I'd found a home here. This time my business-partner-slash-lover is not some gold-digging, man-eating, spanko swindler, but my faithful and genuine sweetheart. Charlene believes in me. She says I have done more to help people lose weight and regain their vigor than any chef in the world. She believes I am the heart and soul of our supper club. (I'm not—she is.) People around here respect me. Simply by walking down the street I often hear someone call out, *Jake!* and I'll turn to see a wide smile, a hand waving, a pat on the stomach. A thumbs up. A pointing finger. *Yo! Jake! You the man!*

I don't mean to say I'm beloved by one and all. A few people who make fat profits off fat customers wish Big's would go away. Merchants of fast food, junk food, processed food, empty calories—they don't *Yo! Jake!* me on the street. Not that I blame them, really. They're invested to their necks in an industry that destroys their customers' health, then along comes Big's to reverse that damage. We rescue their customers,

3

YESTERDAY BEGAN AS one of those days when even your wildest dreams seem to come true. A day when, in near disbelief, you celebrate to the point of exhaustion, then float on a layer of exhilaration into a serene and perfect tomorrow. The celebration involved Charlene on a king-sized bed, followed by my own more solitary contentment, with Jezebel being silly in the kitchen, and later, out on our front porch, with me mulling over topics of sweet summer innocence—fresh vegetables, baseball, the wind in the poplar tree. For a while it seemed these offerings of a quiet southern night would conclude my unforgettable day.

That last part proved to be true—I'm not likely to forget it.

It all started in the afternoon when Charlene's gynecologist confirmed that we are about to become parents, and that you, our darling son or daughter—we still don't know which—will join us in the spring. We celebrated all evening, and finished late last night with a bang, so to speak. A real mattress marathon. At that point, some people need a cigarette. Charlene needs sleep. I need a yogurt smoothie. So I pulled on pajama bottoms and a t-shirt and went downstairs. I was sizzling with happiness. I had no idea what was about to happen on our front yard.

Jezebel followed me into the kitchen. When she saw the blender come out of the cupboard, she dropped into a crouch and froze there. With her eyes and mouth pinned back, she emitted a thin whine pitched so high I could barely hear it. I put the blender on the counter and walked over to the fridge for a tub of yogurt, some blueberries, a bottle of pomegranate juice, and half a banana. I put all that on the counter beside the blender. Jezebel tightened her performance crouch.

I measured everything out, along with a dash of vanilla extract, and—my secret touch—a pinch of cardamom. On Big's menu we list this as Blueberry Yogurt Fruit Shake. (130 calories) We also offer strawberry, cherry, peach-watermelon—whatever is in season.

Jez still crouched there; had not budged one millimeter. A light breeze caused me to look up through an open kitchen window out into the dark night and across the waving hedges toward the bedroom lights of our neighbors up the street. I wondered for a moment why they were still awake at midnight on a Tuesday. I noticed that as the breeze receded, it left behind the sound of insects and the scent of tuberoses. I saw a police car cruising silently down Dogwood. I couldn't hear any sound at all over the din of crickets and locusts, and somewhere in there the taut wire of Jezebel's warm-up whine.

It seemed a shame to disturb the night, but we were about to make one hell of a commotion. I thought of Charlene asleep upstairs, but she was out cold. After a good round of cardio romance, as she calls it, she's fast asleep, about as affectionate as a speed bump in the middle of the bed.

I put my finger on the blender switch and re-established eye contact with the muscled spring coil that right now stood quivering like some shimmering supernatural avatar of my idiot dog. She lowered her muzzle one final notch and when I pulled the trigger she threw back her head and emitted a howl so pained and forlorn that you'd swear her poor heart was about to break. When I paused the blender, she stopped to wait for my cue, and when I started it again she resumed the discordant aria of her miserable life.

I poured my drink into a glass and looked down at her.

Now she held her head high, all dignity and pride. You could see she wasn't going to break pose until I did, so I knelt to congratulate her. She went into her excited body wave, from nose to tip of tail, and pushed into my arms. I rubbed my hand along the tapered, velvety, bone-hard bridge of her nose, up and over the little knot that crowns her head. She looked straight at me and laughed. She was saying, *I was incredible, wasn't I?*

"Sure," I said. "You're a superstar."

I didn't hand her a treat right then. She wouldn't have approved. This was above commerce. She had invented and perfected Blender Opera. This was her art.

You probably know why I'm going on and on about Jezebel. You understand that she was with me every day of her life, from when she was small enough to fit inside my coat pocket, and now I must conjure her from nothing, from stale prison air.

She followed me onto our front porch. It was a sticky August night, but I didn't mind the waft of softness across my face. I could smell our tomato vines all the way out there. The little breeze that had drawn night scents into the kitchen was now strong enough to flip the leaves of our tulip poplar, and to fill the air with a rustling sound.

Sheriff Victor Caraher drove down Dogwood in his cruiser. Nothing odd there. He lives about two blocks away, in a fine old Edwardian made affordable after a young woman was strangled to death in it.

Wasn't it a little late for him to be driving home? I can see that now, but at the time it was hard to imagine a more serene and perfect midnight. Jez stretched out on her side on the front door welcome mat and went to sleep. She always likes to sleep with her back propped against something, especially the wooden step that leads into the house, which means people are forevermore stepping across her to get in or out. Her hind legs twitched as she dreamed about whatever dogs dream about.

I keep a small radio tucked up over the porch frame. I've enjoyed baseball on the radio ever since my childhood on Long Island, when Phil Rizutto and Bill White filled my head with images of Dave Winfield, Ron Guidry, Don Mattingly and that group. Here in eastern Kentucky we get the Cincinnati Reds broadcasts. Older people like to remind me that the Big Red Machine swept my Yankees in the 1976 World Series, but to someone my age that's ancient history, and anyway, once I started to feel at home in Kentucky, I forgave them.

Normally midnight would be too late for a game, but they were playing the Giants on the West Coast, so the three-hour difference meant I picked up the game in the sixth inning, just in time to hear Phillips double in Votto off Cain to make it 3–2 Reds.

Half my mind was on that. Half was planning tomorrow's Special. It's easy to plan a menu in August. Local farmers markets are overflowing with fresh produce, including the white half-runner snap beans so beloved in this society. I'll cook them with onions, a few slices of bacon, olive oil, and— my own touch—a lemon-chipotle drizzle. So there was one of my sides. (60 calories, 6g carbs)

Mackerel has more omega-3 than even salmon, and it's at its best this time of year. Its cheapest, too, but my job is to count the calories and let Charlene count the pennies. I was thinking *maquereau au vin blanc au four* (140 calories, 1g carbs). You might be interested to know that my signature ingredient here is a tiny bit of the powerfully aromatic sharena sol, which you can buy online, often under the name of <u>chubritsa</u>, or summer savory mix. Or you can grow your own savory and then grind in the two essentials, salt and sweet paprika. You can also add thyme, marjoram, fenugreek leaf—whatever. Be creative.

I might bring a melon, tomato, and onion salad in at about 150 calories, if I go easy on the olive oil and feta. (12g carbs)

For dessert, a no-brainer. My peach-yogurt sherbet with nutmeg is already a summer icon with our dieters. (100 calories, 10g carbs)

So there was my Special, a healthy and mouth-watering combo, all for 450 calories, which left a surplus of 150 calories for appetizers or drinks. For a starter, maybe curried edamame (85 calories, 3g carbs) and finish off with an espresso and a square of our own homemade dark chocolate black walnut bark. (50 calories, 1g carbs)

There are several absolute and inviolable rules at Big's, but the most sacred is the six hundred calorie limit. Our accounting system calculates your calorie total right beside your tab. This is but one example of Charlene's genius. You can come in flashing thousand-dollar bills and you won't get so much as a kernel of popcorn after you hit your six hundred.

Sitting there on the porch, I made a shopping list in my head, but didn't bother writing it down. I would do all that in the morning. *This* morning. It's hard to believe that only eight hours ago I assumed that at this minute I'd be at the farmers market on Landon Pike, sniffing tomatoes and talking with people about how much weight they'd lost, or still had to lose. Hearing them say how Charlene and I had changed their lives, even saved their lives. Or the life of a loved one.

My god! Imagine how it feels for an ex-fat woman and her New York City boyfriend chef to hear, day after day after day, that we've changed somebody's life. Yet look where I am now. Now they think I've changed a woman from alive to dead.

You see what I'm doing now, don't you, with all this talk of baseball and fish and white half-runner beans? Believe me, I see it too. I mean, of course I want you to know what our life was like, and what Big's was like, before you were born, and before this scandal destroys everything, but mainly I'm delaying reliving last night. Not to mention how terrified I am of what's going to happen to me, and to all of us, including you. I feel it coming on—that horrible, wasting sensation of my own private gravity field increasing in strength until it's all I can do to open my eyelids, or to breathe. But starting right now, with your encouragement, I'll do my best to gather my strength and get on with describing events exactly as they unfold, no matter how bleak they may be.

I don't know how long I sat in the swing. I heard the Giants pull back ahead in the seventh. I didn't see the police officer, with his gun drawn, take cover behind the cherry tree. I didn't see another one move in behind the jasmine trellis at the foot of the drive.

I did see—could hardly miss—Jezebel scrambling to her feet, all scraping toenails and bumping hocks, as she sought footing on the painted porch floor. She slammed her head through the doggie door and was inside the house in an instant. I had no idea what the hell she was up to.

Before her gate even stopped swinging she bolted back out through it, barking and growling in a panicked clatter I'd never before heard from her. She bared her teeth and went straight for that trellis and cut around behind it in a fluid arc as subtle and trim as a skier rounding a slalom pole. Her lip was curled and I heard her jaws snapping together, then from around the other side of the jasmine I saw a policeman kick up his heels and sprint across the lawn toward the poplar, where now his partner stepped out into the open with his pistol trained on Jezebel.

I still didn't understand, but I screamed and jumped off the porch and over its azalea border into the yard toward the more threatening policeman. There was a loud clatter of shattering glass, and then I heard a gun go off. I dove for Jez, missed her, but saw she hadn't been hit. She slowed, but continued to move in on the two officers, who kept their guns pointed directly at her. Their faces, though, turned toward the sound of broken glass sliding off the porch roof, and their attention shifted to an upstairs window.

I looked up there too and saw jagged edges around a smashed out window, with Charlene's double-barreled shotgun sticking through it.

Sheriff Caraher's big black-and-gold cruiser came roaring up the drive. He jumped out and said, "Whoa, here!" He was unarmed.

Charlene said, "Tell your boys to holster their weapons, Victor. Right now. If they shoot that dog I swear to God I'll drop both of them where they stand."

I said, "Jezebel, come here!" and she did.

Victor said, "Everybody calm down. We're all friends here." His men put away their guns.

I saw Charlene's shotgun barrels withdraw from sight, and she called out. "Friends don't pull shit like this."

Victor shook his head sadly and squatted. "Chum 'ere, girl." Jez wasn't about to go to him, and I wasn't about to let her, so Victor stood, crossed the lawn toward us, squatted right in front of her, and started scratching her head. "You sure do got guts, girl," he said to Jezebel, or maybe to Charlene. "But I got no choice. I have to take him in. A guest out at Lake Roosevelt is missing."

From her perch upstairs, Charlene called down, "What's that got to do with us?"

We all stood up. Jezebel, resigned to some awful fate she couldn't possibly understand, walked slowly up the porch steps, lowered her head against the screen, and pushed her way into the house.

Sheriff Caraher, his head held nearly as low as Jezebel's, said, "Maybe a lot more than you think."

WHEN I SAY I don't know why I'm in jail, I mean I know nothing about the disappearance of the woman they think I made disappear. I'm not saying I don't know her. I just don't know what happened to her. As I mentioned, her name is Angela Van Landingham, and I've had no contact with her for almost three years. They say last week she rented one of those tourist cabins out on Lake Roosevelt, and, even though her car is still there, her bill is unpaid and she herself hasn't been seen for the last few days, so an attendant called the sheriff and they connected her to me.

This was all news to me. Angela Van Landingham is a true blue New Yorker, owner of a successful restaurant (made successful by the acclaimed chef yours truly, thank you very much) and a reasonably wealthy woman. I never knew her to take a full week's vacation, but even if she did it wouldn't be to a lonely lakeside cabin among a bunch of hillbillies. Nothing could be more ludicrous. Obviously it's someone who has stolen her identity.

Whoever she is, I don't know how she might have traced me here. I can't imagine the real Angela Van Landingham following me, even if she knows where I am.

Okay, that last part may not be totally true. What I mean is she certainly wouldn't follow me to be with me, not like she used to be with me. If she bothered to track me down all the way from New York, it would probably be in connection with that little theft at her restaurant, precisely on the day, two years and ten months ago, when I left town.

But if that was it, why didn't she simply send a detective? Why the dramatic midnight capture by local police on my own front porch while I was enjoying a blueberry smoothie and a Reds game on the radio?

All of that is a mystery to me.

I suppose someone will come along later to question me. If I explain all this to them, will they release me? My god, they'd better. If I can't get out of here, who will unravel it? Do they think I can sit inside this prison cell and rescue myself?

I seem to be the only prisoner here. I don't know that for a fact, but I know that this place has been silent all morning, except when the guard brought my breakfast. I could hear the echo of his footsteps in the stairwell for what seemed like whole minutes, moving closer like an old steam train.

When he finally reached my cell he was out of breath, and a good twenty-five to thirty pounds overweight. He didn't seem to notice my quick glance at his waistline—an ever-present occupational hazard, I'm afraid. He paused at the door. The pretense was a search of his key ring, but I suspect the real reason was to let his oxygen intake catch up with his expenditure. Once that balance was struck, he was friendly enough.

"Good morning," he said, and I actually heard myself saying good morning back to him. I wonder if we weren't both thinking, *What a goddamn stupid thing to say* . . . but I don't know. I guess we've all got to get through the day.

While eating from my little metal table I noticed a stack of books there, including *A Day in the Life of Ivan Denisovich.* It was the only one I was familiar with, about a Russian in the frozen gulag, an innocent man. I thought it was kind of weird, to have a prison book here waiting for me, like a Gideon's in some Bible Belt motel. Then I started looking at the others. There was something called *Consolation of Philosophy* by

Boethius, and *Soul on Ice*, whatever that might mean. There was a copy of *Pilgrim's Progress*, which I think I was supposed to read in high school but never did. There was *Letters and Papers from Prison* by somebody called Dietrich Bonhoeffer.

Then I realized: they're *all* prison books. Were all of them about injustice done to innocents? Was this the personal library of the previous tenant of my cell? Did he request these titles because he, too, was an innocent man? Where does that put me? I'm innocent. I am! At least I'm innocent of what they hauled me in here for. Will my story—the story you're reading right now—end up as the next book on this stack?

That's what gave me the idea of writing this prison diary for you. I started thinking that I can kiss goodbye to the next ten or twenty years of your life. Or maybe even more than that. What if I'm gone from your life forever? What if people never so much as mention my name around you?

You see where my mind is running? That's why I'm writing this. I don't want us to be complete strangers.

I have to say, though, given how bleak my breakfast musings were, that the breakfast itself wasn't half bad. Along with a whole pot of dark-roast coffee came a bowl of granola with a banana and some local strawberries already sliced in it, whole milk in a thermos, packets of real sugar or Equal, my choice. Also tomato juice—a sadly neglected morning treat if you're not worried about your sodium intake—and a fresh peach sliced in quarters. Not bad for prison food.

I stood up and stretched, and felt better right away. I don't know if the turning point was deciding to write this for you, or the breakfast, but my change of spirit turned my thoughts to that window up there. Could I get a handhold on the sill, and then grab the bars with enough grip to pull myself up for a peek outside? The sight of a green tree or at least a sliver of blue sky might be heartening.

I jumped as high as I could, but barely got my fingertips on the sill. They came away smudged with a gritty film that must have been accumulating there for years. I needed something to stand on. My only table was bolted to the floor, but the chair was sturdy, so I positioned it beneath the window. By standing in the seat of the chair I could get a secure grip on the window bars, with which leverage I pulled myself up enough to get a foot on the top of the chair back.

I tested it. It seemed strong enough, so I stood to my full height. Through a window pane nearly opaque with a film of black grime, I caught sight of something that caused my knees to buckle and the chair nearly to tip backward. There, way down at street level, stood my sturdy Charlene, holding up a big hand-printed sign that said JAKE THE WHOLE TOWN KNOWS YOU'RE INNOCENT with three exclamation points. Beside her sat Jezebel, her long nose pointed high and sweeping back and forth as she surveyed the upper floor for some sign of my presence.

I knocked on the glass as loud as I could. In fact I tried to break the damn thing, but it turned out not to be glass at all, rather some unbreakable acrylic. I think Charlene spotted my hand, because she raised her sign above her head, lifted up onto her tiptoes like a ballerina, and started shouting. I couldn't hear her voice, but I saw her mouth moving. She pointed in my direction and Jez stood high up on her hind legs, and then, dancing after her fashion in an ungainly circle, began to sing.

I still couldn't hear, and soon couldn't see much either, because tears blurred my view of my beautiful Jezebel, pawing the air, and my beautiful, reborn Charlene, bouncing high on her toes. You were there too, come to think of it. My perfect little family, reaching up as high as possible to diminish the distance between us.

5

NOT LONG AFTER breakfast I heard the hollow scuffing of shoes ascending that deep stairwell. I thought it would be the same guard as before, come to clear away my breakfast tray, but it turned out to be Sheriff Caraher himself. This shouldn't have surprised me. Sheriff Caraher—Charlene and I have always called him Victor—is almost a family friend. Colleague, even, if you can stretch that word to include the work we do for law enforcement around here. Big's has already saved the jobs of four of his people who at first couldn't meet the new physical agility requirements. In a town our size, four policemen is a lot.

We know Victor as a truly nice man, popular with voters even though he's somewhat introspective and low key. Or maybe because of it. He's also said to be the youngest black man ever elected sheriff in the state of Kentucky. He became interim sheriff when old Allard Greer retired, and then voters put him in office on his own. He's up for reelection in less than three months, but this had nothing to do with last night. I refuse even to consider it.

Victor and I have another, more private, bond. In the great universe of male friendship, it can't be all that rare, but for me it's a first. We've both enjoyed a brief fling with the same woman, Yolanda Shanley. Not at the same time, I should add. His ended before I ever heard of Twisting Creek. For Victor, I think she was the halftime show between his two marriages to Shelley. "Half-time show" fits her just right, because she's got those long majorette legs just made for short skirts, nylon stockings, and white boots. (Yes, they still have majorettes around here. I wonder if you'll even know what they are.)

With me, however, she was the pre-game warm-up. I met her almost as soon as I met Charlene. Yolanda works for, and owns part of, our local newspaper, the Guardian. I see her name on a story there almost every day. Still see her in person, sometimes. She's written up Big's on more than one occasion.

Right there you see my problem, almost from Day One in this town. Did I want a reporter interested enough in me to start tracing my back-story?

So, goodbye Yolanda. But as I say, it gives Victor and me an unusual shared experience. Not that we ever talk about it. Never. It's a guy-bond.

So I felt a sense of confidence swell inside me when those footsteps got closer and Victor came into view. He let himself inside, said a quiet good morning, duly took the breakfast tray from the table and slid it under the cell door into the corridor. I joked that with a skill set like that he could bus tables professionally. He smiled his half-smile, which is about the only smile he ever uses. I could read nothing into it.

I asked him what I was to be charged with—I was scared shitless of course that he knew about that trunk load of loot I'd brought in from New York, and which for almost three years has been clearly visible through Big's open kitchen—but he said I wasn't being arrested, only "detained," and even that just long enough for them to determine the nature and "probable cause" of the crime. Until then I was to be "held for questioning."

Here he half-smiled again and added, "This whole thing might be nothing more serious than a tourist running out on her rent. Or," he added, with no alteration to his smile, "it could run the gamut all the way up to murder in the first degree."

At that point I realized I knew nothing about legal

terminology or procedure—nothing except that I should seek legal counsel right from the start. I asked him if I needed a lawyer. His answer gave me my first really good jolt of hope since I'd been taken in.

"Don't you worry," he said. "I've already heard from Charlene. She'll be here by lunchtime, with Leo Akers."

Charlene! The woman is a force of nature. I bet she didn't even bother phoning old Leo; just drove to his house, marched straight into his bedroom, and jerked the covers off him.

Leo Akers is a legend around the state of Kentucky, and he totally looks the part. Well into his seventies, he still sports a full shock of white hair on his huge head. They say he played fullback for Bear Bryant on a UK football team that won a Cotton Bowl back in the fifties. He carries his shoulders in a slight stoop, but walks with such a determination in his step that you get the feeling he could straighten himself and punch your lights out if he wanted. Part of his charisma, I believe, is that his relaxed, Old South courtesy assures you that his strength is purely benevolent, and, should you require it, at your service.

And require it I surely do. Luckily, as with Victor, I know him personally. He and his wife Ruby come into Big's at least twice a week. Ruby is the best seventy-year-old line dancer we have, while Leo and a Japanese taxi dancer named Fumiko have taught the whole club to jitterbug. Leo keeps saying he's retired from full-time lawyering, just taking on the odd case to keep his mind fresh, but the cases he takes are often in the headlines, and he's always the heavy favorite. A prosecutor once told me that if Leo Akers had defended Judas Iscariot, we'd all still be worshipping Jupiter. With Charlene and Leo on the way, I might be out of here in time to fillet mackerel for the Special.

Victor looked around my cell as though he'd never seen it before. "I'm sorry about this place, Jake. We almost never use it. It's basically obsolete. You must feel like you're in isolation."

"It seems too quiet for a prison."

"A simple holding cell. They're doing some work on County, and prisoners are already stacked up in the available cells. I didn't want to stick you in there." He slapped my mattress, sat down on it, and bounced gingerly. "But this might not be much better."

Now my spirits soared. Not arrested, only detained; given special accommodation; Leo Akers here by noon. They *must* not know about New York. Of course they don't know! I covered my tracks there like a pro, and even if I was once a suspect, all that's long been obscured by bureaucratic shuffling. That's an ice cold case. I can practically walk out of here whenever I want.

Victor scooted back casually on my cot to rest his back against the wall. "All I really need to ask you at this stage— you don't even need Leo here for this—is whether you have the home contact details of the missing woman, Angela Van Landingham."

"I can tell you where *one* Angela Van Landingham lived when I last heard from her." I didn't say, When she kicked me out of her apartment, and, for good measure, fired me. "But I doubt she's the one you're searching for."

He did no more than purse his lips, but I knew what he was thinking. How many Angela Van Landinghams can there be? Good question, maybe, but technically speaking neither of us had any idea. For all we knew there might be hundreds in Holland alone.

I said, "It can't be her. It's not possible. The Angela Van Landingham I know would vacation in Paris or somewhere, if at all."

"But you do know one Angela Van Landingham. Am I right?"

A heat rose to my face. It felt like it does when I take bread from the oven. Had he led me into an admission? Would Leo Akers have allowed me to walk blindly into that one?

"Well, yeah, I know *one*."

"That'll do," he said, then thought to add, "for a start."

I gave him her home address, her land line, her cell, her email. Then I gave him the restaurant's address and phone number, and its website. I knew them all by heart. "I don't know if any of that's current. I haven't had contact with her since I left New York."

He wrote it all down carefully on a pad he carried in his shirt pocket. "Okay then, Jake. That's all from me." He stood up to leave.

Before he left there was one thing I had to know. Even if it was foolish. Even if Leo Akers would have silenced me. I needed to get an answer to this question before Leo arrived. This one had to come out uncoded, man to man.

"Victor, will you tell me something before you go?"

"I will if I can."

"What was it in that cabin that led you to me?"

He stopped dead in his tracks and looked out into the empty corridor, as though looking for an excuse to bolt. But the place was empty. It was silent. It seemed the whole town was waiting to hear his answer.

"There was a photograph of you in the room."

I breathed a sigh of relief. "Oh, is that all? My photos are all over the place. You don't know what a rising star I was. I was in cooking magazines, brochures, on websites. New York Magazine once did a story on me."

"This was a photo of you playing tennis."

My modest moment of relief collapsed on itself. I couldn't speak. I knew exactly the photo he meant. I knew where it was taken and who took it. It was before I put on weight. I was serving the ball. My whole body was stretched to its limit. My shirt had pulled up and some stomach showed. Hard, defined stomach muscles. My calves stretching into the serve accentuated my legs—my best feature, according to Angela. I always thought she was joking.

I started, "But still . . . "

He didn't even let me stammer out a response. He's too kind a man for that. He said, "It was a framed eight-by-ten. Propped up on her bedside table. The last thing she would see at night before she switched off her lamp and went to sleep."

Like a lover, I thought. Or an obsession.

6

LONG BEFORE THE appointed time of Charlene and Leo's visit, I moved to the front of my cell and stood with my face pressed against the bars, angling my line of sight as far down the corridor as I could see, and listening almost without breathing for what was becoming the familiar echo of footsteps from deep inside the stairwell. By now all sounds were welcome signals that there was some movement on my case, but my ear was cocked for the footfalls of my steadfast darling Charlene bringing me the best legal mind in eastern Kentucky.

The wait was so long I got worried, and then so much longer still that my mind drifted back to Angela, and that tennis photograph. Although it was taken only about five years ago, it looks older. It's black-and-white, shot with a single-lens reflex. Angela commissioned a professional to take it. He snapped dozens that day on the tennis court. I can still hear the motorized whir of his film advancing. Little did I know that every one-five hundredth of a second was taking me nearer to my split with Angela, to Twisting Creek and Big's. To Charlene. And to prison.

At one time that photo stood on a different nightstand, the one on her side of our bed in New York. It shows me at my best. My dark hair, which I still wore long at that time, is flying backwards from the force of my serve. My sharp face, tanned from many summer days on the court, is all energy and concentration. She used to say that I chose Jezebel because we both have faces like the prow of a ship, and I would blush, because Jez has a striking face. Being compared to her in beauty is a great compliment. But Angela was wrong. I didn't choose Jez. She chose me.

I had a similar photo of Angela on my side of the bed, taken the same day. In it she's crouched, coiled, within a racket's length of the net, ready to drop a volley that will leave her opponent sprawled on the court.

That opponent, of course, is me.

One evening she came home carrying a Chinese vase that she claimed was an antique. That vase took my seat of honor on her nightstand. My picture migrated across the room to the top of her dresser. I later saw the extra distance as symbolic, although at the time I thought she was simply redecorating. Eventually a photo of her standing at the open door of *Le Plat Nourrissant* took front and center on her nightstand, the Chinese vase moved to the dresser, and my tennis photo disappeared into a drawer. Only to reappear, three years later, in a cabin in Kentucky.

I stood there with the prison bars pressing ridges into the side of my face, my ears alert within the silence, wondering: What had become of that picture? Where could it have gone? Who besides Angela could have it now?

Sounds from the stairs interrupted these musings. The footsteps of a person walking alone, judging by the sound— my ears were already a prisoner's ears—and my heart fell. It was my chubby guard from breakfast. He had barely come into sight when I called out, "They didn't show up?"

He took his time answering. Again he was out of breath from the climb. "Oh sure. They're here. Downstairs. I'll escort you." He paused outside my door with the keys in his hand until he caught his breath. "That elevator has been down for a week. They say they'll fix it today. Until then we don't think Mr. Akers should climb all those steps."

"Mustn't kill off my lawyer just yet, right?"

He said nothing more as we passed along the silent corridor. We entered the stairwell and descended into what I abruptly came to recognize as the twisting, tunneled entrance into my own destiny. I was tumbling into some kind of vortex, a drain unclogged, into whatever was to happen to me. It was a dim, gray, concrete-walled plunge into mildewy air, smelling of urine and disinfectant. On the ground floor we passed a window and I got a brief glimpse of a black metal door marked "Visitors Parking," but we didn't stop there. We descended not one more flight of stairs, but two, where my guard directed me into a small room, and left me there alone. I heard him lock the door behind me. Instinctively I looked around for a window— foolishly, since we were deep underground. However, this was not the stark interrogation room I'd been expecting. Rather more like a cozy basement den, with sofa and chairs, a coffee table with magazines, even a potted fern beside a floor lamp.

Soon the lock sounded again and I turned to find Charlene charging into my arms. She almost knocked me back onto the sofa. I wonder if that wasn't her real aim. If Leo and the guard hadn't been watching, you might have thought you were about to witness some passionate lovemaking, or indeed a rape.

After a long hug I pulled her away so I could look at her. I'd never seen anyone more beautiful. Her glowing face, with its rosebud lips, was like a sunrise over water. She was wearing a knee-length white dress streaked in a grapevine motif, with a delicate filigree of green leaves and big purple splotches of grape clusters. In my time Charlene has shrunk from size thirty-two to size ten, and she fills them out just right, all ten of them. She'd sprayed on a gardenia scent. It was as though she wanted to say, "Your hot date is here." I wanted to tell Leo and the guard to take a coffee break while my visitor and I had a conjugal visit.

Leo had other priorities. He came in, nodded, and said, simply, "Jake."

I still hadn't released Charlene, but I freed a hand to shake his. I said, "Thanks for coming, Leo."

The guard left and closed the door behind him. Leo looked at Charlene until she got the hint and followed the guard outside, leaving us alone. Yet at that point, after all that anticipation, nothing much happened. I asked how long they could keep me here without charging me. He said the law allows police a reasonable length of time to investigate any involvement in a crime. I told him that I knew precisely zero about the missing Angela Van Landingham, beyond having been the lover and business partner of a woman by that name before I moved to Twisting Creek. I offered my opinion that this was either a different woman with that name, or an imposter, and explained why. He wanted to know how this imposter might be in possession of my photograph. I rolled out a quick hypothesis that she must have burgled Angela's apartment and stolen it along with Angela's credit cards and ID. If this sounded as lame to him as it did to me, he didn't let on. He only made a quick note of something. I noticed he didn't use what we call a legal pad, but the thin one like reporters use in old movies. In fact he wrote down very little, and what he did write seemed utterly inconsequential. For example when I said that my Angela Van Landingham was more the five-star Parisian hotel type than a Kentucky lake cottage type, he wrote, "Paris."

I hadn't intended to mention the burglary at *Le Plat Nourrissant*, but his expression told me he knew I was holding something back. He reminded me that everything I told him was strictly confidential and could not be used against me, so please be honest and tell him every single thing that might pertain to my case. When I hesitated, he said he didn't think they would hold me here on nothing but a photograph found in the room of a missing person. So then I confessed that I'd stolen a carload of valuable restaurant equipment when I left

New York, stolen it from Angela. I stammered out a quick justification, about how it had been my creativity as much as her business acumen that made the restaurant a success, and I felt entitled to more than a boot out the door.

He answered, "I know your cooking well," and left it at that. He asked for the same contact details that the sheriff had, said he'd be back tomorrow, and left. His face showed no despair, but he at no time spoke the words I hoped for: *I'll have you out of here in no time.* That's how I knew that he thought Victor had run a check on me and found a New York arrest warrant outstanding.

Before that realization had time to coalesce into despair, the door opened and here came Jezebel! She bounded in, leapt completely across that coffee table and pinned me onto the sofa. Seconds after that, Charlene joined the fun. And you know what? I know it defies all logic and reason, but for that brief moment I was the happiest man in the state of Kentucky.

Of all the things I'll always remember about that—let's call it a minute—of my life, that three-way nuzzling and embrace, it might well be the smell that keeps it alive for me. The smell that we can always conjure up, in a micro-second, when we reminisce about a beloved dog. Not wet dog smell, just ordinary sunny summer day clean dog smell. Even now in my head it mixes with Charlene's gardenia to make the entire scene rise up around me, the three of us roaring with delight as we tipped back onto the sofa.

The guard didn't want this to get ridiculous, so he rapped a quick knuckle and opened the door. "I'm afraid time's up."

We didn't give him any grief. Charlene and Jez led the way out, Jez's tail wagging as gaily as if we were all off to the park. Who could believe that hardly twelve hours ago this same dog had faced down two armed cops?

"Charlene," I stopped her. She turned to look at me. "You know what I just now figured out? Last night before Jezebel ran for those deputies, for some reason she charged back into the house. That was to wake you up, wasn't it?"

"She pounced all over me and then ran like hell. She knew her reckless ass needed backup."

They disappeared down a corridor. My guard watched them leave just as I did, and said, "Smart, beautiful *and* brave."

"Which one?"

'Ha!" He said. "I see what you mean."

On the long climb back, my guard showed no wariness that I might ambush him on the stairs. At every landing his breathing became more labored. I climbed a little faster and glanced back. He was boosting himself with the handrail. I checked his height. About the same as mine—six feet even. I slowed, and, as in casual conversation, said, "I don't think I've ever seen you out at Big's."

"Naw," he said simply, not wasting any oxygen.

I called over my shoulder, "Let me guess. Twenty-five to thirty pounds too many? BMI maybe twenty-nine?"

"About."

"You should come on out some evening."

He didn't answer me. He wanted this conversation to end.

I stopped and turned to look down at him. He stopped where he was. He seemed grateful for the break. "You married?" I asked.

"Yep."

"What's your wife's name?"

"Emma."

"Bring Emma along."

"Bring her where?"

"To Big Charlene's Supper Club. Soon as I get out of here, I'll cook you a dinner so good you won't even know it's healthy. First meal's on the house." He was still preoccupied with catching his breath. I added, "Hey, it's Charlene's money anyway, right?"

He smiled. "Right."

"You see what it did for her. Did you know her a few years ago?" He nodded. "Then you can see what it did for her. Me too. I had a BMI of nearly thirty when I first came to town."

"Both of you look real good now."

"You will too. Plus you'll eat well, have some fun, lose that paunch, feel great. Probably perk up your sex life, too."

He waved that off as though it was the last thing in the world he needed help with. Then for no apparent reason his face lost all form. He looked at his feet, grabbed a handrail, and got on with his climb.

I didn't understand his abrupt change—then I thought maybe I did. "You don't think I'm going to get out of here very soon, do you? You think maybe I'll never get out of here at all."

He shrugged, and, without looking up into my face, said, "I really couldn't say. They're dragging the lake right now."

7

ALL THIS ANXIETY has my thoughts bouncing off every wall in this prison. What if I hadn't seen a sign on a flatbed truck? What if that first night I'd eaten fried chicken for dinner, walked back to the motel, watched some TV before bed, and then in the morning moved on toward Mexico? That would seem to be the turning point.

But let me ask you one question. By not meeting Charlene, by missing my chance to help her launch Big's, by never finding a home in this crazy little town—would that balance out where I am now? Not to mention, where would you be?

I know what you're thinking. If I'm playing What If, the place to start would be New York. What if I hadn't skipped town with a car load of Angela's property?

It's impossible to argue against that, but there's still one stubborn little corner of my psyche that disagrees. It may be that in our society's effort to keep things law-abiding, we overlook the healing power of revenge. It may well be that I'm at least a somewhat sane and contented man now, purely because I didn't let Angela go unpunished for exploiting my trust.

In a national debate on this, I'd lose. But folks around here would understand. This is Hatfield-McCoy country. Somebody kills your brother, you go kill their brother. Even in Twisting Creek most people don't adhere to this Old Testament brand of justice. These days if somebody kills their loved one, they'd be much more likely to look to the courts for redress. But they still have a cultural memory for what a satisfying equation *an eye for an eye* is. If everybody knew the facts that led to my New York burglary, in a secret ballot people here would free me in a landslide.

Let's not overlook something else—it's possible that the first time I laid eyes on Charlene it wasn't my boyish good looks or my thirty pound roll of belly fat that won her over, but a trunk load of shining copper pots. Here's how that works. Think back to that evening when I first met Charlene—Big Charlene, she called herself back then—and when Jezebel foretold of the truck driver and his doggie treat.

That driver climbed down from his cab, checked his clipboard, asked Charlene if she was the owner of his cargo, then proceeded to the rear of his truck and pulled out a metal ramp. He climbed onto his flat bed and busied himself with the bungee cords that held the sign in place. Charlene and I followed him up the ramp, for it was clear that one man couldn't steady the whole sign by himself. We held the sides of the new marquee while the driver hoisted the bulk of it onto a hand truck, and together we eased it down the ramp and across a few yards of asphalt toward Big's swinging double-door entrance, and down a dark passageway leading to an even darker area that sounded large and empty. And there we left it—my sign from heaven, in pitch black darkness. Yet even then I knew one day it would snap to life in a blaze of color.

With a pat of Jezebel's head, the driver took his leave. If he'd given her one more treat she would have followed him into his cab and off to god knows where. Even as it was, she walked him to the door and saw him off. Then she came prancing back, her head lifted, enthralled by her own ability to win hearts.

Charlene took me by the elbow and positioned me in the center of a narrow doorway, facing the heavy air of an unlit central area. In my memory she first covers my eyes with her hands, but perhaps that's just me raising the drama to match the magic of the next moment of my life. She flipped a set of switches and light almost sizzled through a truly enormous room. I had to shade my eyes with my hands, but there it was, my first view of Big Charlene's Weight-Loss Supper Club and Taxi Dancing.

It was a construction zone. All the workers had gone home for the day, but their work was evident from front to back. What I saw before me was no mere restaurant. It was a vision. The vision of the woman standing beside me; an idea born in her head and coming to life before her eyes.

She took my wrist and led me inside. "This place used to be a bowling alley, but it's been vacant for a long time. I gutted all the lanes except two in the back. We've already refurbished those. They'll be in an active space over there." She pointed to a wood frame that was in the process of becoming a partition. "Behind that we'll have ping-pong, and what-not. Light activity, that's my goal. Anything to get people moving instead of eating. But not a gym. Only a couple of treadmills. Bowling, obviously. And from just in front of here where we're standing, clear over there to the edge of this hardwood circle, that's going to be the dance floor. We'll have perimeter tables almost the whole way round. Tables here where we're standing. There'll be a little stage over there, for live music, or a host. Usually me. Or maybe a doctor or nutrition expert or motivational speaker. I'll do a little welcome-everybody speech from there every evening. The taxi dancers will sit in a row along the side wall."

"The taxi dancers?"

"Now don't you be thinking what you're thinking, and don't tell me you're not." She pointed to the "Mind Reader" badge on her breast. "They'll be both men and women and they will not be hookers or gigolos or operators of any kind. They'll be normal employees who are here to dance with fat people who otherwise would be ashamed to get on their feet on a normal dance floor. You know why I want to get them up and dancing?"

"Because you can't dance and eat at the same time?"

"Because it makes you happy! That's why people ought to dance. Do you dance?"

"I haven't for a long time."

"That's what all fat people say. So guess what my next question is going to be."

"Why not?"

"No. We all know the answer to that. Because we're fat. What's a better question?"

Then I thought, Oh shit. I think I know what she means.

She said, "See what I'm talking about? Well?"

I was forced to be honest. Something about the moment made it impossible to lie. More likely everything about the moment, from the breadth of this woman's vision, to the breadth of this woman herself, to the smell of sawdust and plaster, to Jezebel taking run ups and sliding on her butt right across that dance floor.

"Well, no," I answered. "I don't suppose I have been very happy."

"See!" she said, as though this was great news. "Now you'll want to see where the kitchen will be."

"Why do you say that?"

"Stop it," she said, and placed her hand on my stomach.

There's one question I'm sure a lot of people in Twisting Creek would never, ever ask, but would love to know the answer to, and that's how much weight had Charlene lost before I experienced my first impulse of lust over her. But I won't hide it from you: it was right then, when she placed her hand on that extra belly I'd grown, and kept it there. It was very nearly spiritual, this laying on of hands, this promise of happier times. I thought it might be something local, a ritual that comes naturally in these Appalachian cults. At that time I didn't even know that her brother was the snake-handling, faith-healing pastor of just such a congregation. I thought of it even without that—the laying on of hands, the human contact that heals. Sexy as hell.

I looked deep into her eyes for the first time. A smile made her whole face beam, but it was her big brown eyes that glistened brightest. She smiled more with her eyes than with her mouth. They slanted back a little at the corners, much like Jezebel's, and I found myself tightening my abs.

Jezebel saw evidence of affection that didn't include her, so she cantered over. She really wanted to jump up on us, but I've taught her not to do that, so what she did was stand on her hind legs and dance in a circle. It's the same trick she was doing outside the jail. She started it after she saw a street-busking poodle do it, and she's been doing it ever since. Her technique hasn't improved very much, but she seems to enjoy it. She's kept it in the act for years. I've never known and will never know whether that's because she wants to do it until she gets it right, or because she thinks it's already perfect, so show it off.

Charlene watched Jez dancing around, said, "Come on over here," and opened her arms. She had no rule against a dog jumping up against her. She smoothed a thumb up Jezebel's nose. "Shoot far! Of course you can be part of this, purty girl."

At the time I thought she said *party girl*. In fact *purty*, as you no doubt know, is *pretty*. You may be familiar with *Shoot far!* too, but just in case: it's Charlene's favorite expression. For the longest time I thought it meant something like "Set your goals high." "Let your reach exceed your grasp." That kind of thing. I'd admired her use of it for a long time when I finally figured out that "far" is how people around here say "fire," and "shoot" is a euphemism for "shit." So every time I was being impressed by her motto *Shoot far!* she was really saying *Shit fire!*, which just sounds really painful to me.

Anyway, I said, "Yes, please. I'd like to see the kitchen."

We walked a few yards into an empty space and she said, "Now. You're standing in it."

"Hang on. You mean you haven't started on it yet?"

"It'll come along in due course."

I thought, No! No, it won't. That's where your vision has failed you.

I said, "If you plan to open any time reasonably soon, you need to get going with this. The kitchen is the heart of a restaurant, and the most complicated part to get right. Also the hardest to undo if you get it wrong."

"You sound like you know what you're talking about."

"I know from experience. I've done this before, you know."

"You want to look at the blueprints?"

"Has your chef approved them?"

"What chef?"

"You really should hire a chef first. Kitchen layout can be really personal."

"No doubt."

"It's important to your success. I should know. I am a chef."

"That's why I'm asking if you want to look at the blueprints."

"Seriously, I am. A certified nutritionist and gourmet chef. CIA trained."

She repeated, "CIA trained?" in a tone that said, *Who do you think you're messing with?*

"Culinary Institute of America." I love this joke. She didn't laugh. She kept her arms folded, so I explained, "The most revered culinary training in New York." When New Yorkers say that, they see no need to add, *and therefore in the whole wide world.* "Plus a semester split between Florence and Lyons. And another between Bangkok and Singapore."

"Uh, I guess I'm supposed to be impressed?"

I wanted to say, *Good god, woman!* But I only lifted my shoulders in a modest shrug. I took my key from my pocket and turned toward the car. Not, I have to say, in an attempt to escape before it was too late. It was already too late.

I popped the lid of the trunk. She took one look at all that lustrous copperware and said, "You're hired."

"Just like that?" I think I managed to present the face of a normal, baffled person, although in my head I heard screaming: *Please don't ask for references!*

"You can start dancing again, too. In fact, you're now officially in charge of interviewing and hiring our taxi dancers."

"Are you joking? You want me to hire the dancers?"

"Just the girls, mind. I'll be seeing to those boys myself."

8

THE GUARD BROUGHT a late lunch: smoked ham and Swiss on whole wheat, with mustard, lettuce, tomato and onion. The sandwich had the look of someone's packed lunch. Written down like that it sounds American suburban standard issue, but the tomato still smelled of the vine, and the ham was firm, bright, moist and smoky. Obviously it was from somebody's private smokehouse. Probably Victor's parents. I'll bet Victor, or possibly Shelley, packed it for me this morning. I imagined Victor telling Shelley, "I'll need an extra lunch today. We arrested Jake Michaels last night."

I tried to imagine the conversation that would have followed, but I came up blank. Would Victor have detailed the case to her, or merely hinted at the circumstances? Or more likely—Victor being Victor—he simply refused to discuss it. He would have stayed tight-lipped, even while Shelley was badgering him for information, and warning him to play his cards carefully this close to the election. Or did her stunned silence mirror her husband's?

I have no idea, that's my point. I'm finally realizing how little I understand about any of this. One second I can place a bet with lockdown certainty that the outcome will be my immediate release, and the next second I know with equal conviction that I will never leave prison alive.

I put my sandwich back down on the plate and took a long look at it. Who prepared it? Where did it really come from? In fact I have no idea. A tray appears. Here's a sandwich. It's unsettling to realize that, after all my years as a chef, starting from today I must eat by the decisions of others.

After lunch I sat in my cell for a while, not knowing what to expect next. I had no real fix on anything—not on what steps I should be taking, or even what steps others might take on my behalf. It was now in the hands of Leo and Victor, maybe Charlene. That was about as close as I could come to a strategy. I didn't even know what to do with my time, other than make these notes for you. If you're reading this twenty years from now, as I hope and plan, my guess would be that the outcome of my predicament is well known to you, so what matters is watching it unfold, maybe learning how it changed me, or didn't change me, or Charlene, or the rest of us involved. Even how it helped to form who you are.

It's strange. I just realized that your interest in this account is the exact opposite of mine. My interest is focused on the outcome. That's all that matters. That's the whole story. I already know, so well, all these people, what they're like, how their characters clash with or complement their personalities. I know who's funny on purpose and who's just funny. I know pretty well who's sincere and who's a pretender. These are the things I want to show you, because that's what I suppose you'll want to know, but that's not what I want to know. I want to know how this ends. For us. For me. From worst case scenario to best case, how does it wrap up? How much of my life is salvaged, how much destroyed?

That's the part you know already. If you could only tell me the ending, I could cope with the rest.

After I learned they were dragging Lake Roosevelt for Angela's body, coping meant an hour or so of brain death. I sat at my little bolted-down table, pen and paper at the ready, yet my thoughts, or the sound those thoughts make inside my head, seemed to grow imperceptibly fainter. They were like music in a song that has no clear ending, the kind where the sound engineer simply turns the volume lower and lower until finally you realize it's over. If you pay attention while people are dancing to a song like that, you'll notice the imprecision at the end, when some people keep going full tilt even after others slow down to an uncertain shuffle, and still others stop dancing altogether. My thoughts faded away and my mind stopped dancing. It stood there on the dance floor, waiting for another song to start up. But none did.

Eventually I rallied briefly with thoughts of Big's. By that time in the afternoon we'd be rolling up our sleeves. Sally, Bryce and Enid are prep cooks today. They'll be there already, sorting through supplies, marinating, chopping vegetables. My line cooks today are Orlando on cold salads, Lacey on sauté, and Laravelle on grill. My sous chef is Rusty. Reliable Rusty. Trusty Rusty. A wonderful sous chef he is, and will be until I inevitably lose him to his own restaurant.

Fumiko and her Asian Mafia are probably there already, being too perfect to be real, making everyone happy to be alive in spite of the facts. Shulin will be with Lacey at the wok, showing her Oriental sauté sauces that I don't even know myself. Fumiko will be handing out espressos, or doing ballet alone in a darkened ballroom when she thinks nobody's watching.

So, no use worrying about Big's. It's in capable, dedicated hands. Charlene's sense of purpose imbues us all with the conviction that we are performing a vital service for our town. She often reminds us that we are the medical workers who rescue fat people from doctors and psychiatrists. She says Big's is the hospital for this stage of their lives, only with better food and a damn sight more fun.

My brain went empty again. It was a void akin to meditation—perhaps therapeutic in its own way, if not exactly optimum strategy for busting out of jail.

Eventually that stack of books entered my consciousness,

so I picked up the Boethius. He turns out to be a late Roman philosopher who was imprisoned for siding with the losers in some power struggle. He knows he's going to be executed, but while awaiting the axe he tries to make some sense of his fate. He gets counsel from "Lady Philosophy", who tells him: *Nothing is miserable but what is thought so, and contrariwise, every estate is happy if he that bears it be content.*

So apparently I should be happy in here, and if I'm not, it's my own fault.

Lady Philosophy also says, *Do you reckon such happiness to be prized, which is sure to pass away? Is good fortune dear to you, which is with you for a time and is not sure to stay, and which is sure to bring you unhappiness when it is gone?*

Well yes, Lady P, I guess I do prize such happiness, and its passing is not sure to bring me unhappiness when it's gone, if, like your buddy Boethius, I'm dead.

I put that book on the bottom of the stack and decided it was just as well I'd never heard of the late great Boethius. I was about to try the next one, *Soul on Ice* by Eldridge Cleaver, when I heard a percussive sound in the corridor. It took me by surprise. Even in my near trance, and certainly while reading Boethius, my ear was receptive to the familiar scuff of feet climbing those stairs, but I had missed the low groan of our now-working elevator. I hurried to peer between the bars and down the corridor as far as the angle allowed.

I waited for the appearance of one of the three people who can help me: Charlene, Victor or Leo. But no. It was Charlene's brother, Lonnie Farley.

I think I've mentioned that Charlene has a brother who is some sort of professional man of God. Charlene calls him a "shirttail preacher." You probably don't know what that means, and I don't either, but I tend not to interpret it as an endorsement. He's a large man, tall, overweight, with soft, fat hands. He has Charlene's ovoid face, exaggerated by a receding hairline. When he's wearing a white shirt and striped necktie, which apparently is all the time, it looks as though his body has ejected a giant egg through the narrow opening of his neck. Folds of skin drape his collar all around, even in back. His kinship with Charlene is clear on first sighting, and would be screamingly obvious to anyone who knew Charlene when she was still Two Ton Tony. Brother Lonnie would seem to be a prime candidate for Big's membership, yet he has never once joined us, and vows he never will. (Charlene promises to help him keep that vow.)

For all their differences, I've never had anything against Lonnie. He's but one of a zillion people who have managed to turn the supernatural into a career, and to my eye he's so transparent about it that he's difficult to despise. And another thing—I have conversations with Lonnie Farley that I never even dreamed about in New York. It's like talking to a space invader. You'd enjoy it too, especially if you know Lonnie at the age he is now. (Not my now. Your now.)

Here's an example. One morning he saw me having coffee on the patio of Fifi's French Press. In fact, he probably sought me out, since pretty much everybody in town knows where to find me at that time of day. Jezebel was with me, as always. She saw Lonnie approaching and ran to greet him. In spite of all the drivel that's ever been said about dogs being an astute judge of character, Jez has a soft spot for him. I think it's because he's more powdered and perfumed and pomaded than most men, and she sees him simply as an olfactory indulgence.

They greeted each other like lovers of long standing, and then he turned to me. He was wearing a white shirt with a Morehead-blue-and-gold-striped necktie. He smelled of something sweet and lemony, with an overlay of tobacco smoke. His big, sloppy, duck-egg head bobbled at me as we shook hands. He helped himself to a seat at my table, and sat there smirking.

He seemed to know what was coming, even to relish the prospect of being bested in theological debate. See, that morning's Guardian had a story on the death of some snake-handling lunatic, slap in the middle of a church meeting not far across the West Virginia state line. A woman, at that. To my mind, that makes her even crazier. It seems her timber rattler took exception to her pious fondling, and struck her just below the ear. She couldn't seek emergency treatment, of course. That would have sent her to hell. It was all in the paper, a front page story. I had a copy right there in front of me.

"Good morning, Lonnie. I hear you lost another customer last night."

"I don't know what you're talking about."

He was lying, of course. His smirk didn't recede one micrometer.

I didn't smirk back. I didn't need to. I said, "You people are like the tobacco industry. You keep killing off your market."

He smiled and pulled a pack of Marlboros from his shirt pocket. But he didn't light up. He knew if he did I would take Jez and walk straight into the café. He laid the pack on the table, and squared a gold Zippo on top of it.

"Want some coffee?" I offered.

"If you're buying, I'm drinking."

"Read this while I order." I slid the Guardian toward him and pointed to the story.

When I returned to the patio with his mug of coffee, he had a cigarette in his mouth. He glanced at me out the corner of his eye, exhaled a big plume of smoke, and made a show of stubbing out the butt even though it wasn't half finished.

He twirled the newspaper around toward me and I put down his coffee. "Mercy," he said. It's the way he pronounces *merci*, and is his way of saying I'm an overeducated and pretentious twat because I list some menu items in French. God, he is such a dick. I didn't respond, so he continued, "I see my name's in today's paper."

I said, "How can you say you didn't know about the story when you're quoted as a source?"

"They asked me to clarify the Bible's stand on handling, and I told them it didn't need no clarification, it's the clear word of God. Then I quoted chapter and verse from the KJV. From that the newspaper got"—he looked me straight in the eyes and quoted without so much as a glance at the paper—"Lonnie Farley, pastor of the Church of the Blood Spilled on Calvary, explained the Biblical basis for such rituals. 'It's from Mark 16, verses 17–18. *And these signs shall follow them that believe. In my name shall they cast out devils; they shall speak with new tongues. They shall take up serpents, and if they drink any deadly thing, it shall not hurt them. They shall lay hands on the sick, and they shall recover.*"

He spread out his pudgy hands and laid them on the table, as though to say, And that was the extent of my involvement.

I said, "Yeah, well, it did harm her, didn't it? And she didn't recover. Isn't that enough of a tipoff that your head is stuck deep inside cloud cuckoo land?"

"Satan's always inside of the serpent. It's faith that keeps him down. Some people can't hold on to their faith. They let it slip, and Satan takes control. That's what happened to this woman. I expect it's what'd happen to you, if we ever got you up in front of the church to take up snakes."

"Not a chance. I'd be the one to recover, because I'd dash straight to a hospital."

"In that case, you're liable to be the one Satan gets— driving at breakneck speed."

That's where we left it, at that compromise position. We sat there for a while, drinking coffee and watching girls walk by. I've noticed that with guys, no matter how completely foreign you think you are to each other, let a pretty girl walk by and for a moment you are brothers.

We did that, not even pretending not to, then he stood up. "Hey! Wait'll you see what I got!"

He ran from the patio as though he'd dropped his wallet in the parking lot. He was only gone a minute, but in my mind it's an extraordinarily long minute, because in my own sequence the next thing isn't Lonnie's return, but Jezebel going berserk and charging over chairs, tables, customers, waiters, and potted plants. I ran after her in time to see Lonnie approaching with a wooden and glass crate held as high over his head as he could reach, and Jezebel leaping to within inches of that level, her teeth snapping, and saliva flying.

I called her back. She obeyed, against her better judgment. After a short standoff of wills, she slid under my chair and laid her head on my feet.

Lonnie set his box on the table. I now saw a strip of masking tape stuck there, with something written in black marker. It was a name: Satan.

I started to ask "What have you got in ... " but then through a wide glass window in the side of the box I saw a twisting rope of something sinewy, sealed in a scaly material I'd only ever seen on urban cowboy boots, a gray and tan scaly pattern that ... *slithered!*

Jesus! I jumped out of my chair and Jezebel interpreted that as release from any previous restrictions. She made tentative dives at that window, while the snake inside lazily turned and opened its jaws wider than you'd think possible, to display its fangs and the milky interior of its mouth.

"Stop it, Jez," I said, but she knew my heart wasn't in it.

"See that?" Lonnie asked. "See that white color all inside of there? That's why it's called a cottonmouth."

Other people hurried over to see why Jez was going meltdown. Someone inside the café responded to the commotion by shouting out the door, "Lonnie Farley go pull your crazy stunts somewhere else."

Lonnie laughed, and left. Jezebel patrolled the patio perimeter until she decided the danger had cleared.

Where else am I going to see something like that? Okay, he may be a thoroughly despicable excuse for a human being, but maybe now you can understand why I don't mind him so much. My darling Charlene holds an alternative position—to put it politely. She thinks he's one wonky synapse away from criminal insanity.

He's several years older than Charlene, a simple accident of fortune that to my mind goes a long way toward explaining the startling differences between them. I've not yet explained to you how Charlene got all that money. I wonder if you know all this stuff already? If not, this seems as good a time as any.

She inherited it. Her parents died together, at home, on the same night, after sharing a meal that included green beans from a jar Mrs. Farley had canned herself. Even though she'd been canning her own vegetables for more than sixty years, it was known that she'd had some mild strokes and had lost some of her organizational skills. Apparently she had forgotten to put the weight on top of her pressure canner. The health department tested all other canned vegetables in her pantry, and found five more quart jars of beans tainted with botulism.

It's weird—these deaths have been on my mind recently because this weekend we will participate in the annual commemoration of that tragedy. Or maybe not, not now. Not me anyway. The tradition culminates on Sunday in a rustic outdoor church service in the Farley family cemetery, where Lonnie and his cult members put on quite a show, complete with fainting, healing, prophesying, and an animal act. This part of the tradition, I don't mind. It's like watching Chinese opera on acid. But the day before, the preparation of the "graveyard" (as they say here), is a full, hard-labor day of undoing the growth and erosion that nature has been working at all year. And it's hot; it's humid; it's way up on top of a mountain that looks more like a jungle until you get right beside the cemetery. It's all sweat-bees and poison oak and briar patches and horseflies as big as prunes. Stink bugs and venomous centipedes. Chiggers. And snakes. Real crawling-on-the-ground snakes, not Lonnie's stage props. It's not at all rare to hear one of the workers shout out, "Got me a copperhead!" and you look around and see one dangling, dead, from somebody's hoe.

(You may be wondering why instead of killing it they don't just pick it up and pet it. If you *are* wondering that, consider yourself a chip off the old block.)

It's ironic—recalling the horrors of cleaning that graveyard, which last year I hated, yet from here, from prison, I know this year I'll regret not being a part of it. Hard to believe, but true. It makes me feel like part of the family, something more important this year than last year.

So . . . Mom and Pop died of food poisoning, and Charlene split the inheritance with Lonnie. The Farley legacy included three large farms across the state of Kentucky. All three farms had lucrative tobacco bases—this was before the tobacco quota buyout—and they all carried herds of beef cattle. Each farm came with a valuable main house, and other buildings, along with antiques of every description. All this went fifty-fifty to Charlene and Lonnie.

(One reason Charlene is sinking her half of her inheritance into improving people's lives is because so much of it was tobacco money. This is just my opinion. She says she never even thought of it before I asked her about it.)

None of this explains how the difference in their ages has cut such a chasm between them. But this does: until one frigid January evening in the late nineteen-eighties, the Farleys were landless and penniless. They share cropped and odd-jobbed. They peddled vegetables at harvest time, and eggs all year round. They weren't starving, but they owed money all over

Buford County. As Charlene says, they could look at their supper plates and know what time of month it was. If all they saw was pinto beans, the month was half over. My theory is that this is why Charlene was, and Lonnie is, fat. A poor diet as a child can do big-time damage for years to come.

Both children had part-time jobs and kicked all their earnings into the kitty. They were the kind of cash-strapped rural family that looks forward to a child graduating from high school to become a wage earner. College was never in the picture. Lonnie went straight to the Air Force, and sent back as much pay as he could. He was at Lackland, in Texas, when, back home in Kentucky, in the dim, sleety dusk of a January evening, his father's car skidded off a narrow county road, through a rail fence and into a ditch beside a cut-down corn field. The story is that when Mr. Farley couldn't spin his way back onto the road, he got out and started walking across that field in hopes of finding a farmhouse with a telephone. What he found instead was what he at first took to be a bundle of rags frozen to the ground. When he saw steam rising from it, he broke it free from the ice and found what he later said reminded him of a garden elf somebody had fashioned out of snow for a Christmas decoration, then thrown out after New Year's.

It was a woman—tiny, ancient, and nearly frozen. Years later, whenever Mr. Farley would tell that story, he liked to add, "You couldn't a-kilt her with a ice pick."

Mr. Farley carried her to his car and positioned her near his heater. He flagged down a truck, which pulled him back onto the road, and headed home with his frozen cargo.

Charlene was eight years old at the time. She says when she got her first sniff of it she thought her mother would tell her father to take it straight to the garbage barrel, but damned if she didn't say straight to the hospital. Charlene says you don't easily forget being that far wrong. The old lady snow elf began to thaw. She regained consciousness. They all visited her in the hospital. She started talking crazy, then made a little more sense. She was intermittently lucid and senile. Gradually they made out that after her husband died she had led the life of a recluse in a farmhouse way out of town, where an old black man who'd worked for her all his life cared for her. His death that frozen January had very nearly meant death for her too.

For the next two years she lived with the Farleys. Even when she died they had no idea how much she was worth, or that they had inherited the whole wad. But all that changed with the reading of the will. From age ten, Charlene knew that her future would include college, and, as it turned out, graduate school and an MBA. Brother Lonnie had other ideas. Additional formal education had never been his aspiration. The prospect of being rich meant that after his four years he could leave the Air Force, and not have to find a job. When an infected jar of green beans made him a wealthy man, he began to manipulate his half of the estate, with the stated aim of never working a day in his life. He dropped a lot of it betting on also-rans at Keeneland and River Downs, then dropped even more of it by purchasing those same also-rans, or others just like them. Once he'd had it with horses, he moved on to cars. He sponsored what he calls, apparently without irony, a Super Late Model Chevy, which crashed into some picnic tables at Tazewell Speedway in Tennessee. He invested in a company that claimed they could produce saltwater-fueled automobile engines.

Throughout it all he was seldom seen without a drink in one hand and a woman in the other. When he'd burned through his entire inheritance, he asked Charlene to lend him part of hers. He sourced his claim on the parable of the prodigal son, but Charlene's charity has other outlets, so Lonnie took up preaching.

In these parts, a history of sin and profligacy is seen as good training for the clergy. Any garden variety church member can stand up and say they've tried to live a life of kindness and virtue, and they recommend it for you, too, but how much thump does that make on a pulpit? The audience wants gnashing of teeth and rending of garments. Tears of repentance loosen wallets. So that was Lonnie Farley's career path: slow racehorses, super late dirt racers, pie-in-the-sky inventions, booze, bimbos, preacher.

You may have noticed that I started out by saying I have nothing against Lonnie Farley. I've already mentioned that I enjoy arguing with him, if only to marvel at the artfulness in the weird shit he comes out with. But then I proceed to describe him as some kind of buffoon-turned-charlatan. It doesn't seem fair—and you're right. It's not. That wasn't me slamming scumbag Lonnie. I was channeling Charlene. She's just so funny when she talks about him that I wanted to give you a flavor of what she's like at her current age (thirty-four).

For my part, when Lonnie showed up at my jail cell this afternoon, I was actually glad to see him, at least once I got over him not being one of my Big Three. To me he comes off very clearly as a sham, and he is in fact a sham, so logically doesn't that make him authentic? Once when I was a student in Bangkok, a street merchant told me his rack of one-hundred baht Rolex watches were "genuine fakes." If I'd known at the time that one day I'd meet Lonnie Farley, I would have bought him one of those Rolexes. I bet he'd wear it proudly.

In addition to all that—let's think selfishly here for a moment. In these parts, Lonnie has clout. Mainstream pastors like Methodists and Presbyterians may think he's nothing more than a pain-in-the-ass redneck and an embarrassment to their trade, but inside the evangelical revival tent, Lonnie Farley has got star quality. Preachers in Lonnie's circle may have a home church, but the most popular ones do guest appearances far and wide, like pop stars. In most of Kentucky, West Virginia, and southern Ohio, when he's the headliner, the crowds stream in with open purses. He's got this one tactic: "Reach into your pocketbook and give God the biggest bill you've got. If it's a twenty, give it to God! If it's a fifty, give it to God! And if it's a Benjamin—the Good Lord *loves* Benjamins. If you give God a one-dollar bill, you're telling Him, 'Lord, I want a cheapskate miracle.' Is that what you're praying for? A bargain basement miracle? Half-price on a close-out miracle?"

On and on. He can really work a crowd. He brings up cripples on crutches, grabs their heads, speaks in tongues, shoves them over backwards, and pretty soon has them doing zumba on stage. He wipes his sweat with red bandanas and sells them as prayer cloths at five bucks a pop. He handles snakes so full of roofies they might as well be made out of rubber. I mean, how can you be more transparent than that? People want a performance, they get one, and they're happy to pay for it. Nobody derides Madonna for flashing the crucifix and getting rich. Or maybe they do, but I don't.

So all I'm saying is the man carries weight around here. I'm much happier receiving him on a "salvation mission to my prison cell" (as he categorized his visit) than have him burning crosses in the square outside the courthouse. I suppose he knows he can't save my soul. Does he know that? By now he should. What I've learned about so many people around here is that saving your soul is their main goal in life. You bring a lost soul to Jesus, you've scored a touchdown. My guess is that, for Lonnie, saving the soul of the New York city slicker who lives in sin with his apostate sister would be like scoring the touchdown that wins the big game. I may be the closest thing in Twisting Creek to a Super Bowl victory.

Today he stood outside my cell looking in, with each hand grasping a bar exactly the way I do on the inside looking out, and said, "We're all of us praying for your early release, Jake. And after that, my next prayer is to get you and my baby sister up in front of my church, in front of the whole congregation, standing before God, then together you reach your hands down in that box of snakes, that you both may take up serpents, and raise them high. Praise the Lord."

Right here a normal preacher would either have tilted his face either upward, heavenward, so to speak, or else down, as in prayer. But not Lonnie. He looked me dead in the eye, with his mouth twisted in his patented smirk. It was a deal, presented as a dare.

He doesn't have a Benjamin prayer of making this happen, of course, but it's his job to keep trying.

I shouldn't stop here, telling you only what I don't believe. You'll be far more interested in what I do believe. In general I see myself as a believer in hard bench science, and although I've never seen any sort of survey to back this up, I'd say most chefs are that way too. All day long we perform scientific procedures. Cooking , like science, is all about five things: ingredients, sequence, method, temperature and pressure. Every cook knows that when we're preparing a soup that requires a teaspoon of salt, and we forget to add salt, that soup won't taste salty. You can pray over it, then taste it, and it'll still need salt. You can wave a crystal pyramid over it, shake voodoo sticks at it, sprinkle magic fairy dust over it, rattle bones over it and invoke the spirit of Vishnu into it, and it'll still need salt. But a teaspoon of sodium chloride does the job. What hope does Lonnie Farley have with a man who does chemistry for a living?

Still, I have to say I was relieved when Lonnie said he'd pray for me, and do what he could to secure my release. I was pleased to hear him say, "I know you're not capable of that kind of evil," clearly leaving me capable of other kinds of evil. Yet in spite of all that, as I watched him walk away, and saw him turn to lift a hand in farewell, I felt lighter, as though a part of me had squeezed through these prison bars and was following him out of here.

I'VE BEEN IMAGINING the perfect time for you to read this manuscript. I've resisted the temptation to imagine the circumstances that led you to find it, pick it up, and hold it now in your hands. Except this one, which jumped into my mind unbidden: You're packing for college, cleaning out your closet all the way back to the rear wall, where you come across a little pile of junk—old toys, pop-up books, maybe baseball cards, stuff like that. Hidden down in that pile is a folder of manuscript pages. You think, *What the fuck is this?* (Watch your language.) You toss it into your backpack and take it away to college.

This is where my original point kicks back in: the perfect age for you to read this is college age. Freshman year, first semester. That's the best. Soon after you leave home. Wherever that home might be, and whoever your family is, the distance will make it more real. College age means you're old enough that I don't have to leave out references to sex, especially to Angela's private kink. I suppose college is where most of us try to figure out who the hell we are and why we got that way. Also a time of acute nostalgia, for both parents and child.

Anyway, let me continue with the story of my very first day in Twisting Creek:

I showed Charlene the great haul of professional kitchenware in the trunk of my old pink Neon, and she asked me to be her chef. Didn't she? That's how I interpreted it. I kept thinking, Does she really expect me to sling tofu burgers in a boarded-up bowling alley and to hire dance partners for fat men? Does she take me for a New York pimp? Am I suddenly supposed to be Kentucky's leading impresario of taxi dancing? Was this prodigious woman serious? Or was this the way hillbilly women pulled the legs of pudgy city fellers?

"I mean every word of it," she said. "I'm serious as a dose of the clap. So it's settled—you're my chef. Next item of business is let's get you fed. And we can all three benefit from a nice walk, can't we, girl?" Jezebel looked up at her and smiled. Charlene took me by the arm, reached around me with her free hand to take Jez's leash, and led the way down a sidewalk bordering the foot of the hill.

I asked her, "Where shall we go?"

"*Where shall we go?* I love that! *Where shall we go?* They're going to love you around here."

"I have my doubts about that."

"'Course they will. No doubt about it, so shush. There's a Tim Horton's about a half hour's walk. On the way I'll describe what this supper club is all about."

I have to admit I enjoyed walking with her this way. For one thing, I felt protected. Here I was, in the land where they shoot a stranger first and later fall on their knees at his graveside to beg God's forgiveness. At least that's the image I had. But Charlene was a local. She was one of them. And apparently she was well-off enough to finance a major construction project. Only then did I start to wonder where her money had come from, and if she was solvent enough to undertake such an enterprise. It was something I would need to learn soon. I wasn't fool enough to get burned twice. (It turned out I didn't learn about the snow-elf inheritance for quite some time, and even then it was Lonnie who told me— about five minutes after I met him.)

But even leaving aside her financial status, I felt safe with Charlene because she was a local eccentric, a self-proclaimed mind reader. A colorful character, probably held in high Twisting Creek regard, for what that amounted to. It almost certainly would amount to enough that I need not fear local gun thugs who get edgy when darkness falls. Having her on my arm was like having a secret amulet, or a diplomatic passport. This was even before I knew she carried a little five-shot Ruger .38 in her purse.

Jez heeled along nicely, keeping in check with Charlene's knee, occasionally glancing up at me to indicate she knew this new setup was exceedingly odd, but it was fine with her if it was fine with me. Even now I recall noting with some surprise that this arrangement was all new to Jez. Angela Van Landingham, on her rare walks with us, never once took the leash, never once took my arm.

The evening air brought a chill with it, and the smell of coal fires and damp leaves made it a perfect evening for a brisk walk. Twisting Creek didn't seem a bad little town. The streetlamps worked—always a good sign—and they were capped to save energy and reduce light pollution. I noticed that the gently sloping hillside to our right contained a city park, with playground equipment, picnic tables, and, up where the hill steepened, banks of shrubbery still in bloom. Those dimmed halide lamps created iridescent islands glowing with pink rhododendrons and camellias, and pale blue hydrangeas.

"This seems like a nice little town."

"It's home. And it's about to get better. You know why?"

"Because some crazy woman is going to open a new restaurant?"

"Because her and her fancy New York chef are about to embark on a historic journey into the dark heart of obesity."

"Very poetic," I said. "I love your spirit. I can already see you'll be an inspiration to people like me who need to take control of our lives."

I noted then for the first time an endearing gesture

that I have since seen repeated a thousand times. When complimented, Charlene turns her face away and reaches out to touch something, in this case Jezebel. She stroked her neck. It's as though a compliment builds up an excess of electricity in her, and she needs to discharge it. "So tell me," I reminded her, "how this whole supper club thing is supposed to work."

"First let me explain the underlying idea. Without that, we don't even get off the ground. One day I was thinking about gambling addicts, and you know what I figured out? It's not gambling that costs them their shirt, not to mention their job and house and car and sweetheart. The problem isn't that they gamble. It's that they lose."

I laughed. Nervously, no doubt. Was she mind-reading again? I had just lost all those things, except my car, such as it was. And I needed to lose that as soon as I could, because its serial number could be incriminating. When that was gone I'd have lost the whole list. Lost it by gambling, too, if you consider that trusting Angela to cut me my fair share of the restaurant was a throw of the dice.

She gave my arm an emphatic squeeze. "Do you see what I mean? If a gambler leaves the casino every night with a pocketful of winnings, is his wife going to say, 'You horrible gamblin' man! I'm leavin' you and takin' the baby!' Hell no. She says, 'Empty them pockets and let's get to countin'.' You can see where I'm going with this."

"I can?"

"Don't play dumb with me, Jake. The problem with fat people isn't that they eat. It's that eating makes them fat."

"And this insight somehow . . ."

"This insight is everything! If you could teach that casino gambler how to beat the house, problem solved. But you can't, because the game is rigged. Same with us. The eating game is rigged against us. Not against everybody. I'm sure you've noticed that. Some people can get supersized and smorgasborded and large pepperoni pizza'd to the gills, and still be no bigger round than a swizzle stick. Nobody says to them, 'How dare you eat a potato chip, you no count sow?' But for us the fix is in."

"True, we're screwed," I said. "It's like a casino where some people get great odds and the rest of us get cleaned out."

"And you know what we're building, Jake?"

I wondered if *we* meant Charlene and me. "A restaurant version of a casino with favorable odds?"

I felt another little squeeze on my arm. "Ooh, I do love people who get it right off."

"So give me the details. You say we'll have dancing girls?"

"We'll have dancing everybody! Listen—it's not complicated. I got the idea one Saturday night when me and some girlfriends went honky-tonking at Zane's, over in Ashland. It was either that or sit at home with my Lean Cuisine chicken carbonara. So I think to myself, *No weight loss today, but sometimes a woman needs to enjoy life.* So what the hell. Girl's night out, and off I go. There's a live band, we're all standing, flouncing and jouncing to the music. I work up a little sweat, and the idea registers with me that what I'm doing isn't only fun, but also aerobic. In fact, I *could* be losing weight, except our table is wall to wall onion blossoms and buffalo wings and barbecued ribs. And all around the room servers are lugging two pitchers of beer at one go, and the smell of pizza is everywhere. So I'm thinking, I could be having this much fun and still be losing weight, if I wasn't surrounded by temptation. That's when it hit me: keep the music and dance and fun, but prohibit the temptation. Sell only healthy food, and set a calorie limit. Cut people off when they reach it. Just like you'd stop a drunk from ordering another whisky. Simple as that."

The more I learned about Charlene's vision, the more fascinated I became. This was revolutionary. What I was hearing was no less than a completely new restaurant format. No existing concept came even close. It was as though I had time-travelled back a hundred years to eavesdrop on Anderson and Ingram as they hatched the fast food hamburger industry. Far greater than that, even. Charlene was not only going to feed people in a new way, she was going to improve their lives. The longer I thought about it, the more I marveled at how fortunate were the residents of Twisting Creek to have in their midst this gloriously innovative and enthusiastic genius, and how fortunate I was to have stumbled upon her at just the right time.

There's more to it than that, though, because she had some pretty good luck herself that evening when Jez and I spotted her sign on a flatbed truck, and decided to heed it. I can say that in all modesty, because when she'd finished describing her plan, I realized that its one weakness lay in the quality of food on offer. She was much more into the entertainment and physical movement side of the club. The bonus I brought to the table *(ha!)* was that I have a philosophy of cooking that plays to exactly the same part of a person's psyche that she was targeting for movement and fun. It's the pleasure center, and it's one thing nature has put there that trumps all the other slaps-in-the-face that life has out there waiting. If your pleasure center is firing, you're happy. A lot of things can propel this energy. Love can do it. Friendship—including a friend of another species. Learning new stuff. Dancing with your sweetheart. Even dancing alone, with earphones, in an otherwise silent room.

And food. Good food triggers immense pleasure—even better, a shared pleasure.

That's what I added to her vision, not solely because I had the skills, but because I know that what people want is a blend of simplicity and complexity that I think of as a melody. That's the key. Temper the complex enough to highlight the simple, while offering enough complexity to keep our attention. Fat people don't have to eat like fat people.

Charlene hadn't quite got a grip on that one. In fact, until I appeared that evening, her idea of a menu would have been a few variations on skinless chicken and a salad. When I wandered in and made it gourmet, we were off and running.

Charlene's premise was brilliant and, like most brilliant ideas, simple. Fat people eat because it's something we are good at. It's often the only physical activity we can do as competently as fit people can. Eating intersperses our commonplace, banal lives with little pleasurable events. How dare anyone ask us to forgo the only fun we're likely to have all day long?

Charlene has the answer: replace it with other fun. Physical fun. Body-based fun. Don't worry if you're not good at it. This nice girl right here wants to dance with you and she doesn't care if you're good at it or not. Because for a three-minute dance, you're going to pay her one dollar.

That was where I came in. I would hire the girls. It was a big responsibility for which I had zero preparation. All the rest of the way to Tim Horton's I mulled over the best way to not screw it up.

Tim Horton's has a few outdoor tables. Charlene looped Jezebel's leash to a chair leg while we went inside to order. I asked for a large vegetable soup with what they called a mini-baguette and a cup of coffee (260 calories) and Charlene decided on a turkey Caesar sandwich on whole wheat, with a Coke Zero. (350 calories).

While we waited, she said, "Just you look at all this other stuff." She swept her hand to indicate one entire wall of display cases filled with maple pecan danish pastries, triple chocolate muffins, cream cheese bagels, and twenty kinds of donuts. And across the room an ice cream parlor. It all looked great. I would have ordered more if I'd been alone. I definitely wanted a strawberry cheese Danish, but I wanted to keep my new job more.

"See," she said. "This is what we're up against. I don't like the odds in this casino."

"It's a rigged game," I said, ripping my eyes from a donut rack drizzled with maple syrup and chocolate sauce.

"Damn right. What you're looking at is what our Supper Club will turn smack dab over on its head. You know what happened with Jesus and the moneychangers?"

"Jesus and the moneychangers. Let me think . . . " I had never really studied much religion. On Sunday mornings when I was growing up my parents would send me off to church, but I'm pretty sure it was mainly because they wanted to have sex in an empty house. And there was a playground between our house and the church, which served the same purpose, as far as my parents were concerned. I had no idea who Jesus and the moneychangers were, unless it was a ring of Mexican counterfeiters, so I made a joke. "Wasn't that where he took francs and marks and everything and made them a single currency? They call it the Eurozone miracle."

She almost spilled her drink. "No, you heathen! He turned the tables on them! That's what we're going to do."

Then she explained the whole setup to me. First of all, it's a club. It doesn't cost anything to join, but you have to be a member. The application form includes a pledge that you are serious about losing weight, and warns you that you will be weighed every time you come in, and that your weight gain or loss will be announced publicly to the crowd, and displayed on a bulletin board. The club is only open in the evenings, so it's entirely possible that people could overeat all day and still come in for an extra six hundred calories, thus never losing an ounce. For that reason every member who comes in must sign an affirmation that they've consumed no more than nine hundred calories so far that day.

Guests of members are allowed. If a member brings an

overweight guest to sample the proceedings, that guest must affirm that even then they're under nine hundred calories for the day. If they're not, they are told to come back another day when they meet that requirement, when they will be welcomed with open arms.

Guests who are not overweight don't have to sign the pledge, but they must stick to the six hundred calories limit just like everybody else.

The essence of the Club is not simply that nobody at the next table is eating coconut cream pie. It's not even as simple as we're all in this together. It's that we're all absorbed in something else, without the distraction, or even the possibility, of overeating. That something else almost always involves moving the body.

Every evening there's dancing. Often the music is live. People around here have a proud musical tradition, so there is no shortage of local bands playing everything from bluegrass to rockabilly to country to straight rock and roll. Friday night is karaoke night. There's even a polka band that comes down from Cincinnati once a month and provides a great show. Sometimes we have square dancing. Down here it's still not a gay thing, although, now that I mention it, the two guys who serve as instructors are a same-sex couple.

It doesn't have to be dance music. Twisting Creek is home to Franklin College, which has a Fine Arts Department. Quite often a student there will come to Big's to perform a violin or piano recital, or some singers will entertain us with opera arias, or show tunes. We'll all sit quietly and enjoy the show, in the reassuring certainty that nobody in the room is polishing off a bacon and cheese sizzler, and that every honest person there will arrive home thinner than they were that morning.

This was the vision that Charlene outlined for me on my first evening in Twisting Creek, and it's worked out more or less as she predicted. We've had some refinements, of course.

We started out charging a cover, but soon realized we didn't need to do that. It only kept out some people who might need help. There's no minimum, either. Nothing on the menu is free, but a cup of that watery coffee people around here seem to prefer is only a dollar. (We also sell good coffee, but not for a dollar.) People are encouraged to eat something, if only because it's hard to enjoy yourself when you're hungry, but it's not required. And Charlene insists that a bargain item is included on every menu, usually an omelet and a salad, or some sort of bean dish. A bowl of our vegetarian three-bean chili (170 calories) has nine grams of protein, nine grams of fiber, and loads of lycopene. The secret here is to drop about a four-inch strip of kombu into each pot. Kombu breaks down the raffinose sugars, and that eliminates most of the gas and makes it easier for us to absorb the nutrients. We sell it with a simple garden salad (5g protein, 7g fiber, 75 calories) for $4.95.

Guests don't have to hire a dancer. They can dance with each other, of course. We've had several romances begin right there on our dance floor.

It was my idea to post a "total pounds lost" board outside, our pitiful negation of McDonald's "Over a billion sold." When we hit the one thousand mark, Yolanda Shanley—that long, low sigh of a woman I was telling you about, the one Victor and I both had a little fling with—she came in and did a story about it for the Guardian, which got picked up nationally. It was a big deal for a while. That's why now we have customers—regulars—who drive in from as far away as Huntington, Lexington, and Cincinnati. Some of these guys will stay until our weekend closing time of eleven o'clock, and not want to drive home that late, so local motels get a bump in business. This is solely due to Charlene's vision and my cooking.

Our biggest wrangle was over alcohol. I said that a glass of wine was necessary to turn a fine meal into a work of art, and a five ounce glass contains only about one hundred calories. Plus it's good for you. But Charlene contends that even one glass of wine lowers inhibitions and makes it more difficult to refuse extra food. Her position—which prevailed, of course—was that it's our job to make losing weight easier, not harder. Also she wanted the church crowd to feel comfortable there, and comfortable to bring their kids in. Banning alcohol solved a lot of legal and regulatory issues, too.

We noticed some surprising turns, as well. For one, women members outnumber men by about sixty-forty. We hadn't predicted that. Also, we have no dress code, yet soon we realized that people were dressing up a little. Was that because a "supper club" sounded classy? Because they knew they might be dancing with strangers?

We started seeing overweight teenagers. Both Charlene and I thought teenagers of any girth would avoid a place that mainly featured old fat people, but we were wrong. We get college students, high school students. We get many of our best workers from this group—prep cooks, bussers and servers. We intentionally overstaff so that all the workers can remove their aprons and have a turn on the dance floor. It seems everybody from the dishwashers to Trusty Rusty shares Charlene's mission of creating lively, rejuvenated customers. There's no sight on earth more heartwarming than an overweight teenage boy coaxing an overweight old lady onto the dance floor. And it's difficult to know who's enjoying it more, the lady, the boy, or Charlene and me, watching from the wings.

And how about those taxi dancers? That's what you're waiting for, right? I know it occupied my own fantasies at the time and I'll bet it does yours too.

10

I APOLOGIZE FOR the abrupt breakaway, but right at that point big things started happening. The biggest of the big things is that I'm out of jail. I'm free!

This whole evening has been an incredible series of events, starting about an hour after Lonnie Farley left the jail and ending just now, at 10:15 pm, when Victor drove me home.

Home! What a wonderful word that is! Just say it aloud and hold it. It's like one of those Hindu mantras that lift you onto a higher plane.

Even better, Charlene won't get home from Big's for another couple of hours. Victor offered to drive me there, but do you know why I chose to come straight home? Because it gives me a nice little time alone with you.

I've realized something. I started this diary to help me cope with prison. Remember, it was only at lunch yesterday— *yesterday!*—when Charlene told me her news, and made my life complete. Yet only a few hours later, out there on the porch, while Jezebel slept by the front door, and the Reds-Giants game moved to the seventh inning, I lost it all. Everything. Every single thing in my entire life that gave it any meaning at all—gone in the time it took for a bullet to miss my dog.

I imagined the worst. I imagined I would never get out again, or that even with parole I could never be a living part of your life. What I learned from my split with Angela is that even dewy-eyed optimists can get blindsided by worst-case scenarios. It's true. Things can go shit-hole in a hurry, and once you learn that, you can never forget it, not deep down. And last night, for me, there it was again. Do you see what I mean? I'm sitting there on the porch swing when *wham!* Out of nowhere cops are trying to shoot Jezebel and I'm in jail, a possible death row candidate.

Even worse things than that are possible, and they're impossible to ignore. Things go wrong in childbirth. Charlene is late having her first, and even in modern hospitals not every new mother survives. And what about her previous obesity? Does that make it more dangerous for her?

Are you beginning to understand? Under those circumstances, this account might have been all you really knew of me, or even of both Charlene and me. That's what gave it impetus. However, now that my life is back to normal, this journal means something different to me. It's as though you and I are hanging out together. Already you and Charlene are together every minute of every day—literally together. You couldn't get any more together. Why should I have to wait until spring to meet you? By asking Victor to drop me here instead of at the club, I have two hours alone with you, and believe me, we'll need every minute of it to give this extraordinary day its due.

The day ended almost one-hundred percent upbeat. I'll get to the "almost" part soon, but let's not dwell on it. It's probably nothing.

As I say, Lonnie Farley had been gone maybe an hour. There I was, still in my prison cell, writing to you about Tim Horton's and taxi dancers, when I heard sounds from down at street level. Even that far away and through that thick window, it snagged my attention. It sounded like someone speaking through a bullhorn, but I couldn't make out the words. I positioned my chair under the window and climbed up to peer down at whatever slice of the street I could see. I saw part of a crowd facing a speaker, who was beyond my line of sight. My first guess was that they were strikers or other demonstrators gathered there for some purpose unconnected with me, but then it came to me as a flash of insight, a dead certain revelation, that Lonnie had rounded up his evangelicals.

I saw a police patrol car drive up with its lights flashing, but no siren. Some of the crowd turned in that direction. Victor exited the passenger side and moved toward them. He was wearing a suit and tie instead of his uniform. He held his hands up in a calming gesture. He walked out of sight and seemed to take the bullhorn. I say that because I heard a different voice come through, even though I still couldn't understand the message.

Maybe five minutes later, I was still perched up there, still trying to make sense of it, when Victor's chuckle directly behind me startled the crap out of me. I almost slipped off that chair back.

Victor said, "You don't have to break out that way. Use the front door just like white folks."

I'm tempted to say that in some grand gesture he flung the door open wide, but he's too calm for that. He did help me gather up my few things, and even put an arm around my shoulder. "Let's get you out of here. We need your help."

On the way downstairs he informed me that every contact number and email address I'd given him for Angela and *Le Plat Nourrissant* was a dead end. The website had disappeared. He'd phoned NYPD for help on their end, and expected to hear something soon.

"I hear they were dragging the lake."

"There was nothing. I didn't really think there would be. Anyway, it was only practicable to drag the swimming area."

"So what's next?"

"Would you mind accompanying me to her cabin? You might spot something that sheds light on the missing woman's identity."

Of course I agreed, and suggested we swing by the house to pick up Jezebel. He said there was no need of that because she was right outside. He asked if I would say a few calming words to the people waiting outside the station.

I got to the big glass exit doors and stopped in my tracks. I saw a group of a hundred or more people there, some holding signs with words of encouragement. They broke into applause when they saw me exit.

I can't even begin to describe how my emotions started roaring around in my head. Tears came to my eyes. I'd never before had such a show of support in a time of need. I'd never addressed a crowd, never had an audience, much less one that had gathered to confront authorities on my behalf.

I looked around and saw Jezebel running toward me. Ever the showboat, she didn't jump up against me, but did her circle dance. She acknowledged the applause of the crowd by sitting on her haunches and offering a brief melody. Charlene walked toward me, carrying that bullhorn. I gave her a shy hug and took it. I'd never used one before. She whispered, "Just squeeze this little red trigger and talk normally."

I collected my wits while I looked over the crowd. I recognized almost every face there. It wasn't Lonnie's crowd at all. It was club workers and club members. (So much for dead certain flashes of insight and revelation.) I let my gaze wander around the gathering, stopping at any random face, and again and again there was somebody I knew precisely how much weight they'd lost since they'd joined Big's. I could tell you to the pound.

I said, "I don't know what to say. Honestly, I'm at a loss for words. Thank you all for this overwhelming show of support. I should tell you that the sheriff says I was never under any suspicion. He's asked me to take an active part in the investigation. A tragedy may have occurred to a visitor to our community, and every one of us will help where we can."

I tried to end with something humorous, saying tomorrow night's special will be a large pepperoni pizza and a pitcher of Bluegrass Pale Ale, on the house. Of course Charlene gave me a dope slap, took the loudspeaker, and said, "He's so full of it. Let's put him back in the slammer." I gave her a longer hug, and told her I was going with Victor to the lake cabins.

Jezebel bounded eagerly into the back seat of Victor's cruiser for the ride out to the lake. She likes car rides, especially in big muscle cars. And trucks. She likes riding in truck beds. Her thrill-of-the-day came when Victor hit the siren. She enjoys sirens anyway, likes the way her voice complements them melodically. This one took her by surprise. To her a moving siren always shifted in loudness, and in pitch from high to low or low to high. The Doppler effect, she got that part. She'd been evolved for it. But being at the very epicenter was novel and pretty damn cool. She looked left and right a few times until she gathered her wits and started to sing.

Along the way Victor seemed to want to apologize for his deputies' overreaction, and did apologize for the show of guns, but stopped short of a blanket apology, admitting simply that he didn't know a better way of handling the case. I told him not to worry about it. It was a tough call.

"Very tough," he agreed. "You know, that's the big drawback of my job. We never truly know that what we're doing is the right thing. We make an arrest. Of course they say they're innocent. They all do. We learn to completely ignore that. But you know what? It might be true."

"It was in my case."

"Like I say. And when that happens, what have we done? Deprived an innocent person of their freedom. You weren't under arrest and you only lost a day, but still."

His tone worried me. The sheriff always seems to be fighting off a tendency toward self-doubt. It's as though his spirit lacks buoyancy. It feels the pull of gravity more than most. He's a big man, three or four inches taller than me. He's got the shoulders of a linebacker, and his wide-brimmed sheriff's hat makes his already large head seem enormous. That, plus the deliberate way he moves and speaks, adds to the aura of heaviness surrounding him.

I know some of his life story. I know that Shelley, his wife, is white. In fact, I know her fairly well, socially. I also know that a few years ago she divorced him for a crew member of some movie they filmed here. She took their daughter, moved to California, and married that guy, only later to divorce him and return to Victor when he became sheriff. And when, I suppose, Hollywood dreaming didn't work out. So he married her again.

Such forbearance is part of Victor's charm, but I didn't think it was my place to be his father confessor, so I tried to lighten the mood. "If you ever need to take a break from police work, that offer of bussing tables still stands."

He ignored my quip. "There is no more precious right in this life than freedom. I'm a black man in an ex-slave state. Most of my ancestors were tobacco farm slaves. Did you know that slavery lasted longer in Kentucky than in the Deep South?"

I thought it was a rhetorical question, but he looked around at me. "Um, no. I guess I've never really thought about it."

"Lincoln's Emancipation Proclamation didn't apply here, because Kentucky hadn't left the Union. We had to wait for the Thirteenth Amendment, two years later. So I don't take freedom lightly. Yet my job is to take it away from people."

"Just those who don't deserve it."

"That's what I'm saying, Jake. You almost never know for absolute certain who deserves it and who doesn't. If you're not caught in the act, modern transportation makes fleeing so fast and easy that a criminal could be almost anywhere in no time at all."

"I see your point." I was simply keeping the conversation going. I had no idea we were moving into that part of the evening I mentioned—the only part that makes me a little nervous.

He said, "What I'd love just once in my career is a murder with a limited universe of suspects. Like in some secluded manor house, on a snowy night when the roads are impassable and telecoms are down. Eight or ten possible killers, no more. All on site."

"Twisting Creek doesn't even have a manor house."

"Back there's my only hope." He used a thumb to point toward my window, so I looked out through it. We were passing the long, tree-lined drive of the grand old Ratliffe mansion, built almost two hundred years ago by the first tobacco baron of Buford County. More accurately, built by his slaves.

Oh, shit. I just had a thought. How did we happen to be precisely on this stretch of road at this point of the conversation? Had Victor calculated this in advance?

I didn't think of that at the time. I was still trying to make light banter. "There are still Ratliffes living there. Maybe you'll get lucky and they'll start killing each other."

He pretended to think it over. "I could drop in occasionally and stir up trouble."

"Maybe they killed Angela. This could be your lucky day."

"Naw, we need a snowstorm. The killer could be in Australia by now." I guess he chose Australia because it's as far from Twisting Creek as any place on earth. "Seriously, Jake. Think about it. Think about how endless the search possibilities are. Take yourself for instance. Suppose you were suspected of committing a crime the very day you left New York, and NYPD made a list of every place on earth that needed to be searched. How far down their list would Twisting Creek be?" Again he looked around to check my reaction. "See what we're up against?"

I didn't answer a word to that, and not much else was said during the rest of the drive to the lake.

Oh—I asked him about the possibility that Angela committed suicide, and he told me that the first officer on the scene thought maybe that was it, because he found an empty pill box by her bed. But Victor doubts this theory. In his opinion very few missing persons are in fact suicides, for the simple reason that suicides usually want the people they leave behind to feel guilty, so they leave a note, or find some other way to make it clear they killed themselves. Those who kill themselves to provide insurance money for their loved ones have to set it up to look like an accident. The last thing they want is an inconclusive case.

"Angela had no loved ones to worry about. Plus she owned a profitable restaurant."

Victor shrugged. "Maybe she didn't. It seems to be missing too." Then without even turning to look at my reaction he asked, "Why do you refer to her in the past tense?"

Jesus! Was I shocked! But I recovered—adroitly, if I do say so. "She's been past tense for me for nearly three years."

He permitted himself a half-smile. "I had a wife like that once. Then my past tense became my present tense all over again." He was cracking a joke. God, was I relieved!

"Not to mention your future tense," I said, and that's where we left it. I almost said, *Past pluperfect subjunctive*, but it's an old joke, not even very funny.

To reach the cabins, you drive New Lake Road down the hill, almost to water's edge, then turn left onto a gravel road that curves away from the lake, through a stand of evergreens, and then back toward the lake again, where a wide, unobstructed private beach has been created. I'd been out here before, so these "cabins" were no surprise to me. They're more like resort cottages. They're still not the kind of place Angela would ever dream of visiting, but they're not primitive shanties. They have mod-cons with all the trimmings, and those beamed ceilings and knotty pine walls that people here consider the height of home décor. In fact, our basement den on Dogwood has a similar interior.

We passed all the other cabins. Angela's was the one on the far end. According to the desk clerk, she'd requested it "for privacy." I told Victor, "I hope you're checking him out, and the other people who work here," but he only lifted his eyebrows in what I took to mean a polite, *Of course.*

We spotted her cabin from a distance. It was roped off by yellow police barrier tape. I asked, "So do you consider this an official crime scene?"

"No, not yet. It's in a gray area. To be honest, if it was just some local guy's wife run off for a couple of days, we might not be making such a big deal out of it. But with a tourist . . . " He didn't finish the sentence.

Now I noticed a car parked out back, a silver Malibu. "I never knew her to have a car. In the city, smart people don't."

"A rental," he said. "Virginia plates."

A sheriff's deputy in uniform sat fishing at the end of a wooden pier. He jumped up when he noticed us, and hustled toward the drive.

"Nobody been around here all day, sir. I had a clear view from that spot." He pointed to the end of the pier.

"Clear view of them big bass," Victor said. He raised his eyebrows at me and started for the cottage.

For now we left Jezebel with the deputy outside, while Victor and I walked up the split log stairs to the front porch. I stepped into a cabin without a hint of disarray, and I felt my heart jump. Even before I opened the bedroom door, I knew what I'd find there: Angela's silk pajamas, neatly folded on the bed, the left side. Her side. Silk ballerina house slippers carefully paired on the floor. On her nightstand, an empty glass and an antique pill box with a fat, pink cherub on the cover. And beside that—me. Furiously serving a tennis ball. If this wasn't Angela's bedroom, it was some sick copycat version. Or somebody who'd been coached.

"Look familiar?"

"Yes. My god. It certainly does. But still, it can't be her. Of all the vacation spots in the world, why would she come here?"

"Evidently because you're here."

"But you say she was here for three days before she went missing. Why didn't she contact me? And how would she even know I was here? I sure didn't tell her. I never wanted to see her again."

"So you had bad blood between you?"

"Bad blood? She fired me and dumped me. She cut me out of my fair share of the restaurant. Is that bad blood?"

"Bad enough for some to want to take revenge."

I wanted to say, *Shit Victor! I did take revenge. Third degree larceny revenge.* My god, I wish we lived in a world where I could have said that, and we could have rolled around laughing on the little cabin floor. All I could say, though, was, "Not my style." Then I thought to ask, "Do you still consider me a suspect?"

He dismissed that with a wave of his hand, and I felt better.

He said, "Let me explain how the suicide theory works. The woman is depressed. She can't sleep. She swallows the last of her pills, but that doesn't help. Maybe she even tries to overdose, but wakes up the next morning anyway, surprised to be alive. She still wants to die. She removes her pajamas, walks out the door and down the pier, and steps off into the water."

"But you already dragged the nearby lake and found nothing."

"I'm saying, it's one hypothesis."

"Why the water?"

"Our bloodhound followed a scent to the end of the pier."

"How did it pick up the scent?"

"Starting from the bed."

"But of course she walked the length of the pier. Whoever stayed here would do that."

"There's a possibility it was an old trail."

"Sure it was. And why would she come to Twisting Creek?"

"To punish you for something?"

"Hey, she's the one who dumped me."

"Maybe in her mind you caused the breakup. Maybe her restaurant business took a nosedive when you left."

"Then where's the note? You said . . . "

"Maybe there's a message but you haven't got it yet. It could be in the mail, or an ad in the paper." He seemed to be thinking this through as he spoke. He took out his note pad and wrote something.

I said, "Here's why that theory is wrong. First of all, it wasn't morning. It was evening. She always laid out her pajamas before she went to bed. Laid them out just like that. She always took one sleeping pill at bedtime, with a full glass of water."

"It really doesn't matter, morning or night."

"Oh, yes it does. She wouldn't be swimming at night. She was terrified of dark water. And even if she wanted to kill herself, she wouldn't do it by drowning. She was a strong swimmer. She was a real jock. Forget drowning. Forget suicide."

Victor paused to look over the room. "Yeah, I don't buy it either. I just wanted to hear what you thought."

"Here's what I think. It's a frame. She wanted to punish me for . . . as you say, for the failure of the restaurant. It's true that she was the owner, but I was the reason people came in and paid top dollar. So she somehow managed to stage her disappearance in order to incriminate me. To cause me to go through exactly what I'm going through now. Her cunning little plan is working."

"It would be a criminal act."

"Then let's catch her criminal ass." Then it came to me! YES! That's the way to extricate myself from both crimes. We nail her for stalking and harassment, but I don't press charges, in exchange for her dropping the larceny charge. See why I say I've had a great day?

Victor said, "It still could be some hired stand-in. Let's find out what Jezebel knows."

She bounded through the yard, still thinking, I suppose, that we were on an outing to the lake; thinking, if I know her, that those ducks on the water would benefit greatly from a big dog swimming behind them. But something went wrong when she reached the door, and in the bedroom she lost all sense of play. She whined and started sniffing the bed. She jumped up on it. She didn't even look to me for permission, just went for it. She placed her nose directly against the coverlet on Angela's side. She buried her nose in the pajamas, then looked around the room for me. I saw worry in her eyes. She was asking, *This lost smell of a lost woman from a lost life—what can it mean?*

I squatted and clapped my hands. She rushed to me and pressed her face as hard as she could into my shoulder. It's her stance of highest emotion. At times it means she can hardly bear to be so happy. It can mean she's absolutely mortified about that garbage on the kitchen floor. It can mean almost anything that overwhelms her. This time it meant, *I don't want things to change ever again.*

I stroked her neck. "Don't you worry, puppy. Everything is going to be just fine."

Victor didn't need to ask. We knew now, beyond all doubt, that the missing Angela was my Angela. He said, "Maybe Jezebel can pick up the trail."

"Good idea." I held Angela's pajamas under her nose. "Where is she? Where's Angie, girl? Find Angie."

She bounded onto the bed again, as though to double

check, jumped back down to look under the bed, then began sweeping the room in wider and wider swaths, with her nose almost dragging the floor. I held the door open for her as she expanded the hunt down the steps and into the gravel parking lot. Her tail was high, flicking like a machine. When she reached the grass border, the tail slowed, and sagged. She made forays into the grass but kept returning to the gravel, her nose always to the ground.

Victor said to try the pier, so I called her over that way and pointed down its length. She trotted down the full length and gave the ladder a perfunctory pass before rejecting it. She hurried back, past the Malibu to the empty parking place, and made a few frenzied passes before stopping dead still and looking up at me. Her eyes said, *Here I lose her.*

I sat down on the edge of the porch and patted the floor. She jumped up beside me and laid her head in my lap so I could give her fine face a rub.

Victor sat down on my other side. "Seems to me she's telling us that our missing lady left in somebody's car."

"Seems that way."

"Could have been a taxi," he said, and wrote something on the notepad he kept in a shirt pocket.

I said, "Here's one thing though—Angela wouldn't go anywhere without her phone. Did she leave one behind?"

"It's in the drawer of her nightstand."

"Can I see it?" I asked.

"Wait here."

When he returned he had three plastic bags of evidence from the nightstand: the Victorian pill box, the empty glass, and her iPhone.

I recognized it immediately. It still had her fanciful rainbow-patterned silicon case. I told Victor, "That settles it. She's been abducted."

"You're sure?"

"Angela did not leave here in a taxi. You can check with the taxi company, but they won't know anything. She's been taken against her will. I'm sure of it."

"How can you be so certain? There are no signs of a struggle."

"I'm certain because I know her. That phone was like an appendage. She would never willingly leave it behind. She thought of her phone just as I think of this mutt." Jez closed her eyes while I stroked the soft hair under her neck.

"Then somebody's either holding her against her will, or killed her."

It was overload. We stopped speaking for a while. Under different circumstances this could have been an idyllic spot. A refreshing land breeze had replaced some of the humidity with cooler air from the evergreens behind us. The lake air now smelled of pine. I noticed for the first time that the park had erected a bird feeder in the front yard, surrounded by a mounded flower bed. I couldn't believe I'd missed it earlier, but now that I focused my attention on it, I saw that the reds were crimson, the yellows golden. The butterflies were livelier and more satiny. The aroma did not evoke funeral parlors, but summer mornings at my grandparents' house. All this against the blue lake and the sun starting its slide down into it. If my short stay in jail did nothing more than prepare the ground for those moments of exaggerated perception, it was time well spent.

I watched a yellow warbler land on the feeder. Jezebel's ears flinched at its liquid trill, but I kept stroking her neck and she kept her eyes closed. She'd had a traumatic few minutes.

Now the deputy came up and sat beside Victor, who asked him, "How's the fishing?"

"Look, Sheriff, I really never took an eye off this place all day long."

"I don't doubt it. I know you don't have to watch the

bobber the whole time you're fishing. I'm more interested in what's for supper."

"Oh. White bass. Pan-fried, I guess."

It's funny how you think of one thing when you're trying to think about something else entirely. My mind had already started to look through its files for white bass recipes. In fact, the very word in my head at that moment was *cornmeal*. But then I had a thought. "Wait a second. Didn't Apple bring out a new iPhone last year?"

Victor's eyebrows pinched together. "Seems like maybe they did."

"Yes, I think so too. And if so, Angela bought one the minute it went on sale."

"How do you know that?"

"Because I know Angela. It would have been an event. The release date would have been marked on the kitchen calendar. She would have paid one of the waiters to stand in line for her."

"Well, if that's true . . . "

"It means she planted this old phone in her nightstand in order to mislead us. There could be no other reason. It means she's having some fun. Criminal fun."

"It's worse than criminal," Victor said. "It's starting to piss me off."

11

I JUST GOT a call from Yolanda Shanley—she's the local
reporter I mentioned before, the woman I almost had a little
romance with soon after I arrived in Twisting Creek. She asks
if she can meet me here at the restaurant within the hour. I
suppose that means she wants to do a story on my big prison
ordeal for tomorrow's newspaper. This is going to turn out to
be great publicity.

I'm laughing my ass off. Why? Because I'm such a goose!
Angela used to call me a panic-manic, and I can't really argue
with that. It seems I overreact on both ends. Either everything
is wonderful, or the whole world's in free fall. Are you a little
like that? If so, you got it from me. If you're more balanced,
you got it from Charlene.

From just past midnight yesterday morning until about
five o'clock yesterday evening, the panic part held my brain
by the balls. There I sat in jail, thinking I'd better hurry up
with my prison memoirs so you would have some idea who
your father was before he got himself executed. Yet now look
at me. It's one day later and I'm back at Big's, sitting at my
favorite work station—a corner two-top table facing the
shining dance floor, across from the row of chairs where our
dancers sit. We're still a couple of hours from opening, so the
dance floor is empty. The dancers' chairs are empty too, except
for Fumiko's hat and bag. She always gets here early. She says
she wants to learn everything she possibly can while she's in
America, so she often turns up long before opening time and

helps out in the kitchen. Today she swung by my table to give me a big welcome-back hug. In fact, before that she gave me a formal Japanese bow. I guess in her country getting out of prison merits one.

Fumiko is such a doll. She and her little Asian gang are all students at Franklin College, and they are the heart and soul of our taxi dancers. There are five of them altogether, no two from the same country. They tell me that's by design, because they came to America to learn English and with each other they can't use their own language. They were already an established study group, and, I think it's fair to say, good friends. Then Fumiko spotted our ad in the Guardian, and they pounced on it.

In addition to the Japanese Fumiko, there's Shulin from China, Laneth from the Philippines, Jai from Thailand, and Minh, from Vietnam. Those five girls all showed up together the first week we posted job openings—to be precise, it was my ninth day in town—and without my Asian mafia I can't honestly assure you that Big's would have enjoyed its runaway success. Their infectious cheer on the dance floor sets the tone for the entire enterprise. I'll tell you about all of that right now in a minute. First let me set the scene. By this time of day you can usually find me right here, with my laptop, and with my little yellow menu notes scattered out. Eventually Fumiko will bring me a square of dark chocolate and an espresso. I don't even have to request it. I just look up, and there she is, with her deceptively shy smile. We always finish with a ritual. I say, *Arigato*, as she has taught me. She smiles, and says, *No*.

According to her, where we would say *You're welcome*, Japanese people typically say the word that literally means *no*. So every time I say *Arigato*, she says *No*. It's an inside joke she never tires of. Then, with a quick bow, a sort of abbreviated curtsy, she hurries away.

She runs everywhere. I don't think I've ever seen her walk.

I love to sit back, sip my coffee, and watch her dart through the double doors into the kitchen. And I love the moments that follow, when I survey the polished maple emptiness in front of me, so soon to burst with life, happiness and hope.

Kitchen sounds and smells reach me through the great serving window, but right now I can't see anyone back there. Jezebel is lying on the floor beside me with her eyes closed and her chin resting on her front paws. She's not asleep. She may be trying to sleep, but her ears twitch with every sound from the kitchen, and her nostrils flare at something. Personally, all I can smell is garlic, onions, and coriander in the chopper. Sometimes I wonder whether Jez recognizes how little I use my nose. I've read that a dog's nose is ten thousand times better than ours. She probably considers me nose blind. I expect she feels sorry for me. Likely she considers herself my guide dog.

I can hear my prep cooks hard at work, especially Orlando on salad station, practicing the spicy Thai papaya salad I taught him. It takes practice because you have to put shredded green papaya into a clay mortar, only a serving or two at a time, and bruise it just right with a pestle. My idea is that if we omit the peanuts we'll save both cals and carbs. We can add some chopped arugula for that nutty flavor. And if we substitute salt and a squeeze of lemon for the fish sauce we can list it as a vegetarian selection. Some of our teenage girls are asking for more of those, and this should be a nice addition to our menu. It won't be real Thai *som tam*, but it will be flavorful, especially since our back yard garden now produces both the arugula and the little Thai peppers they call mouse turds. We'll list it as Piquant Papaya Salad. (85 calories)

I can't believe how thrilling it is to be back at work. Only one day away and I could almost weep to be back where I belong! That means it wasn't the time away that matters, but the perception of permanent dislocation. So much of what is in our heart comes from how we envision the future. Does everybody else already know that? Why was I so late to catch on?

In the space of one day I went from chef, to brand new prospective father, to murder suspect, to amateur detective, then back again to chef. My attitude now is that my direct involvement in the Van Landingham case has ended. If something new comes to light and Victor needs my help, of course I'll be happy to provide it, but now at last I can turn my attention away from this extraneous business and concentrate on filling you in on the real story of these past three years: starting Big's and finding my true soulmate.

You know, my plan here is not at all to advise you on life's great questions, and I will not fall into that trap. (Of course when I say that, you know what's coming next is the exact opposite.)

With me not "on ice" anymore—yes, that's what it means—I can hand these memoirs over to you when we dump you at your college dorm, and you'll be just the age for one or two little gems of wisdom on the subjects of love, and business.

As for love, I don't believe in the term I just used, "soulmate." It makes it sound like there's only one such person in all the world, when in fact there are tons of wonderful people out there and I suspect we meet many potential soulmates along the way. Unfortunately our tendency is to try to lay claim to as many of them as we can. Then we lose the one we had. My advice to you is to find one and stick to him or her. That way you can share all the stages of life, from whenever you meet, right through middle age and then retirement and infirmity. You'll share more memories, have more to laugh about. It'll be more fun, and deeper fun. The kind of fun that goes straight to your heart.

As for all those other "soulmates" you can't have, I think there should be a separate category for special people we could have loved and cherished all our lives, except we already had one person to love and cherish, and one is the optimum number. I don't know of a word for that separate category, but there must be one in some language. (I'll research it between now and when you head off to college.)

One more piece of advice and then I promise I'll stop. This time about business. Of course I have no idea what you'd like to do with your life, or even if Big's will exist in twenty years, but, judging from our early success, Charlene and I might possibly have created a successful business model that can expand and expand and keep expanding into every city and town in this country where people are overweight. Which means, everywhere. We could franchise this thing, see? We don't have any such plans just yet, but we've got great press all over the region, and a venture capital group from Cincinnati has already made an inquiry. What if by the time you're old enough to tackle a career, Kentucky's most famous exports aren't tobacco, bourbon whisky and fast-food chicken, but Big Charlene's Supper Clubs, where people eat great food, hear great music, dance like monkeys, and turn their lives around?

If that happens, and it all falls to you, and maybe to your siblings, my advice is: don't get too rich. Keep your prices low enough that everybody can feel welcome in your clubs. Make enough profit to keep yourself solidly middle class, but be content with that. In my view, for anybody with an American middle class standard of living, if they're still unhappy, more money won't fix it. They need to look elsewhere for the solution.

That's it for the sermon. Now I want to tell you about the start-up of the club.

My first three nights in Twisting Creek, I stayed at the Days Inn just off the Interstate, and during that time workers partitioned off and furnished a section of the gym area for me to use as a temporary bedroom. Living on the premises allowed me constant oversight of the kitchen installation. It also allowed me to ditch that awful pink Neon. I sold that thing for scrap the minute I could. A junk dealer paid me two hundred for it, and off it went on its journey to recycled reincarnation. I'll never forget the conversation with the junk dealer.

He asked me, "Whoncheeselitstidajunkinit?"

At first I thought the guy was Ukrainian or something. "I'm sorry?" I said.

"What fur?" he asked.

"Huh?

"Whachee sorry fur?"

"I mean I didn't understand your question."

He repeated, "Whoncheeselitstidajunkinit?" Which I eventually worked out meant, *Why don't you sell it instead of junking it?*

I told him, "I wouldn't sell that monstrosity to my worst enemy."

"Say whut?"

I rephrased it for him, "Because it's a piece of shit."

"Yeaeezangshoresuk."

I got the cash and walked away, puzzling it out piece by piece until I came up with, *Yeah, these things sure suck.* I realized that if I was going to stick around these parts I was going to have to install a sort of Google Translator in my head.

With my potentially incriminating car safely on its way to the crusher, I began to prepare for the opening of Big's. My early duties were divided into three categories: overseeing work on the kitchen, preparing menus, with calorie and fructose content, and interviewing women as taxi dancers. The first two tasks were pure pleasure, but that last one stressed me no end. See, I knew that if even one of my hires turned out to be a temptress prepared to use what the Good Lord gave her to vamp money off fat men, then I could destroy the whole dream. One bad decision here and we're finished before we start. Even if she only had the look of a seductress, or only the suspicion of it, we were sunk. I needed prim, pure, vestal virgins who were nonetheless perfectly willing to dance with fat men for money. They needed to be attractive and insistent enough to entice shy men onto the dance floor, but too wholesome to encourage more. If I could have found a willing group of good-looking nuns with nice legs and nimble feet, I'd have hired the whole convent.

We placed an ad in the Guardian, and I must admit that my first attempt was so poorly worded that the initial applicants seemed to think they were responding to "Wanted: Hookers. Crack whores with skank tats preferred. Swollen faces and cigarette burns optional." One woman with a big haystack of blond hair said, "I'm the hottest dancer in town and I'll prove it. Sit down." So I sat down. She sat down in my lap.

12

SORRY AGAIN—UNSETTLING INTERRUPTION. I still can't quite get my head around what just happened. I was totally unprepared for it.

Right at that point Victor came in and walked as fast as I've ever seen him walk, straight to my table, and sat down. He said, "What bothers me about this whole case is . . . "

"And good afternoon to you, too, Victor," I said, trying to be funny. I was still in a good mood from thinking about my lap dancer.

He didn't respond to that. Jezebel stopped pretending to be asleep, stood up, and eased away from him. She had always loved Victor, but, after the gunshots in our front yard, still had her doubts about him. He leaned down and scratched behind her ear. She seemed to interpret this as an apology, and pinned her eyes back to signal forgiveness. She flattened her ears when he squatted in front of her, and let him stroke her nose.

Then he looked up at me. "Don't you agree? There's something out of kilter here."

"Like what, exactly?"

With my foot I scooted a chair out for him. He groaned when he sat down, like an old man, with a hand on each knee, but said nothing. He couldn't find a phrase to describe what it was. To me, if someone can't put it in words, it means it's a feeling rather than something they've thought out. It was unusual to watch this man striving to retrieve a feeling. That had to indicate something in his past, maybe as far back as childhood. I know this for sure, not because I'm insightful and wise, but because of his next sentence:

"It reminds me of being with my grandmother."

Strange sentence. But, sadly, he explained it. And therein lies the great twist.

"My grandmother is small, with a ball of shining white hair. If she sits facing away from you it looks like a bright full moon stuck there on top of her neck. She and her friends make each other's clothes, so you can imagine what they all look like. She didn't get a great education, and her eyesight is troublesome. Oh, and she smiles all the time. On sunny afternoons she'll doze off on a park bench, and smile in her sleep. So all this, plus her being black, together it makes a lot of white people speak to her as if she's slow-witted. They talk slower than usual, and plainer. They take on an accent that's more old-timey, more like everybody had, back before schools came to this part of the state. My grandmother doesn't seem to mind such condescension, but she notices it. I think that's as far as it gets with her. She notices it. I've asked her about it, even as a tiny child. How come they talk funny to you? All she would ever say was, They only just tryin' to be helpful."

I said, "Victor, I know you've got a point in there somewhere."

"They thought she was slower than they were, so they made it easy for her. This case reminds me of that. Don't you see it yet? They think I'm slower than they are, so they're making it easy for me. We found your fingerprints on a drinking glass in Angela Van Landingham's bedroom. Did I tell you that?"

I was too stunned to say anything. I thought he was joking. I actually took it lightly. I didn't even think to say exactly what you've probably already figured out—that it was a standard water glass like you see in every motel bathroom in America, and the very same style we use at Big's. I had one on the table in front of me. Fumiko had brought it with my espresso. Even so I didn't think to suggest it.

Victor noticed it, though. He nodded at it and said, "Don't worry. I'm familiar with your classy table settings. But think about it. Would you leave a perfect set of fingerprints at the crime scene? Wouldn't you wipe down a place after you'd finished? Of course you would. Then she leaves her phone behind to make it convincing, but she's too attached to her new one to leave it behind and make it truly convincing. Why? She thinks the sheriff won't know the difference. And if that's not enough, there sits your photograph, staring at me. Jake, what caused her to make such a huge mistake? Was it because I'm black, or because I'm a hillbilly?"

"Oh, hillbilly, by a long ways."

"You sure?"

"Hunner-ten percent."

He gave me a look of surprise. "Pete Rose, right?"

"I always hated that bastard."

"Yeah. But he's our bastard."

Do you see how far behind I am at this point? While he's busy teasing out a whole new layer to Angela's intrigue, I'm doing Pete Rose imitations.

He wasn't finished. "And oxycodone, for pity's sake? We found some in her car. Would a well-to-do New York lady be caught dead with hillbilly heroin?"

"Maybe she planned to sell it. She'll do almost anything for money. I should know."

"No, no. Wrong. All wrong. She wanted to make sure Barney Fife recognized a crime scene when he saw one. She didn't want anything to trip me up on my way to arrest you. It's people talking slow to my grandmother. That's exactly what it is. They only just tryin' to be helpful."

He waited until I caught up. Yes, I could follow his argument now. He made a good case for fabricated evidence. But then he exposed the next layer with this question: "Is your

Angela the kind of woman who could think up a scheme this audacious, then turn right around and underestimate me that much? See, it's the irregularity of it that tips me off."

I had fallen behind again. "Tips you off to what?"

"To a scheme devised by more than one person."

"Are you actually saying you think it's some kind of conspiracy?"

"I am. That's exactly what I think. And if Van Landingham herself is one of the conspirators, who is her accomplice? It's my job to figure that out."

13

VICTOR LEFT MY table as abruptly as he had arrived. He said
he wasn't really here to talk to me anyway, but to Charlene.
Fumiko had spotted him and was bringing him an espresso on
a white salver, but he didn't notice her until he stood up. He
thanked her and carefully took the cup, leaving her standing
there holding a glass of water on a tray. Her puzzled gaze
followed him as he left the restaurant area toward a corridor
that led to Charlene's office.

Fumiko's face never betrays much emotion, but I could see
she was troubled. She loves Big's almost as much as Charlene
and I do. We are her American family, this is her home in a
distant land, a happy home that in a major way she helped
create. But what she fears now is good fortune turning in
its cycle toward ill. I smiled at her and shrugged it off, and
without changing her expression she returned to the kitchen.

Within five minutes she was back. This time she could
hardly mask her worry. Her voice was a warning whisper.
"There's a reporter asking about you in the kitchen. What can
we do?"

"Is she beautiful?"

The unexpected levity of my question provoked a laugh.
"Yes," she said. "So, so, so."

"Then show her in, why don't you?"

"I worried . . . "

"No need. I'm expecting her." She smiled and hurried
away. "Oh, Fumiko?" She turned toward me. "She's not nearly

as beautiful as you are."

She held her arms stiffly at her sides and trotted toward the kitchen. Before pushing through the doors she looked back at me and called out, "Smooth talker." She said something to someone in the kitchen, and soon Yolanda appeared.

Yolanda Shanley is a sweet-flowing river of a woman. Her long brown hair parts in the middle and flows in waves down her shoulders. She often goes for the upmarket cowgirl look, and she's long and lean enough to carry it off. Today she was wearing a cotton work shirt in pastel plaid, with the sleeves rolled above her elbow and the shirt tails tied under her ribs. Her skirt was low-waisted enough to expose her stomach, and yes, I did check her bellybutton for jewelry or a tattoo, but there was none. The hem of her skirt was fringed, cut at an angle, and showed maybe just a bit more leg than was strictly professional. She was wearing red-dirt cowgirl boots, and carried a matching bag.

If you're wondering how a small-town journalist can afford to dress like that, considering both not getting fired and paying for those outfits, you should know that the Shanley family owns the Guardian. With Yolanda's long legs and social standing, it's no wonder half the men in Twisting Creek have had a crush on her. Including me, on the rebound, of course, for maybe the first week I was in town, until I remembered that in my situation I didn't need a reporter interested in exactly what baggage I might bring to a relationship.

She made a joke about me being a jailbird. She said I was looking fine, that my stint in the Big House apparently didn't do me any harm. So we had a chuckle, then quickly went through the it's-been-much-too-long routine. When Yolanda makes small talk you might think she's flirting with you, but I don't think that's it. She's just so beautiful, and so nice, that you think it's flirting, you want so badly for it to be true. She sat down and took a letter-sized envelope from her purse, but didn't draw attention to it right away, because Fumiko appeared with coffee.

Once we were alone, she picked up the envelope. It didn't look new—it had soiled edges and a flatness about it, like happens to letters left a long time at the bottom of a drawer. I noticed that it was addressed to The Guardian, in the jerky handwriting of a child just learning cursive, or of an adult who never really learned it very well. She held it out to me.

"Read this."

First I asked, "What is it?"

"You may know that part of my job at the Guardian is to lay out the op-ed page, and part of that is handling the Letters to the Editor section. We get mail from some real crackpots, stuff we would never dream of running, and I have a file where I save some of the stranger ones, or funnier, or whatever. Just for my own amusement."

"I take it this is one of those?"

"Oh, before you read it, I should say that I did think about showing it to Victor, but decided to come straight to you. I don't think there's any way that anybody could consider this to be evidence of any kind, but still . . . read it."

"Evidence? What kind of evidence?"

"Read it first. I'll explain after."

It said, *What kind of a man would call hisself a preecher of the gosple of the lord but still yet goes around junk yards looking for car parts for his hower.*

"For his 'hower'?" I asked.

"He means 'whore.'"

"Oh, I see." I guess I saw. I mean, it may have been mildly interesting to a researcher of cultural anthropology, but I didn't see what made it worth a special trip to Big's, and least of all what it had to do with me.

Yolanda asked, "Does it mean anything at all to you?"

"Well no, I don't suppose it does. Not really."

"The reference to a preacher ... who do you think that might be?"

"Ah," I said. Still, we all know that Lonnie Farley has a history with women. Buying car parts for one doesn't seem so damning. It's not like he emptied out the church treasury and took her to Victoria's Secret. I told her exactly that, then asked, "When did you get this?"

"Last winter."

"What am I supposed to see?"

"Think about it a little longer. Reread it."

Why not? So I did. *What kind of a man would call hisself a preecher of the gosple of the lord but still yet goes around junk yards looking for car parts for his hower.* "I think I get who it's referring to. Is that what you mean?"

She only said, "Do you know any junkyards around here?"

"Why?" It was the only word I uttered. I knew even then it was grossly inadequate, but at the same time I knew what she was hinting at, and I felt my whole life start to unravel. You might just think that's hindsight, in light of what occurred a few minutes later, but I'm telling you that even before Charlene and Victor emerged, in fact right now, I felt the first stitch pop loose, and the ends fray.

Yolanda said, "Jake, I'm not here to scare you or anything. I told you already I'm not showing this to Victor. I only suspect it may be important—but I can't figure out how."

I nodded and smiled. It was a pitiful attempt at a thank you. I said, "I don't think I can figure it out either. There's not much there."

"But I know something more. This is what made me suspicious. I got this letter in the mail one afternoon about three o'clock. But before that, on the morning of that same day, I arrived at my desk to find a lady already there waiting for me. She was dressed for cold weather—that's why I remember so clearly it was winter. She had on a heavy gray cloth coat, and a headscarf. Not the Islamic kind you see on the news these days, but the old-fashioned American style, before women started wearing ski caps and such. This woman looked like an apparition from the nineteen-fifties, like some kind of museum piece from those days. She was wringing a handkerchief in both hands. When I got face to face with her I saw that she was real pretty. I got the impression that she was wearing that get-up to conceal just how pretty she was. She introduced herself as Mrs. Sidney Cantrell. That's the way she said it. How long has it been since you heard a woman introduce herself as Mrs. plus her husband's name?"

"I don't know that I ever have."

"You can see why this made such an impression on me. She told me her husband had mailed a letter to the Guardian, but now regretted it. She asked me not to publish it. She was obviously on the verge of tears. If I'd delayed any time at all before assuring her we wouldn't run it, she would have broken down. I'm sure of it. But I told her not to worry, that I hadn't even received the letter yet, and when I did I wouldn't use it. She cheered up a little bit, but the poor thing looked so vulnerable, like there wasn't much improvement she could hope for. She blurted out a garbled explanation, about what a good husband he was, at heart. It's just somebody put an idea in his head. She told me, 'Just because a man asks about a car the same model as I drive don't mean nothing.' She claimed she hadn't so much as spoken to 'that other man'—referring to that preacher—for over two years. But when Mr. Cantrell drank, he dragged out old subjects, and next thing she knew he was half-crazy. She said he knew now he shouldn't have mailed that letter.

"I told her that if she ever felt the need to find shelter, just call me anytime, day or night. I gave her my card. I watched out my window as she walked across the parking lot. Jean, one of our cleaning ladies, was on her way back from the dumpster.

I watched them chat for a minute before Mrs. Sidney Cantrell got in her car and drove away."

I asked Yolanda, "Did she ever contact you again?"

"Never. But when Jean came into the building, I asked her who she was. Jean said that at one time they'd both belonged to the same church, Lonnie Farley's church, and everybody suspected this woman was his mistress, because as soon as she joined, she started wearing nicer clothes and so on. By and by, things went wrong, the woman left the church, and before long married some other man."

She left it there for a rest. She sipped her coffee, looked around approvingly at our décor.

"That's some story," I said. I kept trying to understand what made me so sure this junkyard information was going to undermine my whole life, but I couldn't break through to the final connection until Yolanda said, "I saw her get in her car."

"What kind of car?" Although I already knew the answer, knew it in my stomach.

"A Dodge Neon."

She went on to say that she remembered the car I drove to Twisting Creek, in fact drove to the Guardian the day I arranged our first classified ad, the day I met her. She said she was very, very sorry, but it was impossible to forget a pink Dodge Neon.

This disclosure sent my mind pinging wildly among many varied, sometimes contradictory, scenarios. Lonnie Farley? Searching for my car? But why? What did he hope to find? A serial number? A license plate? Was he trying to dig up my past? Did he think he could track it that way?

Luckily I could rein in my runaway speculations thanks to one key decision I made my first week in town: my Neon isn't here anymore. It isn't anywhere. I sent it to be crushed. I congratulated myself on my foresight, and told Yolanda, "By now my car has been reincarnated as a bunch of bicycles in

China, or something."

She said, "Or maybe not. Did you take it to that scrap yard on Landsdale Pike?"

Hell, I don't know where I took it. I looked down on the table, where all my yellow menu stickers now seemed as foreign to the scene as a life not lived. I lifted my shoulders. "I hitchhiked back to town. That's all I remember."

"I ask because I phoned around for a pink Neon, and they have one."

"Intact?"

"Intact."

Had the bastard kept it for salvage? I was still working that around in my head when I looked up and saw Victor and Charlene walking towards me. Victor said, "We're on our way to my office. Shouldn't be too long."

I asked Charlene, "What's going on? Will you be back in time to open?"

Charlene motioned me to come near, put her lips to my cheek as though for a kiss, but whispered, "They need a formal statement. Somebody out at Lake Roosevelt said they saw me near that woman's cabin."

"Good God. When?"

"The day before she disappeared."

14

THIS MORNING I woke up asking those big questions again, just like in my prison cell. *Where am I? Why am I here?* Of course what makes that crazy is I was in my own bed at home on Dogwood. When I stretched my hand down to pet Jezebel, I really did find Jezebel, and when I reached behind me for Charlene, a woman's voice said, "Not now."

You see why I'm a panic-manic? Are you starting to understand now? *I'm* not what's fucked up. Life is fucked up. You see the evidence. I'm up, I'm down. I get great news, then a freight train runs over me. Is that me lacking ballast? Or is it fortune and misfortune playing blind man's bluff?

Anyway, I apologize for complaining to you about that. What I should be doing instead is helping Victor puzzle out who Angela's co-conspirator is. That's what I've spent this whole morning trying to work out. I lay in bed a long time. Usually I hop right up, but not this morning. Charlene apparently reconsidered her "not now." She turned toward me, laid her head on my shoulder, and mumbled, "On second thought, what did you have in mind?"

I didn't have anything in mind. I was only making sure I wasn't back in jail. I breathed a short laugh and stroked her hair. Soon I felt a twitch of her head that meant she'd fallen back to sleep, so I eased my arm free and slipped out of our bedroom.

Jez followed me out. I let her into the back yard, put some food out for her. By the time I was ready to go she was waiting for me by the car. I think she looks forward to mornings at Fifi's as much as I do. She makes her rounds of the tables and lays her head on people's laps until they feed her bits of croissant. She especially loves children. If a child is crying she'll trot straight over and nuzzle it. Every single time she does it, the kid starts laughing. It's really something to see. The agency for this transformation seems to be nothing more complicated than her sincere desire for it to happen. It's so simple. I don't know why we all can't master it.

This morning my plan was to do my deep thinking over coffee at Fifi's, as usual, but I surprised myself. I watched Fifi's go by on my left and kept on driving. I'll admit that these new developments have got me too stirred up to relax on Fifi's patio and accept the well-meant comments of friends and acquaintances there, but it's worse than that. I couldn't even present myself face to face with a server. I couldn't bear the presence of another living soul. I wanted to be alone, absolutely alone. I needed to withdraw from my wildly oscillating life and find a place of tranquility where I could work out my next step. I needed to hide away somewhere nobody would even think to look for me, so I switched off my phone, kept driving and ended up out here by Lake Roosevelt.

It's mid-morning. The breeze off the lake is humid and the air carries the threat of a scorching afternoon, but right now it's perfect for a lover of clear summer days. Sunlight slants through the tall trees behind me and sparkles the otherwise shadowed surface of the water near the shore. Morning birdsong is winding down, and a lone cicada has started. I think that's a cicada's impatient buzz. I'm sitting at a picnic table on the far side of the lake from the tourist cabins. It's a few hundred feet across the water, so the cabins look quite small, in panorama like a traditional rustic village in miniature, as in a window display at a crafts shop. Even so, I can make out bright flowers showing through white picket fences, and some geese cruising the shoreline. The cabin on the far right would have been Angela's. It all looks far too perfect to be the setting for her undoing. Maybe mine, too.

I guess I'm not absolutely alone after all—Jezebel is with me. If she senses my trauma, I can't detect it. She started by bounding onto the picnic table for her pantomime of the heroic collie statue. From the corner of her eye she checked to see if I was smiling or not. I was, just to be, you know, courteous. She hopped down in one big leap and happily sniffed along the shoreline for a few minutes, and now I hear her exploring the woods in back of me. It undermines confidence in a person's ability to predict anything when you recall that Jez is a city-bred dog, born to a life of Central Park, groomers, professional dog-walkers and car trips to ocean beaches. As a consequence of my escape from New York, she's now a dog of forests and creek banks and swimming in a quiet lake.

Yet here I sit, needing to escape once again. I'm not sure what Jez would think of that, but to me I'm spellbound by how complex the world becomes when you're hit by the notion that you could live in any part of it. My international experience is limited. I studied for a few months in Europe and a few months in Asia, and that's it. Only four countries, at that. Will I be forced to go abroad again? Will later chapters of this narrative take you to wine bars in Prague and Budapest? Or to tortilla stands on a beach in Mexico? Or one of those conveyor belt sushi places in Japan? Will I eventually value worldly experience as fair compensation for losing my little family? My god, that would be the ultimate tragedy. But, if it happens, will I confess it to you?

No, unlikely. I'd simply stop writing.

How can I get these pages to you if I leave town? I've already worked out a solid plan to deal with that. I'll send them to Fumiko. We talked it over and she doesn't mind a bit. She'll be happy to do it. If we lived more stable lives I suspect she would look upon you as a godchild. She'd remember every birthday, get your size right every Christmas, make rice balls for you, and at any time show up at the door unannounced to take you out somewhere, if only for an ice cream in the park.

If you're wondering why not send them to Charlene, I can tell you honestly: I still have a deep dark secret from her. She doesn't know about my burglary. I want to keep that quiet for now. Later, perhaps. Much later. Let us be an old married couple first.

Fumiko makes much more sense. I physically mailed her the first, handwritten part, in other words the pages I wrote in jail, and I've emailed all the rest. Every new entry, I'll send it straight to her. She says she'll scan the handwritten parts and file them with the emailed documents, all in one folder. She's promised not to read them. She laughed and said it was too much like extra English homework. Her sense of propriety will stand in her way, too. But she'll keep them up to date, saved in a couple of places. When the last one gets to her, she'll add that on, and that's that. The end. Then she'll hold it for twenty years.

I revealed to her my dream of having this presented to you as you start your freshman year, your first day in the dorm, so if that day happens to be today, check your email. Or whatever people check in twenty years. No—forget that. This is Fumiko we're talking about. She may decide to jump on a flight from wherever she is to wherever you are, and knock on your door in the dorm. You'll open it and you'll see a forty-four year old Fumiko. She could even be wearing a kimono. God, I hope so. She'll bow from the waist and you'll notice she's clutching a brown manila packet to her chest. Fumiko, in middle age. You, in college. These are exhilarating visions, and more painful that I can possibly say.

You know what drives me fucking nuts? If I could have remained underground for barely two more years, my second escape would have occurred automatically. To be precise, in another twenty-seven months, the statute of limitations on my burglary expires. Have I told you that? Leo Akers called to tell me. I almost wish he hadn't. It makes it all the more painful, knowing how close I came. It doesn't seem too preposterous a dream, does it? Lay low for twenty-seven months, just keep on keeping on, and by your second birthday all my burdens fly, fly away.

Well, by then you would be my burden. You and your terrible twos. What a lovely exchange of burdens.

You're probably wondering how serious I am about heading for Asia, or maybe revisiting the old Mexico plan, or some other route that would remove me from your life, and from Charlene's. I suppose you're right to question the strength of my loyalty, given that Victor could solve everything, in my favor. All this while I spend two years sunning myself in Puerto Vallarta, then on your second birthday Daddy shows up, a free man. So you're asking me if I'd even consider leaving you.

The answer is . . .

Okay, I started to say it's an unequivocal no, but maybe I'm being foolish. Until Angela turns up to exonerate me of all suspicion in her disappearance, I could be looking at a lot more than two years in Puerto Vallarta. And what if she turns up—as a corpse? Now we're up to life without parole in Eddyville. Or there's another way to get out of Eddyville—with a needle in my arm. I guess if I'm honest I have to say I will resist leaving you with all my might, and that's where I'll leave it for now.

It'll be far more productive to spend this morning on specifics. If Victor is right and Angela has a co-conspirator, I need to help figure out who it is. One thing I've noticed is that when I write things down for you, I seem to understand them better. I make connections that go right past me when

I merely think it through on my own. So maybe you can help me unravel all the threads.

I need to put myself inside the mind of Lonnie Farley. If he's the accomplice, I need to scheme it the way he would. If Lonnie really was the "preecher" looking for my old car, and if he did in fact find something inside it that set this series of events into motion, how many different ways can it play out? And is there even one possible outcome that can keep our lives intact?

Let's say it was Lonnie. What could he have been looking for? One answer, the simplest one, is that the jealous husband Mr. Sidney Cantrell knew what he was talking about, and Lonnie was still boffing the pretty Mrs. Sidney Cantrell. He really was helping her repair her car, and merely happened to stumble over something of mine.

It occurs to me that one bit of leverage I have on Lonnie is that there's a jealous husband lurking out there. A mean-ass one, from the sound of it. I can probably stir that up, if I have to.

But what did Lonnie find in my car? Obviously something that linked me to Angela. But what could that be? I was careful to clean out the glove compartment. Did I miss something? Some of the paperwork from the dealership? Under the seat, maybe?

Precisely what he found isn't nearly as important as why he was looking for it, and from Yolanda's description of the abject Mrs. Cantrell, and the information from the cleaning lady who knew her from church, she and Lonnie had long since parted ways. That means his search had nothing to do with her and everything to do with me. He specifically targeted my pre-Twisting Creek history. But why?

Oh, shit. Remember what he said to me in prison? That his one constant goal is to lead me and his wayward sister back into the fold? That he prays for the day when we lift the evil viper with our own hands and raise it high over head, an offering to the Lord? Wasn't that it? Or something equally bizarre? What if he suspected I was hiding out in Twisting Creek thanks to some fairly serious transgression? Lonnie may be a fruitcake, but he's shrewd. He notices that I always rebuff his apparently innocent questions about my past. He notices that I give vague generalities to his specific questions. He even says, "You're the mysterious one," and I make a joke of it, saying women go gaga over a man of mystery, or sometimes I pull out my "CIA trained" quip.

Could that be it? He's decided to blackmail me into salvation? And Charlene along with me? Bag two major trophies with one shot, a double-barreled triumph that will transform his reputation among mainstream Christian denominations from fringe cult leader into a true saver of souls?

Alternatively, or rather additionally, what if while making contact with Angela he learned that she's looking for me, and with a vendetta? By this time surely he's figured out that she has money enough—and motive enough—to pay him handsomely for the whereabouts of her hated ex-chef and lover. As I look across the lake toward Angela's cabin, and around this quiet, isolated spot, it comes to me that only Lonnie could have devised this place as the venue for Angela's intrigue. She would never in a million years have come up with this spot. Operating on her own, she wouldn't even have stayed at a local motel. The Hyatt Regency in Lexington or Cincinnati, that's more her style. Force me to drive to meet her. She would want me to come crawling. Sitting here I can clearly see Lonnie's hand in all this.

I suppose I know the question in your mind—and you're right to ask it. What about Charlene? Why do I hesitate to consider her? Wouldn't she be inclined to sharpen her claws and go after any rival who crossed over into her territory? We know she's got an impulsive side. Or maybe I should say a decisive side. She was quick to slam that shotgun of hers through the upstairs window when she thought Jez and I were in danger. And anyway why does she even own a shotgun, when we live in the quietest, safest neighborhood in town? I've wondered about that myself, even before the shooting incident. I once questioned her about it. She said that her father gave it to her, so she kept it, simple as that. And it's true that against the police she didn't fire it at anyone. She used it—wisely, as it turns out—as a distraction, a game-changer. Still, some people might argue that she was quick on the trigger. Not to mention her threat to drop two deputies in their tracks.

And what about that cute little Ruger she carries around? Her father sure didn't leave her that in his will.

The main argument, though, is that Charlene was spotted here at the lake, right? The very day before Angela went missing. What was that all about? As far as I know, Charlene never comes out here to stroll the lakeshore. What business did she have out here? How did she know Angela was here, when I didn't even know it myself?

The last you heard, Charlene was on her way to Victor's office for questioning. Let me tell you how that went down.

She wasn't gone all that long. She was back at Big's in time to deliver what we jokingly refer to as the Invitational. The Invitational is the part of the worship service of some churches when the pastor calls for fresh converts. Charlene's invitational is more of a short motivational talk. She takes the microphone and welcomes everybody, reads off the up-to-date weights or BMI's or waistline measurements of our guests. She might give a quick science lesson on fructose and insulin, or the hormones leptin and ghrelin, or comment on results of new scientific studies into obesity. She talks about her own experience, stressing that the journey back to fitness ought to be fun. Occasionally she makes members aware of skin removal treatments and costs and clinics and so on. For the most part, though, she's the friendly hostess, announcing the evening's musical program, and assuring everybody that she's enjoying herself immensely and hopes they are too. No doubt her primary appeal comes from simply standing there, looking great.

As usual, I didn't get a chance to sit down with her—we stay too busy for that—although I managed to buttonhole her outside her office to ask how things went at the station. She said, "How about after we get home?" She apparently saw consternation in my eyes, for she added, "Full report—I promise."

It was almost midnight when we left Big's. We both should have been exhausted, yet on the drive home she kept glancing up toward the clear night sky, and once we pulled into our driveway told me to stay in the truck. Jez jumped down from the truck bed, Charlene let her into the house, locked the door and came straight back. She drove our main road out of town. I didn't ask why. She turned up a narrow valley called Wade Fork, and a few minutes later took a hard right up a steep, pot-holed, one-lane dirt road pinched tightly between two hills. Here they call this a holler, meaning hollow. We passed a couple of empty shacks, then the road became little more than ruts left over from an old logging trail. I'd never even seen this particular hollow, much less followed it all the way to the mountaintop. We kept jolting along at a snail's pace, picking our way uphill. A doe and her fawn watched us from behind some trees, but they didn't seem too perturbed. I started to think Charlene had completely lost her way. Nonetheless, she seemed to know where she was going, so I remained quiet. I sensed she was following a plan.

Once we had made the crest of the mountain, the terrain leveled out in a small clearing. She stopped the truck, killed her headlights, took something from her purse, and said, "Come on."

The night was as dark as blindness. At first it seemed like a total blackout. I knew there was a flashlight in the glove compartment, but when I opened it she said, "We won't need that."

"It's too dark for a walk."

"We're not on a walk."

When she left the truck and closed the door, the night was so black that I literally didn't know where she'd gone until I felt the front end jolt and knew she'd sat down on the hood. I got out and climbed up there too. Up close, I put my hand out and found her lying stretched out, with her head propped up against the windshield. I joined her, feeling the warmth of the engine penetrate the back of my shirt and on down my legs.

"I think I saw one," she said.

"One what?"

"A shooting star."

"I missed it."

"There'll be more. Lots more. It's the Perseid shower."

I know almost nothing about the night sky. "Like a meteor?"

"A meteor shower. I heard about it on the radio. Tonight's the peak. Give your eyes a few minutes to get dark adapted."

We lay that way for a long while. The silence on mountaintops is thicker than in town, anytime. It forced us to be silent with it. We spoke in whispers. *Over there. Nice one.*

We lay like that for at least a half hour, then she said, "Remember when we first got out of the truck, how little we could see?"

"I couldn't see a thing. The inside of a casket would look just like that."

"But now look up, down, around, everywhere. What do you see?"

I did as she asked. The sky itself was like looking out over the crowd at a rock concert, when everybody fires up their lighters and lifts them up high. Off to the side I could easily make out trunks of the trees that lined the clearing, and up close I could see Charlene's profile in silhouette clearly enough to appreciate how beautiful she is.

She gave it time to sink in, then said, "You can see a hell of a lot, can't you?"

"Yeah. Everything seems to have its own glow."

"You realize the moon has already gone down, don't you? We're too far from town to get light from there. So the light we can see, where does it come from? Have you ever thought about that? I never did."

"About what?"

"About where light comes from on moonless nights. It all comes from distant stars, far beyond our solar system, way out there." I saw her hand sweep through that starlight, in an arc from horizon to horizon, until it came to rest on my shoulder. "Yet it's right here with us now." Her finger traced the arc of my forehead, my nose, down to my chin. "Your face is glowing with starlight."

I wanted her to knock off the astronomy lesson and tell me what she'd told Victor, but I tried to be patient, to let her develop it her way. Anyway, I knew it was on her mind as much as it was on mine. Our love is just as important to Charlene as it is to me. I've never doubted that. Those three things—the light show among the stars, the immensity of our love, and the fresh threat of prison—seemed to swirl and meld together in my thoughts, forming a silent passage into infinity.

My neck started to cramp. I sat upright. She seemed to interpret this as a call to get on with it. I heard the rustling of paper. She said, "I guess we will need that flashlight after all. No—I'll get it."

The light from inside the car reflected momentarily off the weeds at the side of the clearing, then it was dark again and I felt her sit down beside me. She directed the light onto her paper. It was folded in a square. The side I saw said only

"Bradley Michaels."

I started , "You know Bradley is . . . " but she cut me off.

"Four days ago I found this in an envelope somebody slipped under the door at Big's. The work entrance, not the main door. I opened it immediately. Maybe I should apologize for that, I don't know. But look—'Bradley'? In a woman's hand? I'm opening it, no question. I've got something to protect here. Tooth and claw."

"Can I see it?" She handed it over to me and shined her light on it. It said, *SURPRISE! It's me and I'm at Lake Roosevelt Resort, Cabin 12.* "That's it?" I asked. I turned the paper over and back again. "This is why you were at her cabin?"

"I wasn't at her cabin—exactly. I was merely walking nearby."

"But why?"

"To check out my competition, see how beautiful she is. I simply waited for her to walk past me. I knew she was going to be a knockout, and I was right—she's really beautiful."

I put my arms around her. "Point one: she's not beautiful compared to you. Point two: you have no competition."

She laid her head against me, and I felt a tear against my neck. "I've been so afraid . . . " She couldn't finish.

"Of losing me?" I let the rise in my voice tell her how ludicrous that was.

Now that the subject was out there, tears rained down. "But Jake, you knew me back then. Back when I was as big as a house."

"What the fuck are you saying, woman?" I said, trying to make it sound hillbilly, and put the light on my own face. I wanted her to see the comedy in my eyes. "You knew me when I was the Pillsbury doughboy, too. We don't give a good goddamn about that. Do we?" I moved the spotlight to her face. Her nose was dripping, and she was trying to rally a smile. "Well, do we?"

She sniffed and moved in for another hug. "I don't really know."

"Of course you know. Or else know it right now." I handed her the light so I could take off my t-shirt, which I used to dry her face. "Okay? Tell me you know it for sure."

"I guess so."

"No fair guessing. Charlene, we're perfect together. How could life ever get better than this? I love you like I never thought possible. I didn't even know this category existed. I never want to live another day of my life without you."

I said it that way on purpose. *Never want to live* rather than *Will never live*. Even then my mind hadn't fully cleared itself of life without parole at Eddyville. But ignoring this technicality, it's the truth. God, it's the truth. I never want to live a day without her.

She started to cry again, not sobbing any more, more like trembling, as though from a chill, although I felt a skim of sweat when the mountain breeze blew against my naked back. She buried her face in my shirt.

I said, "And how about me? Where does your Pillsbury doughboy stand?"

She spoke into the shirt, "You know where you stand."

"In that case . . . " I took the flashlight back and coaxed my t-shirt away from her. I wanted to see her face. Her eyes were puffy and her nose was a mess. "Wait . . . first blow your nose."

"I don't have a tissue." She sniffed.

"On my shirt. Here . . . " I held the shirt against her nose, as a parent might help a child. As, come to think of it, I hope I will have occasion to do for you some day. "Blow. Come on, give it a good one. Maybe your average hillbilly suitor wouldn't notice, but where I come from a man is reluctant to propose to any woman with snot spilling out her nose."

She buried her face, wiping and blowing with gusto, but when she pulled the shirt away her eyes were wet once again, this time with laughter. I have to say . . . I hope you can see this in your mind . . . your precious mom on this dark night of tears and fears and shooting stars . . . her flashlit face . . . I have never seen a sight so beautiful in all my life; am unlikely ever to again.

"Propose what?"

"You're going to start with the snot again, aren't you?"

"I might."

"Is it a hillbilly tradition?"

"I hope so."

"In that case, Charlene Farley, will you do me the honor of becoming my wife?"

"I will," she said, "on one condition."

"What condition?"

"You do me the honor of becoming my husband."

We kissed. Her lips were soft and salty. Neither of us seemed willing to leave that spot just yet. We resumed our position on the car hood, with our heads on the windshield. Soon our eyes were dark adapted again, and the light show seemed to be for us alone.

On the way home she said, "Old Perseus sure knows how to throw a meteor shower."

I thought of a good one. "That's just the start. Now you have a bridal shower and a baby shower ahead of you."

"We don't have time for all that, Jake. We need to get moving on the marriage ceremony."

I asked her why the hurry. I thought I knew why. I thought she was referring to you, but her answer surprised me.

"Because that way we can't be forced to testify against each other."

Sorry again about the abrupt breakaway, but right then Jezebel started barking like mad about something way back in those woods. I called her, and here she came charging toward me with something colorful in her mouth, streamers from it flying behind her. I thought she'd found something to make a game with. She laid it at my feet like it was some lavish offering. My wacky dog had brought me a bra. A dirty red silk bra.

At first I almost laughed. But then I noticed Jez wasn't laughing. There was no play in her eyes. Instead there was consternation. She gave the bra a quick sniff and looked at me, urging me to do the same. She doubts I can detect a hint of the key scent, but she can't tell me any other way. When I bent to pick it up, her feet drummed out an excited little dance. I looked closely at the bra and saw a small dainty green bow on it, with the initials AP. Immediately I switched on my phone and called Victor. "I'll wait for you here at the lake," I told him. "Bring extra men."

15

Two things have happened in the meantime, and honestly I'm not sure which one to tell you about first. You might think, "The most important one. Tell that first." However, the kicker is I don't know what's important and what isn't, and won't know until I learn how this whole wretched business ends. Which, as I've said before, is what I am dying to find out, but cannot, while you almost certainly know it already. You may legitimately say, "That's not relevant, Dad. Get to the other part." Or you may see nothing in any of it, except bitter futility, because you know where and how I ended up. Instead of that, try to think about it from where I am at the moment, in the midst of it all, totally confused. Only then will you appreciate what a soul-twister this is.

I'll tell you in the order they happened.

I was sitting at the picnic table when Jez ran up to me carrying Angela's very expensive Agent Provocateur red silk bra. I knew there was likely to be more evidence back in those woods, maybe even a body. I also knew it would take Victor and his men at least fifteen minutes to get there. This was my chance to search those woods alone. I held the bra in front of Jezebel's face. "Where did you find this, girl? Show me where."

She turned on a dime, sniffed briefly around her feet, then covered ground faster than I might have thought prudent with her nose buried deep in high grass, and, beyond the border of the picnic area, skimming the forest floor. Along the tree line, a sign from the Kentucky Nature Conservancy helpfully explains that you are entering one of the rare patches of old growth forest remaining in the state. In fact, they didn't really need to tell us that, because a few steps into the woods the atmosphere deepens into mystery and reverence. You leave behind bright, humid air, filled with the smell of sun-warmed grass, and enter a dim world scented with dark green foliage and tree bark and mulch. The temperature drops a few degrees and the sound shifts its source from below, where your own feet were hissing through meadow grass, to the wind blowing through treetops far overhead. This is Kentucky as the Indians knew it, as Boone and the pioneers would have found it. Here are the ancient basswoods, beech, hemlocks, and oaks, the great pillars rising to a thick, dark canopy high above, alive with birds and squirrels. You feel you ought to pause and reflect on how small your own life is.

Luckily, Jezebel holds no similar impulse towards contemplation. Her mind and nose were on the job. I watched her as she retraced her trail with such certainty, with so few backtracks, until it dawned on me that she was following her own scent, but in the direction of its diminishing strength. It seemed to me a brilliant strategy, a stroke of genius, but I suppose it's as second nature to her as it is for us to know we're walking towards something because it looks like it's growing.

I often lost sight of her when her path took her into a clump of trees. She would stop to look back for me, then once I was in view, off she'd go again, completely absorbed in her task. Eventually I saw her watching for me, but this time she didn't plunge ahead. She stood nearly motionless until I was by her side, then with her nose she indicated the patch of mulch at her feet. I noticed it had been churned up. The further along I looked, the more disturbed the ground was, and I realized this was where Jez had been digging.

Now it occurred to me that by entering the area before Victor arrived I could only disturb the scene further, that I really had no idea what I might be searching for, and that I had no good reason to be there ahead of legal authorities. If questioned on it, I guess I could say I hurried to save Angela's life, on the theory that she was lying there breathing her last, but that sounded far-fetched, even in my own head, so we turned to retrace our steps all the way back to the picnic area. I was nearing the edge of the clearing when my phone rang. Through the trees I saw Victor and four uniformed officers already leaning against the picnic table. Victor had his phone to his ear. I didn't bother to answer mine. I waved and said, "This way."

"So you've returned to the scene of the crime," Victor said.

"Not funny," I told him, and held out the bra. "This is what she found."

"Who's *she*?" asked a deputy.

"*She* is she," Victor said, pointing to Jez, who claimed the limelight by tilting her head back and singing a low note. "A better question is, How do you know it belonged to our missing person?"

"See this logo?" I said. "That means it's an Agent Provocateur product. Angela's favorite."

"Surely she's not their only customer."

"This bra probably cost two hundred dollars. How many visitors come out here and toss away two hundred dollar bras? And if that doesn't convince you, I saw recognition in Jezebel's body language. Just like at the cabin."

"Right, men. Let's go with that. We're going to do a grid search." He told two officers they would walk the x-axis, and the other two the y-axis. He asked them, "What do you think we're looking for? What might be the object of our search?"

"A body," one man said. "Or other articles of underwear."

"Right as far as it goes," Victor said, as a mentor might. "But it doesn't go far enough. What else?"

After a long silence one man answered, "Anything."

"Correct. Don't go in with expectations. Find what's there. That's this stage of the mission. Find anything that doesn't appear natural to its environment. Assessment of validity comes later."

The deputies started their methodical search through the pine needle floor around the spot where the bra was found. Jezebel followed a meandering trail of her own. Victor stayed beside me at the edge of the clearing.

He said, "You know that drinking glass they found beside Miss Van Landingham's bed with your prints on it? We questioned pretty much everybody on your staff about it."

Actually I knew about this already. Several people told me about it, including Fumiko.

"What's the name of the girl who brings people coffee? The Japanese girl."

"Fumiko."

"Does she always bring water with it?"

"Espresso should always be served with a small glass of water."

"On the day before we took you in for questioning, when she went to clear your table, the glass was missing. At least that's what she says. Any ideas?"

I tried to think of something helpful, but drew a blank. "Not really. The ballroom is almost always open."

"Even when nobody's in there?"

I shrugged. "People need access. Musicians sometimes set up early. Delivery guys with large boxes. We're pretty loosey-goosey about it. There's nothing much to steal."

"Sounds like someone stole a glass. Somebody who knew where you sit and drink water."

"That's pretty much everybody."

His half-smile said he knew that already.

Jezebel stopped at what amounted to no more than a rise in the forest floor, looked around for me, and started barking.

I let Victor lead the way. He squatted beside it and carefully flicked away leaves until he saw a glimpse of red. With his pen he lifted a pair of red silk panties the same color as the bra.

"Recognize these?" he asked.

I saw AP on the waistband bow. "Same brand," I said. "I suspect there's a matching garter thingie buried around here somewhere."

He raised his eyebrows at me. "You guys really had some fun, didn't you?"

"All of it perfectly legal, I assure you."

"In New York City, maybe." He stood up, momentarily showed me his half smile again before his face went hard. "Would she have got all fancied up like this for a normal day out? Or does this mean she was expecting a lover?"

"AP was everyday wear."

"How about the garter belt?"

"No. No, not that. If you find that, it means she was ready for action."

He nodded in his earnest way, and looked around. "All the ground between these four trees has been disturbed recently. Do you think it was Jezebel?"

"No, definitely not. If it was, she'd have dug out those panties."

"Probably so." He surveyed an area of scattered leaves. "We had no sign of a struggle over by the cabin, but we sure got some out here in the woods."

One of his deputies said, "I reckon she led a lover out here for a little nature study. Lots of women like it better that way. My girlfriend does."

"That's your trouble, Raymond," Victor snapped at him. "You open your mouth before you open your brain. After your big hot date in the woods, does this so-called girlfriend of yours ever throw away hundreds of dollars' worth of underwear?"

Another officer said, "His girlfriend don't even own no underwear."

"Who the hell told you that?" said the first.

I interrupted them before somebody got mad. "Not Angela. Angela would never in a million years have willingly had sex in the woods. Especially not with a perfectly good bed just a few minutes away."

"That settles it," Victor said. "This is not some vindictive ex-girlfriend messing with your head. And we need to drag that lake again."

For a long time nobody said anything. We all knew that this new evidence was of an entirely different order than a tennis photograph and planted fingerprints. Nobody wanted this underwear found, ever. Then I said, "So what're we looking at? Kidnapping?"

"At this point kidnapping is about the best we can hope for. Looks like we add rape to the list. Even murder?"

I asked him, "If it's kidnapping, why am I not getting ransom demands?"

"You didn't get the first note either. Maybe that's happening here."

"Surely you don't mean Charlene?"

He shrugged. "Somebody. Somewhere. Let's hope so. If there's no ransom demand, we're searching for a corpse." He turned to look me in the eye. "One day when I was still in training a thought hit me and almost spun my head around. It was so out of left field that . . . I don't know . . . it changed my whole attitude toward law enforcement. It changed everything."

He paused there and looked me in the eye until I asked, "What was it?"

"You know how in any other crime, say rape, or kidnapping, theft, anything—the victim is the one at the emotional center. They're the ones most enraged about the injustice of the crime.

But now change the crime to murder, and what happens? In a murder investigation, the victim is the least interested person of all. The victim could care less. So now who takes center place?"

I nodded. I knew exactly who it was—it was the investigator. It was Victor. If Angela was murdered, her rage must fall to Victor. She had bestowed it upon him. That's why it changed everything.

I finished my part of the search in time for me to reach Big's at my normal time, mid-afternoon. (That's where I am now, but it's nearly midnight.) I entered, as usual, through the kitchen, greeted everyone already there, stopped by my office to get my laptop bag—I do have a proper office, though I use it more as a storeroom—and swung through the double doors into the empty ballroom. I only half noticed that someone was following me. If I'd thought about it I would have assumed it was Fumiko, simply because she's always here, and often follows me places, sometimes with a question, or a suggestion (for example, adding kombu to our chili beans was her idea) or to ask if I need anything. So when I reached my usual work table and turned around, I was shocked to find that it was Lacey Fouch, one of our line cooks.

Lacey never says much of anything beyond good afternoon and good night, but she's a real cog at Big's, a tireless worker I hired straight out of training. She's from a hellish place they call Rat Row. I've even seen her house—or hovel, more like it. One time Charlene and I drove past it. Purely by accident. We were just driving through. Neither of us had any idea Lacey lived there, but there she was, sitting beside a small child on a set of rough plank steps leading to their front door. The scene was just what you'd expect: a mostly bare dirt yard with sparse patches of grass. Chickens pecking for food, a good-sized dog stretched out under a tree. A couple of plastic tricycles turned over on their sides. Garden tools stored under the porch floor. Lacey seemed to be helping the kid with homework, or a coloring book, or something. Whatever claimed her attention was a lucky break, because it meant she didn't see us pass by, and doesn't to this day know that we know how poor her family is.

I hired her for her first real job. Backed by Pell grants and Perkins loans, she'd just completed her associate degree in culinary arts at Sullivan University, in Lexington. The remarkable thing is that once she'd made it out of Rat Row, she wanted to return. As far as I know she's the only wage earner in her family. She came to me with glowing references from Sullivan. The main reason I hired her, though, was she was fat. She was alternate Charlene, the twenty-year-old Charlene might have become, absent the inheritance from the ice gnome.

You see what this means, don't you? Even then, almost three years ago, I was so awestruck by your mom that I hired a cook, simply because she reminded me of her.

Never have I regretted that hire, not for the job she does— she recently earned a promotion to wok—or for the weight she has lost. She looks great now, seems happy, and I have a suspicion that someday in the not-too-distant future I'll lose her to Trusty Rusty and the future they devise together.

So anyway, I put my laptop bag on the table and turned to find Lacey standing there. She held her hands folded against her apron. She wasn't smiling, but didn't look angry either. I couldn't begin to guess what she wanted.

"Oh, hi, Lacey. You startled me."

She gave a pained smile, but still couldn't bring out the words.

I tried again. "Is everything okay back in the kitchen."

"Things are fine. They're great, really."

"You're doing good work on sauté. I know how stressful it

is. Do you enjoy it?"

"Oh yes, sir. Thank you."

I motioned for her to sit, and started to say *What did you
... ?* but she sat down hard and before I finished my question
she said, "I don't even know if this is important, or nothing
but a bunch of gossip." She bit her lip and looked down at her
hands, folded now on her lap. "No, it's not all gossip, I know
that much."

"What then?"

She still couldn't bring herself to look at me. "I don't think
I've ever told you and Charlene how grateful I am to you for
... I can't thank you enough."

Clearly she was fighting back some strong emotion. I told
her, "We're the ones should be thanking you, Lacey."

She was losing the fight. She bent her head and a tear
rolled down her cheek. "I can't stand the thought that you all
are in any kind of trouble. Why would anybody do such a
thing?"

She looked at me as though if I had the answer I should
tell her right now. I said, "God knows."

"Like I say, this might be nothing more than a coincidence
and not have any connection at all, but I couldn't live with
myself if I didn't say something, and then it turned out it did."

Following our discovery in the woods, I was desperate for
anything. "Please tell me what you know."

"Where I live up on Rat Row, the house right behind ours
is where my cousin lives. She and I are the same age. And she's
been dating—if you can call it dating—more like running
wild with—this man she calls her boyfriend."

"You mean he's not really her boyfriend?"

"More like another loser Sadie's picked up—Sadie's my
cousin. She's had plenty of practice, and they all only end up
bringing trouble to us all. And now here's another one."

"Do you know his name?" She nodded delicately, almost

imperceptibly, but didn't speak the name, so I said, "Good. Go on."

"He disappeared for four or five days. The same days as that missing tourist. Sadie says she doesn't know where he was, she only knows he wasn't anywhere she could find him. On the third or fourth day I started to think how lucky we were if he dropped off the face of the earth, but then this morning she comes over to my house, grinning and prissing around, flicking her hair back out of her face. Then I saw why. She was wearing earrings. Ten o'clock in the morning and she puts on earrings to walk the twenty yard path to my house. Expensive ones, too. Looked to me like real gold and real emeralds. Is that the green one?"

"Emerald? Yes. Birthstone for May. How did she locate him?"

"He called her from a bar and she went there to meet him. She said he was real drunk, buying drinks for people and stuff. He told everybody he loved her and she was the best ... blankety-blank ... in Twisting Creek. And he gave her those earrings."

"The gold part of those earrings—did you notice its shape?"

Of course she did. And of course it was entwined hearts, set with an emerald at the join. Identical to the ones I gave Angela three Mays ago. God! I can see them so clearly! I also see that their reappearance can spin my life in many unpredictable ways. I can even see it's the key to it all. What I can't see is the only thing I'm begging to know: will it unlock the door, or lock it?

"That's not all, either," Lacey said. "He says there's going to be a lot more where that came from."

At that point I gave up. Events had obliterated my most intense efforts to ride out the storm. From here on out the storm was in complete control. I said, "Lacey, maybe you should talk to the sheriff about this," and picked up my phone.

"I really don't want to get too involved. It could get . . . "
She stopped there.

"I'm sure you can depend on Victor to keep your name out of it."

Victor came straight over and is with her right now, back in my office. I have no idea how that's going to turn out. Can't do anything about it anyway.

16

HEY, LOOK—I KNOW the question you've asked yourself a dozen times by now, and that I have stubbornly refused to answer. Trust me, I'll get around to it. The thing to remember is how little time Charlene and I have had together since the moment I learned about you. Between me being in jail, and us working, and me helping Victor, that leaves very few available hours for Charlene and me, and most of those, if you want to know the truth, were sex. In other words, your question required a consensus answer, which I didn't have. However, Charlene and I talked about it on the way home from the Perseid meteor shower, so now here goes:

Are you *bambino* or *bambina*? That's the big question. Are you *pu-chai* or *pu-ying*? *Mon fils* or *ma fille*? That's usually the first big question on parents' minds.

Of course that's my question, not yours. You've known the answer all your life. Your question is whether I know right now if I'm addressing my son or my daughter.

No, I don't know, not yet. Here's what's going to happen, as I understand it. In a couple of weeks, Charlene will get an ultrasound, which may, providing you are stretched out with full frontal nudity (if, in other words, your screen debut is rated R) this ultrasound view should reveal your gender. Not that it matters to me, not one snip. I'm going to love you like crazy, and the whole fatherhood gig along with it. Providing I get out of this mess I'm in. But leaving that aside, here's what happens next. If the ultrasound technician can't determine your gender, then that's it. You'll remain a mystery until you reveal all, on your birthday. In your birthday suit—perfect choice of outfit for a birthday party. But if the ultrasound does resolve the question, the technician will ask us if we want to know. And we need to be ready with our answer. That's what your mom and I talked about on the drive home and again last night.

So, at this point I don't know if I'm addressing my son or my daughter. Luckily in English I can simply say "you" and "your" without violating any rules of grammar. I won't know for at least a few more days. At that point I'd say sure, go ahead, tell me right away, but Charlene isn't sure she wants to know. I don't know why, exactly. Maybe she's simply keeping alive the traditional time of revelation.

By now I've given it more thought, and if I can persuade her, here's what I'd like to do. We'll swear the ultrasound tech to secrecy—even from us—but have him or her write your gender down on a note paper and seal it in an envelope, which I will then hand over to Trusty Rusty. He (also sworn to secrecy) will bake enough cupcakes so that each guest at the wedding reception will get one. All the cupcakes will be completely covered in pure white frosting. But here's the thing: to the cake underneath, Rusty will have added pink or blue food coloring, depending on what the ultrasound shows.

Apart from the ultrasound technician and Rusty, nobody—including Charlene and me—will know if you're a boy or a girl until, on signal, everybody bites into their cupcake to reveal pink or blue. Then they'll all shout "It's a girl!" or "It's a boy!" I guess if it's twins we'll get loud responses of disagreement. Whatever color the cupcakes turn out to be, we'll feel like we're all taking part in the big revelation. Doesn't that sound like fun?

It sure beats the alternative method, where Charlene holds you up behind the visitor's glass at Eddyville Maximum Security, and says, "Meet your kid."

17

YOU'VE HEARD ME mention Leo Akers several times. As I said, in legal circles around here he's something of a legend. Now I'm sorry to say he's my lawyer. Or rather, I'm glad he's my lawyer, I'm only sorry to say it looks like I need him. Again. Until a couple of days ago if anyone had asked me to describe my relationship with Leo, I wouldn't have called him a close friend, not like Victor. More of an acquaintance than a friend. We never see each other socially outside Big's. There's no compelling reason for this, unless it's because he's twice my age. Although Leo and his wife Ruby are Big's regulars, Leo is more of a good customer than a good friend. He's a fun customer—don't get me wrong. He and Fumiko started that jitterbug fad going, with fifties' rock 'n roll, and now almost everybody gives it a try, including Charlene and me. A lot of us are getting good at it—Charlene has perfect curves for twirling—and it makes us all laugh, even when only watching through the kitchen serving window. But that was pretty much the extent of my interaction Leo here at Big's, until this afternoon. That's why I was so surprised to see him standing there at those double swinging doors, well before opening hours, leaning his long frame forward into the kitchen, asking if we could speak privately.

I was already there, in the kitchen, supervising the mayhem that characterizes the prelude to a busy night in a popular restaurant. I've never been the kind of high-handed *chef de cuisine* who barks out orders and berates underlings.

I've worked under enough of those to know they don't bring out the best in their staff. In fact, I find a calm demeanor and an occasional hug promote efficiency and creativity. Even so, to an outsider, the run-up to opening bell can look and sound chaotic, with pots and pans getting banged around and everybody darting from work station to equipment cabinets to food storage and back again. There's a good deal of playful bumping and loud threats with butcher knives, enough so that when Leo walked in unprepared for the melee, he stopped himself at those double doors. Jezebel, who can go anywhere in Big's she wants except the kitchen, was standing beside him, peeking around the door. When I spotted Leo standing there, still dressed for work in a UK-blue sport coat and tie, he was taking in all the pandemonium, and seemed ready to retreat.

I walked over to him and shook his hand. He asked, "Is there a quiet place where we can talk?"

As you know, my usual workplace is the corner table by the dance floor, but today's band, the cheekily-named Big Boned Boys, was already setting up. They've become our de facto house band. They manage to combine authentic early rock and roll, from Buddy Holly and Bo Diddley, with bluegrass, and you should watch the joint start jumping when they crank up *Peggy Sue*, when those violent tom-tom paradiddles propel even the most sedentary guest to stand up and bound across the dance floor. There has evolved a house custom where everybody joins in to sing "Oh Pe-he-gy, my Peggy Sue-hu-hu." And there's another oldie about people all over the world dancing in the streets, where our Big Boned Boys change the line "Every guy grab a girl" to "Every girl grab a guy." At that moment, originally Fumiko and her Asian Mafia would charge across the dance floor to grab any man not dancing. Soon the other taxi dancers followed their lead, until now pretty much every woman in the room starts gyrating and tugging at some man's arm.

God, it's one of the great thrills of my life, to witness the daily reawakening of Charlene's vision, her miracle of happy fat or ex-fat people having fun and taking control of their lives.

I don't know if you got the full meaning of the name Big Boned Boys. That wasn't their name when they first played Big's. It was Darrin and the Polecats or something stupid, but when they figured out what Big's is all about, they changed it. Big Boned Boys is meant to sound naughty—that's undeniable—and there really is a Big Bone Lick, Kentucky. In fact, it's a state park, right next to Beaver Lick. God, what an innocent age it must have been when those names got handed out. But the main joke in Big Boned Boys is that fat people often deny being fat, saying instead they are "big boned."

Charlene keeps hoping a girl-group will turn up, named Big Beavers, but no luck so far.

Anyway, the commotion in the ballroom meant that for privacy Leo and I went into my underused office. Jezebel followed us and lay down beside my chair while I cleared a stack of *Saveur* magazines from a chair for Leo. Fumiko showed up—how she does this no one knows—I hadn't even seen her yet today—with two espressos.

Leo sipped at his coffee. I could tell he didn't want to say what it was he'd come to say. Hardly moving, holding the demitasse to his lips, he could have been modeling for the cover of a Big's promotional brochure. He's a large man for his, or any other, age, with a St. Bernard-sized head and wide shoulders that stretch the seams of his sport jacket. Now that his paunch is gone, he again looks every bit the Cotton Bowl fullback that he once was, gracefully aging. He started by apologizing for "sticking his nose in," as he put it. Aren't lawyers' noses supposed to poke around unexplored places? I suppose he was hinting that I had probably thought the whole mess over and done with, and he was sorry to inform me otherwise. Little did he know that I have been bouncing wildly back and forth, from deep denial to mentally booking a flight to Guadalajara.

He continued, "For some ungodly reason I'm always picking up bits of scuttlebutt from down at the courthouse, and in your case, once I finally fit all the pieces together, what I surmise is that there are at least two people itching for Sheriff Caraher to settle this case by labeling it a crime and making an arrest."

"Which two people?"

"Mayor Ball and DA Reynolds."

"Uh-oh," I said. Neither Charlene nor I know either of them very well. As a general rule, I know only the fat or ex-fat around town, and both the mayor and DA are thin. Reynolds, in fact, looks anorexic. Apparently her burning ambition to throw the book at everybody in Buford County and then move on to state office in Frankfort burns up plenty of calories. I'm completely apolitical, but Charlene's a lifelong Democrat, which will do me no good at all with that ruling clique. "And what do you mean, 'label it a crime'?"

"Abduction. Murder. Anything to show movement in the case." I gathered that what Leo was saying, without saying it, was that Victor is under intense pressure to arrest me. Who else could it be? Let's take a look at Victor's list of possible suspects. Except there is no list. There's one name: Bradley Jason Michaels.

I asked Leo about that, point blank, but he demurred, saying instead, "As I mulled over the mayor's position, I kept asking myself a real tough question. Can you guess what it was?"

I gave him a long look. "You're not referring to that New York thing, are you?"

"No, but that's a good point. I needed to rule that out first. This will be good news for you." The way he said it made it sound like it was the only good news I could expect from him.

"Reynolds told her assistant that it's too bad you're so squeaky clean."

"Wow! That is good news. How can you explain it?"

"I can't. I was convinced the sheriff knew, and was biding his time. But now . . . maybe not. Can he really sit on that and hope to keep his job?"

"Maybe so," I said. "He runs kind of a one-man show down there."

"I don't know," Leo said, and added, in his quaint, old-timer's way, "It bumfuzzles me."

"So shall we get to the bad news?"

"What I find instructive about the mayor's eagerness for an arrest is who's responsible for it. Who do you think would be eager to damage your reputation?"

Besides Angela and, now, Lonnie, I had no clue, so I guessed, "Lonnie Farley?"

"Powerful people in this town rightly see Lonnie Farley as a lower class con-man who poses no threat to anyone. Anyone who doesn't prance around carrying rattlesnakes, that is."

"In that case . . . "

"Think about it like this. Here was my starting point—follow the trail of dollars."

I tried to think of who might be losing money because of this. "Well, it's more newsworthy because she was a tourist. Maybe cabin and motel owners?"

"I thought of that, and asked around. But no. They love you. A lot of Big's customers come from out of town."

"Oh, I see!" This was totally not good news. Twisting Creek is the county seat of Buford County, which has a population of almost forty thousand. That means it has its fair share of fast food places. McDonalds, Hardees, KFC, IHOP, Taco Bell, pizza places, a couple of notch-above places like Red Lobster and Chili's. Dunkin' Donuts. I've already told you about Tim Horton's and that ice cream shop that's there with it. There's one of those fake Italian chains, all tomato sauce, salt and sugar. I can't even remember its name. They're all here, fighting for forty thousand sales.

Leo asked, "What do you see?"

"All the folks eating at Big's aren't eating somewhere else."

"Not only when they're eating here. We're talking *ever*. It amounts to a boycott. Ruby and I used to go to Pizza Hut almost every Saturday, and we'd have take out KFC maybe once a week. Sometimes twice a week. Now it's more like once a year. How much would that . . . ?" His lips moved silently as he calculated. "With us alone, Big's costs the fast food industry three or four thousand dollars a year. And we're not even the heavy users. Some of our members used to eat like that every single meal. Multiply that by every member you have. You've dug deep inside those guys' pockets."

"Come on, Leo. I can't believe KFC and Pizza Hut are worried about little Twisting Creek."

"Not corporate. I mean the local owners."

"I'm supposed to feel guilty about that? Let them serve better food."

"That's the thing—they can't. They're chains. You probably know the financial structure of these franchise places. The local owners get low start-up costs, and first-class marketing, but then have to send huge sums to corporate headquarters, and keep the crumbs for themselves. Their typical profit percentage is in the low single digits. A McDonald's senior coffee pays the local owner less than two cents."

"And these local owners are the ones pressuring to have me arrested?"

"I doubt they phrase it so bluntly. More like, 'We're losing business because of the publicity involving a tourist.'"

"But you think that's bogus?"

"I called around to several motels—all doing well."

"And how do you know it's the franchise owners?"

"I'm not at liberty to divulge my methods. That's how private appointment logs manage to stay private."

I felt the heaviness of everything in me, felt it droop toward the floor. This town that I've adopted, and that I thought had adopted me—they want me out. Gone from their midst. Everybody here who makes a living selling obesity, they want their customers back. If it means I go to jail, fine. Return the lost dollars, return the lost pounds, and go away.

The screws are tightening around me, much as they are around Victor himself. If it becomes public knowledge that he's trying to shield me from a felony arrest, he'll never work in law enforcement again. He may even be liable for prosecution. Can't I do something to prevent that?

"But surely, Leo, all those chain owners didn't form some kind of secret society to abduct Angela."

"Of course not. Somebody else did that. But you've got a truckload of enemies who've seized the opportunity to rid themselves of you, and Big's along with you."

"I'm at a complete loss," I told Leo. "I honestly don't know how to respond. I've known for some time that this is out of my control, but I didn't think I had enemies on this scale. And Victor in trouble too. It's getting to be too much for me to bear."

"Son—you're not alone. Not yet. Tell me once and for all the honest truth. Did you have anything to do with the disappearance of Miss Van Landingham."

"Nothing at all."

"Swear it on the Bible."

"I don't have a Bible," I said.

I looked down to where Jezebel was lying beside me, her head resting on crossed paws. Among the many tragedies that will result if things go wrong is one thing I can't bear to contemplate. Even before Angela's disappearance I refused to let it cross my mind, and now . . . my god it's heartbreaking.

The canine life span. Why don't they live as long as we do? Who came up with the cockamamie idea that they should die at about age twelve? And if I go to jail, she'll be gone before I get out. I'll never see her again. It could happen tomorrow— my last moments with Jezebel. It could happen today. Or in the next two seconds. My remaining time with darling Jezebel. Two seconds. One second.

I was ready to cry. I mean, seriously cry. I felt my chest get ready for a jolt, that feeling anybody who was once a child will remember.

Jez somehow sensed I was looking at her. She does this all the time. She started up her little relaxed pant, nearly a chuckle, smiled her eyes, and stood up. I raised my right hand, placed my left on her head, looked at Leo, and said, "I do so swear."

He laughed, bless him. "Then if you have any notion of what course of inquiry I can pursue, you'd better tell me now. Because frankly, I'm as puzzled as you are."

Jezebel walked toward Leo. She's always liked him. She seems to like older people, for whatever reason. She touched his hand with her long nose, causing him to lift it and stroke her face. She glanced over at me, to see if I got the message. She was saying, *Trust this man.*

"Okay," I said. "It seems likely that Charlene's brother Lonnie might have found my old car and somehow connected me with my old life and Angela. Another thing—a local man was seen with a pair of earrings that almost certainly belonged to Angela."

"What's this man's name?"

"I don't know. Victor probably does. At least he interviewed someone who saw the earrings. He doesn't yet know that Lonnie found my car."

Leo thought for a moment. "You can't inform Victor about what Lonnie knows, can you?"

"Not without opening up about New York."

"Yes. It would amount to a confession that Victor would be bound to act on."

"I can't involve Victor in that. Not yet."

He looked at me for a long time. I had the vivid impression he was going to scold me for letting a third degree larceny complicate his efforts to extricate me from a possible homicide. He gave Jez a healthy pat on the rump and looked her in the eye. "In that case, old girl, we need to figure out a way to hold Brother Lonnie's feet to the flames, don't we?"

18

I WILL NOT go back to jail. I'll do a runner first. I've thought about this a lot since Leo's visit yesterday. Since even before that, I suppose, but especially since Leo informed me about the growing pressure on Victor to arrest me. I try to tell myself: that's political pressure, not pressure of evidence. My good friend Victor Caraher won't bow to political pressure.

Or will he? He's up for reelection this November. That's three months away. What if the local political establishment speaks out against him? He's already got a built-in opposition, being an African-American in a county that's over ninety percent white, where in the last election President Obama got less than forty percent of the vote. Victor beat the odds, and almost everybody seems to like him, but still, how will that support stand up against local fat cats and fat merchants?

How about his wife? I've already mentioned that Charlene and I know Shelley Caraher socially. She's white, did I tell you that? A blond, blue-eyed, and what they used to call statuesque, white woman. Somehow I think that matters here, in this description, although I don't have a clue why. She's fun at a party, still looks great, has half a brain. She wears high heels a lot, and seems happy. But let's face it—she dumped Victor once to move to Hollywood, and only came back to him after he became sheriff and bought a fine old house in Bedford Woods. Gossip has it that the real reason he humbled himself and remarried her was because he missed Alyssa, his nine-year-old daughter. Will Shelley stay with him if he loses his job? Loses it protecting a man who, according to the bulk of the evidence, is the prime suspect? Shelley's still got the goods to attract a fresh mate. When Victor sits alone in the dark and contemplates his choices, does it come down to my freedom versus his job and family? What kind of chance do I stand in a trade-off like that?

Let's think about that. Maybe my chances aren't all that horrible. We know Victor is a man of principle, and he values freedom above all else. He would never arrest someone he knew to be innocent, not for all the world. Right? He just wouldn't.

Someone he *knew* to be innocent. That's the key word. Right now, though, he doesn't know I'm innocent. He feels it in his gut. He wants to believe it. But he must also consider that I'm on the run from New York. I still worry that Victor knows about that for sure, and is sitting on it. If that becomes known to the people who want Big's to fail, certainly that in itself will be the end of Victor's career, and quite possibly his family. And Big's. And my freedom. Total catastrophe for all involved. All except the likes of KFC, Pizza Hut and Burger King.

Apart from Victor's gut feeling, right now about the only thing on my side is that pair of earrings, but even that's not exculpatory. That boy can say simply that he found them somewhere—like what I said about the bra out at the lake. *I found them on the ground and gave them to my girlfriend. So arrest me.*

No. I'm still the one in the crosshairs. I will say to you right here and now that I am very, very sorry to be forced into this, but there's no way I'm going back to jail. I simply cannot do it. The decision isn't even in my power to reverse. I can't sit in my cell and write prison philosophy like Boethius and that crowd. I'd be the guy who makes bed sheets into a noose and hangs himself from a light fixture. I already feel events closing in on me, feel them as a pressure on my chest, just as I did the blackness of my prison cell that first morning. To be honest, it's all I can do not to run straight to the bus station right now. Thankfully, the magnetic pull of Charlene and you and Big's and my wonderful little life here, is strong enough to overcome the impetus to flee. You can't imagine how polarized my urges are. I must go. I must stay. No, I've got to haul ass to Mexico. No, my heart is here.

Some odd consequences come to my mind as I contemplate my choices. If I do a runner, I'll certainly take Jezebel, although Charlene will almost as certainly stay with Big's, which means you will stay in Twisting Creek. Which means you will never meet Jezebel. This wonderful companion won't be part of your childhood.

Look—what can I say? I could let remorse eat me alive, but if my arrest is imminent, I'm out of here. I do promise you this, though: when I reach some place of safety—assuming there is one—I will do all I can to bring you and Charlene to me. Everything in my power. But I also have to say, in all candor, that when push gets to shove, I'm gone. Feel free to curse my name. Label me whatever you want. Coward, weasel, fraud, hypocrite. I won't contradict you. But also call me: fugitive.

Luckily, I'm not there yet. There are still some things I can do to ward off Armageddon. The big one at the moment is to hold, as Leo put it, Lonnie's feet to the flames. Although, as I think about it, that phrase has it more or less backwards, since I'll be the one feeling the heat, until the result, where, if my analysis of Lonnie Farley's motive is right, my method will produce the crucial information. Meaning, I learn what Lonnie knows about Angela's disappearance.

(You know what I have to do to get that, don't you? Do you think I'd be doing shit like this if I didn't love you?)

I suspect Lonnie, too, is eager to get on with our exchange, because yesterday there was an email from him to Charlene, bcc'd to me, reminding us that tomorrow, Sunday, August 15, is Memorial Day. Of course that isn't America's Memorial Day. It's the day Lonnie and his congregation at the Church of the Blood Spilled on Calvary hold religious services to commemorate the passing of Mr. and Mrs. Farley. Could the timing of Angela's disappearance and this church service be a coincidence? Maybe—but it's a big one and bears thinking about. To be precise, it was on August 16, thirteen years ago, that the elder Farleys had a big helping of beans and botulism for dinner, and now, every year on the Sunday nearest that date, Lonnie moves his congregation to the makeshift outdoor church that lies alongside the small family graveyard way up almost on top of the hill that locals call Farley Mountain. This ritual brings with it the subject of Lonnie's email—Saturday graveyard clean-up. The day before the church service, Charlene and I meet up with Lonnie and any members of his church he's somehow coerced into devoting a dog day Saturday to hard physical labor.

Charlene never goes to the Sunday service, of course. She wouldn't be caught dead sitting there with people who jump up from their benches, wave their arms in the air and blurt out sounds in tongues, and then take the stage and lift rattlesnakes over their heads like Wimbledon trophies. "Speaking in tongues," in case you don't know, is when a religious fervor entices people to make speech-like utterances that correspond to no known earthly language. Supposedly they can understand each other. It would be a simple matter to test that hypothesis, but I doubt anyone's ever done it.

Anyway, Charlene thinks they're all batshit crazy. She says they should put on Spock ears and speak Vulcan. Your mom is an uncompromising realist, as you will soon enough see for yourself. Your dad, however, believes weirdness of this magnitude merits watching up close, so I've attended a couple of his big tent meetings and last year I attended the Farley

Mountain Memorial Day service. This is where he breaks out Satan and his fellow reptiles. Maybe that was enough to make Lonnie think I'm a potential convert. He may think that my occasional attendance is enough to throw doubt on all the barbs I've aimed at him and his religion. Come to think of it, he probably thinks my belief in science is as much a pose as is his religious posturing. He wants to think that he and I are doing our own private scorpion dance. You noticed he didn't cc that email, he bcc'd it. He thinks his maneuverings will work out perfectly, providing we all keep our secrets intact. He believes that when the stakes are high enough, I will join him on stage to take up snakes and speak gibberish, and then he can notch his salvation gun for the biggest prize in Twisting Creek.

Funny thing is, he's right. If I can work up the courage, it will happen tomorrow afternoon. But right now let me tell you what happened today, Saturday.

As I said, Charlene attends the Saturday graveyard grooming. She sees it as a dutiful way to honor her parents, not to assist her brother. We left home almost as the sun rose. On our way to the truck she tossed me the keys and headed for the passenger seat. Every time we've driven anywhere since I proposed marriage to her, I'm the driver. I have no idea why, but I think you may find it an interesting change. I know I do. This morning it meant I drove the truck to the top of Farley Mountain—my first time driving up one of these rough hollows where the "road" is more metaphor than anything. We bumped along slowly, bouncing violently enough to draw squeaky protests from the metal springs in our seat. I did fine behind the wheel.

Jezebel, who had automatically jumped into the back of truck, where by now she rides just like any other canine native of these parts, was being jostled about pretty strenuously. She started whining at the rear window, so I stopped and let her in the cab with us. She sat upright between us, like the guest of honor.

Even at that time of the morning, hardly an hour after sunrise, we weren't the first ones to reach the top of the hill. Most of Lonnie's cult members pitch in and help, and we saw four of their cars already there, parked on a slant just beside a wide and sagging wooden gate that marks the entrance to the Farley family graveyard. The trunk lid of one car stood open, and as we got closer we saw a man leaning into it, looking for a tool or something. He was repairing the broken hinge. He took his cap off to wipe his forehead on his sleeve, saw us get out of the truck, and greeted us with his lifted cap.

It was hot already. Morning sunshine pulled steam from the thick vegetation, and the call of insects had more sizzle up here, far above human incursion.

The burial section itself occupies about half the space of a flat piece of ground near the crest of the mountain. The whole "flat", as it's called, is surrounded by a barrier that's mostly a rock wall, except the front portion, which is a zig-zag split rail fence. Lonnie says it's been there all his life. It looks as old as Daniel Boone.

Even though the graveyard sits on a mountain ridge, the view from the top is almost entirely disappointing. Tall trees and a jungle of secondary growth restrict sight lines all the way around, except one rocky point that doesn't have anything growing on it, where you can walk to the edge and scan the coal-scarred mountains far up and down the creek. By this time of summer, Twisting Creek Valley is a tattered green fabric covering the waves in the earth's crust, with a gleaming silver ribbon running down the middle.

Inside the enclosed area, the near half is devoted to a primitive sort of outdoor church arrangement. There are about ten double rows of rough plank benches, warped, full of splinters, and, when we got there today, covered with dead leaves and debris. Cleaning all that away was part of why we were there. In front of the benches, there's a raised wooden floor for the preacher and pulpit. It's wider than you might think it needs to be to accommodate one preacher. That's because preachers of Lonnie's sort tend to pace frenetically back and forth; also they need room for an altar, and, when the snake cages are brought out, room for them and the people who brandish the evil serpents.

On the ground just off the right-hand corner of the stage there sat a "zinc bucket" of water, with an old-fashioned metal dipper down in it. Every person who turned up on this hot August day to help clean off the graveyard was going to need a lot of water, and we'd all be drinking it from one vessel. It seems whatever impulse it is that makes people like the Amish want to live in the past, it's still strong in Lonnie's people too, and, interestingly, only in church services. Most of them— probably all—have cable TV, and you already know Lonnie has Internet, because you know he sent me an email. But here at the graveyard, it's water from a dipper. Maybe it's fitting if we all infect each other, while honoring a man and wife who died of botulism.

Past the benches and the preaching platform is where the graves are located. These are not flat, grassy burial plots, but mounded bare-earth graves. After a year's neglect, they form a grisly memorial to the souls they enclose. Rain cuts deep gullies in the mounds, and everything is covered in weeds. Fallen tree branches are everywhere. Add to that the things I mentioned before, the copperheads, black widows, centipedes, poison ivy, prolific thorn vines. It's like some evil inner sanctum where death hides out, and once each year we must trespass there.

That's what we were here to set right. By the time we left, this place would be a showpiece of pride in ancestry. First we dig out all the weeds, rake fresh dirt over the mounds, clean the markers, then for a final touch we prop fresh wreaths near the headstones. There are several others buried here, not only Mom and Pop Farley, who occupy the two newest graves. It's easy to see that the Farley money started with them. They have a big double-wide polished granite headstone, with their names and dates engraved, and with the enigmatic epitaph "Death Loves a Shining Mark" outlined in a sort of filigree wreath of palm and laurel branches. We wash this down with dishwashing liquid, and soon it sparkles like new.

Of the other twenty or so graves, some have weathered slate tombstones, where the inscriptions are minimal, and are wearing away. On some even the names are hardly legible. Even older than those are burial sites marked only by two sandstone rocks stood on end, one at the head and one at the foot. No words or markings of any kind. These are the final resting places of your great- and great-great-grandparents, great aunts and uncles, and distant cousins. So far, between Lonnie and Charlene, the occupants of all those plots are known, but surely family memory will run out in a generation or two, and they'll all be forgotten. Maybe that's as it should be, I don't know. It's interesting to think—this just now popped into my head—the responsibility for remembering all those names and relationships will eventually fall to you. Pull your socks up.

One sad observation is that when you go back to the time of the sandstone markers, many of those graves are tiny. Some measure only about a yard between headstone and footstone. I can admit to you that the sight of these lost children affected me very differently this year than last year.

Graveyard clean-up is such a long day that I don't even try to make it to Big's on time. If by the end I'm exhausted, I don't go in at all. That's what happened today. Trusty Rusty takes charge, no big deal. That's why tonight I'm writing you from home, alone. I forgot to tell you that. I've got a small writing table set up here on our screened-in back porch. Charlene's got a lot of rattan things out here, all painted white. It looks very southern. Sorry—I meant wicker. Graceful and very Old Kentucky. The ceiling fan's on, low. I can hear rain on the trees in our back yard. It's only just now started, not yet a downpour. Tomorrow's outdoor service may well be under threat.

Charlene is at Big's, though. She likes to be there as emcee, so she left the graveyard early and took the truck home. I said I'd get a ride into town with Lonnie.

By the time the sun started dropping behind the mountain ridge, spreading welcome shade across the flat, we'd nearly finished the job. A couple of Lonnie's people were still raking near the fence and repositioning fresh wreaths on their metal tripods. Jezebel was digging at one of those old graves. I suppose she somehow sensed a treasure trove of bones down there. She got a sniff of something and really ramped up her efforts, her front legs tearing at the fresh dirt, which she sent streaming backwards. I spoke her name sharply, and her paws slowed to a meticulous tamping, as though she was only trying to be useful.

Lonnie had come up with a plastic bottle of water from somewhere, and sat on a rear bench, taking sips and looking at the sky. I looked up to see what he was looking at. There was a cold front moving in, a wedge of gray cloud slicing across the mountaintop. Only now I realized that the cool relief I was feeling came not only from a setting sun, but from this new weather pattern.

I went over and sat down beside him. Jez followed and stretched herself comfortably lengthwise along the bench beside me. Lonnie offered me a sip of water, which I accepted, then nearly spit out across two or three benches, because it wasn't water after all. It was vodka. Apple, I think. I contained myself and swallowed as normally as I could. His eyes crinkled back into thin wrinkles of a smile. If his face weren't so fat, I doubt I'd have recognized it as a smile. I managed, "Very refreshing."

He took it back for another swig, looked up at the advancing gray line of cloud cover, and said, "I hope that don't rain out tonight's game."

This knocked me back a bit. I'd mentally and prematurely finished his sentence with *tomorrow's service*. "Game? You mean the Reds?" I was starting to realize how little I knew about Lonnie's life.

"They're at home tonight. That front is heading straight for Cincinnati. Usually it's the reverse—we get their weather."

I scanned the skies. "Hard to predict."

He said, "The Lord sends rain on the just and on the unjust. *Matthew 5:45*."

"And on the Reds and on the Cardinals. *Sports Illustrated*."

He smiled, took another sip, and passed it back to me. I now noticed that his eyes were starting to exhibit an alcohol shine. I took another drink with him. What the hell? Probably safer than drinking water from that communal dipper.

I continued, "I didn't know you were a baseball fan." One of the many wonderful attributes of baseball is that it provides a rare opportunity for people like me and people like Lonnie to talk about something and be on the same plane. It's somehow exempt from all the churchy dogma. Nobody from Lonnie's side ever says "The Good Lord laid down the supreme sacrifice bunt," nor does the opposite side ask, "Where was your god when Jay Bruce tried to score from first on a single?" No, it's mostly "Chapman was lights out again," or "Arroyo was hitting the corners all night long." I don't know why sport is a blind spot, but I'm grateful for it and was happy to take advantage of it with Lonnie.

"Been a Reds fan all my life," he said. "Mommy and Daddy always had a game on. Back then it was mostly radio around here."

"Charlene's hates it." He gave me a look that I interpreted to mean, *What would you expect?* I said, "We should drive up and catch a game sometime."

"You and Charlene?"

"Me and you."

I think he was surprised to hear me chum up that way. He nodded and handed the bottle back to me, but didn't say anything, so I continued, "Did you ever go to a game with them?" I tilted my head toward his parents' grave.

"Huhn-uhn," he said. "First they were too poor, then they were too old."

"Ah. Too bad." I knew where I wanted to steer this conversation—I wanted to talk about me handling a snake in exchange for what he knew about Angela, but I was having trouble making a smooth transition. The idea of *exchange* in a baseball conversation gave me an angle. I asked him, "Do you think the Reds should trade a reliever or two for some help on the bench?"

"I wouldn't mess with that bullpen."

He had no idea where I was going, and I knew I'd made the right move. "Maybe. But sometimes a good trade can benefit both sides."

"Like Josh Hamilton for Edinson Volquez?" One of the worst trades in Reds' history.

I laughed. "No, more like if one man needs a favor, and another man needs some information, they can work something out."

"I don't get what you're drivin' at."

"For example, one man wants to boost his image among local church folk, and another man is looking for someone. Let's say, a woman." He didn't answer me, but I could tell his brain was in high gear. "Don't you think they could work something out?"

"A woman?" he asked. "What kind of woman?"

"A city woman. The kind you find in junkyards."

"In *junkyards?*" He took a long drink from his plastic

bottle. "What does that mean?"

"A woman who turns up in a rare old car, like a Dodge Neon, maybe."

This time he didn't pass the bottle, just took another pull. "I always said you're a man of mystery."

"I can keep my mouth shut when I need to. Are you bringing your snakes to tomorrow's service?"

"Does Charlene know about the information you're interested in?"

"Nope."

"I want Charlene here too. She needs to witness this."

"Not a chance, preacher man. This is between you and me."

"And Satan."

"Who's Satan?"

"My favorite cottonmouth."

"Of course Satan," I said. "He's the guest of honor."

19

Hᴇᴍɴ ꜱɪɴɢɪɴɢ ᴡᴀꜱ already under way when Jezebel and I—minus Charlene—pulled up at the graveyard gate. They sang in draggy, droning, languorous, voices. The style seemed to appeal to Jezebel, who raised her muzzle and joined in a chorus. I cleared my throat at her, cutting her song short. She shot me one of her *You need to lighten up* looks and made her way to a bench at the rear, where I joined her.

Lonnie was on his preaching platform, with one hand clutching a hymnal, and the other cupped over his ear. I don't think he saw us come in. His face was tilted toward the heavens and his eyes were closed. His snake box tagged "Satan" was sitting on what I took to be an altar. If so, it seems like an unsuitable place for Satan, but I'm not going to argue doctrine with them. Some people along the rows had their own snake boxes sitting on the bench beside them, but apparently as the headliner I got first go at center stage. Then, one by one, moved by some spirit or urge, others will move onto the stage. At least that's the way it always happened before.

Me? I'm doing the minimal required for an official snake handling experience and then hauling my ass back to the rear bench, where I can watch the action in comfort and safety. There's no doubting that as spectacle it's seriously riveting. Somebody is apt to die right before your eyes, a self-inflicted death by a person who to all appearances had no wish to die. Someone who already has prepared a big pot of chicken and dumplings for Sunday dinner, and has a banana cream pie ready for the oven. But somebody who won't get dessert this Sunday, or ever again, all because they tempted a wild and amoral creature to do what's in its nature.

Couldn't they accomplish the same thing with a hamster? And why do they do it? I have no idea, but I know why I'm doing it, and that's good enough.

Some people smiled and nodded to me as I walked past. For the second year running I had joined them in the Saturday graveyard cleanup, and down here, you do backbreaking outdoor work together, you both give and earn respect. I was surprised—still am—to find that I had grown fond of some of these people. If I needed somebody to help dig my car out of a ditch, or "carry me" (give me a lift) to the hospital any time day or night, here sat quite a few volunteers. I have no doubt of that.

Probably at that moment I needed to feel kinship with them. All through the service I kept reminding myself to stay calm, maintain my poise, focus on the end result, when I would place my hands inside the cage where Satan the cottonmouth lay snoozing away—preferably in a coma—and lift him up for the congregants to see.

Lonnie's self-esteem would inflate beyond measure, and maybe his income along with it. My act of faith would confirm him as a true miracle man, the fisher of men who could really haul in the big ones, even smarty-pants New Yorkers. It would show those snooty downtown First Baptists and Methodists that the snake handling practice so heartily recommended in Mark whatever-it-was, was no outlier to the Bible, not some crackpot cult gig, but a tenet as central to Christianity as John 3:16. And if they shied away from such a practice, maybe they needed a little lesson in faith, the kind Brother Lonnie Farley provided over at the Church of the Blood Spilled on Calvary, and that even gourmet chefs can understand. Then I'd carefully replace Satan in his cage, tuck him in if necessary, retreat to my rear bench, and await my return on this bizarre bargain.

That was the way I imagined it all the time I sat there on my rear bench, alone but for Jezebel, who lay asleep lengthwise, just like yesterday, only this time under the bench instead of on it. I suppose she changed spots in response to the rain, which now had returned as a fine mist, but which overnight had been just heavy enough to dampen the "pews" (as Lonnie insists on calling them) while leaving the ground underneath relatively dry.

Was that the reason? I wondered about that while I sat there ignoring Lonnie and his sermon. As well as I know Jezebel, and she knows me, there are so many questions I'll never get an answer to. There could be other reasons. If I could only ask her, she might say, *Oh, because it's softer under here.* Or, *I didn't feel stable on that narrow bench.* Or, *I like the feel of the cool (warm?) earth against my side.* It could be something totally out of our realm, like, *There's a wormy aroma down here that's really relaxing.*

So you see what my mind was doing. Running around with its head cut off (Charlene's expression). Anything to avoid thinking about Satan's gaping mother-of-pearl inner jaws, but it was a hard vision to shake. For a while I tried to think about my core menu. A very popular dish is my spin-off of Lebanese chicken livers, pan fried in olive oil with yellow peppers and onions and annatto. (180 calories) We list it in a menu section labeled *Not for cholesterol-restricted diets.* All our chicken is free-range, all from local organic producers. Still, should chicken livers be part of our menu? I tried thinking about that. Anything to avoid a mental video of me reaching my hands down into a cramped, glassed-in box, where long, white fangs ache for release.

It's odd, though. Sometimes when you're trying not to think about one thing, your mind will hop straight over to another thing you don't want to think about. Like right now

I remembered something Victor said in my cell that first day. He said none of Angela's contact info was live. He said he expected to hear from NYPD very soon. And that's the last I heard of it. Did they respond? What did they say? Why hasn't he mentioned it to me since? Why haven't I asked him?

Okay, I think I know the answer to that one: because I don't want to know. I'm in denial about it, just as I was in denial of Satan sitting in there, coiled and hissing at me. When your whole brain is pockmarked with regions you can't bear to contemplate, that could be a sign it's time for a change.

But then again, a change was just what I was trying to effect here, on this mountaintop, with all these weirdly normal people. By this point in the show most of them were on their feet, waving both hands in the air, speaking in odd ways— though for *Hallelujah* and *Praise Jesus* and a few others, they switched back to English, maybe for my benefit. Change was why I was here, right? Or rather, reversing a change that's in progress, which amounts to the same thing. If I can learn Lonnie's secrets, I'll be back in control of events. At least potentially. Am I right? When I wrote you from jail I think I said I needed to get out of there because I couldn't unravel this from inside. This is what I was referring to. This is my chance to restore contentment to our lives. All I have to do is pick up that snake.

I've done a little research about this. The cottonmouth, or water moccasin, as people here call it, doesn't rattle a warning, therefore isn't a rattlesnake. (Maybe I'm the only one who thought it was.) It's of a different genus, although, like the rattler, it's a pit viper, meaning it has two slots in its face, between the eyes and nostril, and these openings (pits) can sense heat the way you or I sense sound with our ears. Their heads are shaped like arrow points, and have bony ridges that hood their eyes, so that they can't be seen from above. In other words, when I open that box and look down into it, I won't know if Satan's eyes are watching my hands or not. But does that really matter? Its heat pits will see my hands moving in on it. And the cottonmouth is an aggressive species. The badass of the swamp.

I'm spending all this time describing my thought processes because this is one instance when both you and I know the outcome. We know I didn't die of snakebite, or else you wouldn't be reading this. I could be in the hospital, writing from there. You don't know where I am, but you know I'm not dead. In any case, no, I'm not in the hospital, and I didn't get bit.

It was far, far more serious than that.

I don't know exactly what I heard. I guess my brain registered a change in Lonnie's delivery of the sermon, and I noticed some faces turned toward me. Maybe my heat-sensing pit picked up the signal. I don't know. But I saw Lonnie take Satan's cage from the altar and bend over to place it on the floor. When he stood back up, he was looking straight at me.

My legs picked me up and delivered me to the platform. That's the best way I can put it. I can't remember any act of will involved. I simply arrived on stage, facing the crowd, with the snake box at my feet. Lonnie had retreated to the far edge. His arms were fully extended over his head, and his hands flitted like birds. He smiled at me, gave a nod to the box. I leaned over and opened the lid.

First thing I notice: This isn't the Satan I'd seen at the café. That Satan was thick and sinewy, covered in a grid of small pastel scales, light colors, mostly tan and gray. This snake has big black diamonds and white connecting stripes. It's much smaller, both in length and girth. Lonnie has switched snakes on me.

Why? I had only an instant to consider the question, and no answer came to me. My brain mustered one thought and it stuck: the most poisonous snake in America is a little one. I couldn't even think of its name (coral snake—later it popped into my head). All I could think was small equals lethal.

Lonnie saw me hesitate. He lowered his hands long enough to make a lifting gesture with them, and to clap a few times, like a third base coach. Then he started up again with the hallelujahs. After still more hesitation, he nodded toward the cage and gave me a full smile. It was a smile meant to convey, *Don't worry, it's all good.* I leaned down and put my hands towards the snakes' body and—do you believe in miracles? No? Well then, explain what happened, starting in my fingers and radiating up my arms? I looked at Lonnie and let fly with my own Hallelujah, as heartfelt as any ever uttered.

HALLELUJAH! What my fingers felt was cold air! I looked carefully at a bed of grass where the snake lay, and I realized it wasn't level with the cage floor. This was a false bottom. Brother Lonnie had a layer of ice buried under there. *HALLELUJAH!*

I picked that snake up. No more lifeless snake ever demonstrated the power of the Word of God. It seemed to be suffering rigor mortis. Yet even as it rose from its confinement and the congregation erupted into shouts and tongues, something else started happening out on the edge of my awareness, where, through a clatter of claws on wood, and ladies screaming, Jezebel charged past people and over pews, leapt onto the stage and jerked the snake out of my hands before I had time to react. She gave that thing a series of neck shakes and slapped its flaccid body against the floor like a whip. She dropped it, crouched at it, barked at it, made up-and-back feints. The snake moved and once again Jez had it between her teeth, slashing it back and forth. Now I recall puppy Jezebel doing that same thing, to a stuffed toy, or a pillow. This was what she'd been training for.

The snake, once nearly frozen, was wide awake now. Blood was oozing out its sides but it would go down fighting. Wide jaws opened and moved toward Jezebel's throat, then that heartbreaking sight, the black-and-white arrowhead closing on her neck, striking, attaching, hanging there.

With a vicious jerk of her neck, she pulled it loose. The fangs were buried so deep that they and the top half of the snake's head remained stuck in her neck, while the body of the snake hung limp from her mouth. She knew the act was over, so she leapt onto the altar and went rigid in her Monument to Canine Virtue statue. Everyone froze and stared at her. Lonnie too. Me too. The crowd had gone silent. Jezebel was silent. The mountainside was silent.

Finally my muscles released and I grabbed her up in my arms and ran to the truck. I bounced that thing down the hill like a bowling ball. Jezebel was trying to look out the window and kept getting jostled. She looked around to scold me three or four times. Finally we hit the asphalt of an almost empty county road where I could really pick up speed. I also managed to call Charlene at home and tell her to alert Kyle Taybert at our animal clinic that I was bringing Jez in with a rattlesnake bite.

Only when I finished that call did I realize I'd driven almost to the town's first stoplight (which I ran) and I looked around for Jezebel at the window, but she wasn't there. She was lying stretched out along the front seat, with her head draped over my leg. She flicked me an upward glance before she closed her eyes. I felt a twitch in her softening body. She was falling asleep.

I stroked her face and ran every light. I kept thinking, *She's going to die in my lap* and *that is only fitting because I did this to her. I killed her as a direct consequence of my actions in New York.* If I hadn't robbed the restaurant, Angela would never have hunted me down. Jezebel wouldn't be lying here depleted while snake venom attacks her brain and her blood cells. The responsibility is all mine. These moments will haunt me until my own final breath.

Time after time I spoke her name. She released a sigh of deep contentment—I felt it in my hand. Imagine how precious that sensation will be, for as long as feeling lasts. I kept thinking—no, it wasn't thinking. I kept wishing, wishing for prayer, wishing for someone to pray to. But it wasn't belief. It was more like disbelief that this was happening. I disbelieved that at age eight weeks she ran up and sang to me in a park. I disbelieved I'd ever burgled a restaurant or ever heard of Angela Van Landingham. All I believed in now was speed. I drove like mad, as though I still had some say in the outcome.

Kyle Taybert lives upstairs from his clinic, so as soon as I turned the last corner I could see him already waiting in the parking lot. When I stopped I sent gravel flying, and Kyle got the passenger door open before my wheels stopped skidding. I carefully lifted Jezebel's head from my leg, and slid out the driver's side. Behind me Kyle shouted, "Whoa!" and then Jezebel shot right past me. She circled the truck to greet Kyle—he gives her treats—then came back round to me. She used her lively-but-polite gait. I asked Kyle, "Shouldn't we try to keep her quiet?"

He had found the half snakehead in the floorboard of the truck and was inspecting the fangs. "Um, I think that may not be necessary." He held them up to the light. "These are clean. I don't think they broke the skin." On her neck I indicated for Kyle the general area of the fangs' entry point. He peered down into all that dense hair, but saw no wound. He scratched her behind her ears. "That's why you evolved that thick ruff, isn't it, girl?"

We went into the examination room and an exquisite thing happened. Jezebel hopped from the floor to a sofa to the arm of the sofa and onto the examining table, where she froze in her statue stunt, nose straight out, tail straight back, eyes straight ahead. She held it until she couldn't hold back a smile, so she broke pose, came at me laughing, and buried her head in my shoulder. She was saying *This has been the funnest day ever.*

20

VICKI YAPITA-CROSBY IS a Big's regular, a success story, certainly. Nothing like our biggest loser, but she was only thirty or so pounds overweight when she joined. She's a stalwart who uses her position as psychologist at Franklin College to bring in others who need help far more than she did. She's got the Andean look of her forebears, with a broad, burnished face, high cheekbones, eyes like drops of black paint, and a low hairline that forms a widow's peak as sharp as a spear point. When someone is talking to her about a serious matter, her face signals concern by lowering her hairline even more, until her forehead is a thin band of wrinkles, but when the conversation lightens, her face is quick to animate, and when the music starts, she moves straight for the dance floor.

Until this afternoon, Vicki's main attribute in my mind was the way she asks Charlene for the microphone during the "Invitational" and advises our members to seek the kind of self-renewal that does not require a complete rift with the past. She says that the decision to reform one's life frequently brings with it a rejection of the former self, which in turn hardens into self-loathing because we can't really divorce who we are now from who we once were. And self-hatred is pre-determined defeat. That's more or less how Vicki puts it, and she illustrates her point with some examples from her own experience as a counselor.

She takes it upon herself to explain this to our members perhaps once a month, or more often when a batch of new members comes along. She says something like, "The person you once were is not your enemy. He or she used to be your dear friend. They were with you in happy times, and they stuck with you through hard times. But people change. You've moved on. Think of your old self as a good friend who sometimes dared you to choose behavior you'd really prefer to avoid, and now you've moved to a town far away, and you're free from their influence. But you loved them once, you love them still, and they'll always remain in your heart."

None of that had ever occurred to me. I guess I don't think like a psychologist. To be perfectly candid, the first time I heard Vicki say that, I thought, "Pure psychobabble. I left myself and moved to another town? Who came up with that nonsense?" But I glanced over at Charlene to get her reaction and saw that her eyes were damp. Since then I've checked out the listening guests, and more than one has wiped away a tear. And guess what? It took me an embarrassingly long to time to say, *Wait a second, Jake. Didn't you leave your old self and move to another town? You even changed your name. You weren't 'Jake' in New York.* And then maybe a little redness came to my eye too. Vicki had reached a place I didn't even know existed. This feat of psychology was what I thought of first when I thought of Vicki Yapita-Crosby—until this morning.

That patchy rainfall that tantalized us all weekend materialized not long after we left the vet's yesterday, and delivered a steady downpour all night. Today was also wet, so I didn't go for a run or to Fifi's either. By late morning I was on a stationary bike in Big's gym section, and Charlene was on a treadmill. Jez was lying in the opposite corner with her head on her paws. She wasn't asleep—one eyebrow popped up occasionally when somebody came in. The gym has a really thick soundproofing door to isolate it from the restaurant area, but it stays open much of the day. First I saw Jez lift an eyebrow, then her ears, then her head. Only at that point did I hear someone deep inside the restaurant call out, "Jake!"

"In here," I said. "In the gym."

It was Vicki. She rushed through that big gym door and hurried toward me. She was near tears. She said, "Oh my god Jake—I had no idea . . . " but then she spotted Jezebel, who had stood up at the sound of her voice and was looking at us from her corner. Vicki shouted "Ooooh!" or the equivalent, and made a sharp turn toward her. She squatted and pulled Jez into a tight embrace. Jez looked up at me as though to ask, *Any idea what this woman's up to?*

No, I had no idea. I dismounted the bike. Vicki looked back toward me, a wide grin on her face, and asked, "Where did you find her?"

"What do you mean?"

She was burying her face in Jezebel's ruff. I heard her repeat, "Where did you find her?"

I know it sounds random now, but I repeated it too. "Where did I find her?"

Still squatting and holding Jezebel by the neck, Vicki turned an expectant face to me.

"Well," I told her, "one day in New York I was walking in Riverside Park, and there she . . . "

Vicki's face lost its shine. "No! I mean today!"

"Wait a second. You must be . . . what exactly are you asking me? She hasn't been lost."

"But the message . . . " Now she stood and walked toward me. "Could there be more than one Jezebel around here?"

I had no answer for that, so I asked, "What message?"

She bent her head and held it in her hands, with her fingers touching her temples and her thumbs under her chin. "I'm sure I read it right. Okay. Let's see. I just now drove back from a trip to Louisville. I thought I could make it home without a final pit stop, but I needed gas, and I really needed a break, so . . . you know that GoMart station just up the freeway? At the

exit to Buffalo Run? I went in to use the restroom and there was this strange message saying HELP
FIND JEZEBEL."

"Jeez, that's strange. In a restroom at Buffalo Run?" I asked myself if this had something to do with yesterday, if possibly some snake handling resident of Buffalo Run had witnessed Jezebel's production of Death of Satan and wanted to condemn her for it. Or maybe praise her for it. Canonize her. You never know with these guys.

"Yes! Right at that exit. It was even weirder because it wasn't a printout or anything. It was written on the restroom mirror, in red lipstick."

Red lipstick. The thought went through my mind that Angela wore *only* red lipstick. Red underwear and red lipstick. And then I saw an alternate meaning. Maybe it wasn't asking people to help locate a missing Jezebel. More than likely it was *Help! Find Jezebel!* Why Angela, or anybody else, would have phrased it that way isn't something that at this point I can puzzle out to any satisfactory conclusion, but it makes more sense than anything else I can think of.

I called Victor. He was in his car and on his way even before he hung up the phone. He'd also dispatched a car to the GoMart at Buffalo Run. He got to Big's about five minutes later and once he got here and heard what Vicki saw and how it might be read, he changed his mind about his deputy and called him off.

"How long ago did you find that message?" he asked Vicki.

"I came straight here. I've been here about ten minutes."

"The Buffalo Run turn is no more than twenty minutes away—so roughly a half hour ago?"

"Thirty to forty minutes," Vicki told him.

"That place has a little grocery store too, right?" Victor asked,

Vicki said, "Mostly snacks and drinks."

"And cigarettes. What we need isn't a uniformed officer, but a woman nobody would connect with either Big's or the Sheriff's Department." He went straight for his phone, and we heard him say, "Hey, Yolanda, how would you like to get in on a story?"

I couldn't hear her part, but obviously she agreed.

"All right, then. This needs to remain completely private for now. Here's what we need. Drive as quick as you can over to that GoMart at Buffalo Run. Act casual. Buy something, make normal conversation, then go into the ladies' room and see if there's anything written on the mirror. If there is, make sure you're alone and take a picture of it. Whatever you do, don't let anybody see you do anything that looks like an investigation. Here's the key question: try to find out when the bathroom was cleaned. And if the message has already been wiped off, find out the last two cleanings. See what I mean? To bracket the time of the message. They might keep a cleaning log on the back of the door or on the wall near it. If so, take a picture of that." He paused a moment and then said, "That might work." He asked Vicki, "Was the bathroom clean or dirty?"

"It was fine, I think."

He told Yolanda, "It won't be very dirty. If you tell them it's for a newspaper feature, say it's all about how clean our area's public restrooms are. Ask for their cleaning schedule." Again he waited while she said something, then he answered, "Sure, interview the cleaner if you can. Ask them if they ever find weird things in there. But keep it all normal and friendly. Arouse no suspicion." He paused and laughed. "Sure, someday I'll tell you just what the hell is going on. But right now, hurry." He rang off and told us, "She says she's already in her car."

Vicki said, "Maybe somebody could tell me too just what the hell is going on?"

"I promise to do exactly that, someday. But right now

what I need from you is complete silence on this. Okay? Not a word to anyone."

Charlene said, "Sounds to me like she's still playing mind games with us."

Victor didn't respond directly to that, not even with so much as a glance at me, but I'm certain we shared the same thought: *That underwear was no joke.* Instead, he said, "She's telling us to search for her, not for her corpse."

21

I'M AFRAID I got a bit ahead of myself with that GoMart discovery. It was big news—wonderful news—so I suppose it couldn't wait, but another reason I inserted it ahead of this part is that in the aftermath of Jezebel's encounter with an eastern massasauga rattlesnake (as it turned out to be) my mind was too disturbed to continue. It was as though my brain had been dropped into the bowl of an industrial dough kneader and the hooks were tearing into it from every direction. How close I had come to losing her! By whose hand? Not Lunatic Lonnie's, that's for sure. As you will hear, his hands were silky clean. He comes off as the fucking hero here. No, it was me. I almost killed my beloved puppy, all by putting myself in a position where I need information from a morally twisted con man.

First though, here's the latest on the GoMart story. Yolanda was able to pinpoint a forty-five to fifty minute window when Angela might have been there. Victor has collected the security video. Deputies are keeping some kind of lookout, although keeping it undercover is more important than trying to overreach and make it airtight. So far they think it's still secret. The actual cleaner signed in as Humberto, but there's no Humberto working there. They haven't figured out what that means.

That's it. That's all Victor has told me about GoMart right now. As for us—Charlene, Jezebel and me—after we left the vet's yesterday, and before we needed to open Big's, we stopped for a nice, long romp in the park. Obviously if I want to keep my NYC felony secret from Charlene, I can't tell her about my Faustian bargain with her brother, so I tried to obfuscate on just exactly how Jez had come so close to a serious accident. "Somebody who didn't know what they were doing opened the snake cage and it came out and a split-second later Jez was on it." True enough, for a letter-of-the-law interpretation, by my god how much truth can you omit and still have it be true?

Then, after I made sure the kitchen was in good hands, I slipped away quietly and drove through steady rain out to Lonnie's house. I was eager to know what he knew, and to parley that into a strategy, and that into action.

Lonnie lives precisely where he grew up, by the creek at the foot of Farley Mountain. One smart thing Lonnie did while he still had money was to buy the little farm they'd rented all those years ago, and replace the old shack with a modern log home. It's tucked away up a county road, just around a wide bend in the creek, so if you know where to look between the trees you can see it up ahead for maybe half a mile. That's a long vista for around here. The thing to look for is a wraparound cedar porch with a green roof. One corner of it fits into a bend in the creek, where he has lined the far bank with ornamental cherry trees. It can be very pretty at times, especially in the spring when the trees blossom. You'd never imagine the kind of man who lived there.

When I cleared the curve, I spotted the house, with Lonnie rocking on his porch. Sitting way out here all by himself, wearing a short-sleeved white shirt and a tie. When I turned into his yard and got a good look at his face, I knew he'd been drinking. His eyes had that shine again, and even his rocking motion had a hitch in it, something not quite relaxed and normal, that I would soon find echo of in his snappish mood. I parked the truck and rolled down the window.

"She's fine," I told him.

He only nodded his head.

"The fangs couldn't pierce all that hair on her neck."

"I could'a told you that."

"How did you know?"

He gave me a disgusted look and reached down to the floor for a green Seven-Up bottle. "Because it was a goddamn eastern massasauga rattlesnake, that's how. Who do you think put it there?"

"I don't know. Maybe Moses?" In all honesty, that was nothing but a quip. I had no idea what he was talking about.

He repeated, "Moses?"

It was odd having a conversation through the rain like this. Maybe he felt it, too. With the bottom of his pop bottle he gestured the offer of a drink. I climbed out of the truck, sprinted through the rain, and took the chair beside him.

"I could sure use one." I took a good sip and asked, "Is that apple?"

"You don't like it, I got a ten-dollar bottle of Old Crow in there."

"No, this is fine. Hit's the spot."

"Why the fuck Moses?"

See, this was new, too. I'd never heard him use foul language, none at all, not even hell and damn, much less G-D's and F-bombs. And I should say here that all through the belligerent conversation to follow, that Seven-Up bottle keeps passing back and forth.

I said, "Didn't Moses do something with a snake in one of those old movies?"

"Old movies? That's religion to people like you. Like they can't put anything they want in a movie."

I didn't even offer the obvious comeback. I'd nearly killed my dog that day, through my own moral failings. We listened to the muffled drumming of rain on the porch roof, and watched it run down in long, beaded streams through the gaps in the shingles. Finally I asked, "What's an eastern Mississippi rattlesnake?"

"*Massasauga*. It's the least poison rattler there is. Little short fangs. I raised it since it was a baby. Called it Blackie and handled it like a kitten. It wasn't going to bite nobody."

"Well, hey . . . I didn't know any of . . . "

"And I fed it a fat mouse before church. *And* it was on ice. There was more chance you biting that snake than that snake biting you. Hell, I'm the one saved your dog's life. Not some animal doctor."

"It was her hair that saved her. Still, Lonnie, leaving all that aside, I did fulfill my part of the bargain."

He looked at me as though I'd just asked him to have sex with me.

"YOUR part of the bargain!" I could see he was ready to rise up out of that chair. "YOUR part of the bargain made my church into a circus act and killed my Blackie to boot!" He paused a moment, apparently to calm himself. "That snake cost me two-hundred and seventy-five dollars."

My first reaction was: this is so typical, in the end it all comes down to money, only he wasn't making eye contact the way he would have if he'd just named his price. He was looking through the beaded curtain of rain, off into the shade of the wet trees across the creek. The loud rush of water swirled through the creek's sharp double bend.

"Two-seventy-five," I said. "That's a lot of money."

He was quieter now. By contrast to what had just passed, he spoke in a whisper. "Black market prices, see. 'Cause they're scarce. Endangered in some states."

Jesus Christ. I didn't know what to say. Add illegal animal trading to the long list of things I detest about Lonnie Farley. It occurred to me that if he stood up all bolshy, I'd stand up too and knock him off the porch. God, I could, too. Easily. He's old and fat and slow. I wanted to watch him splash in the wet grass. That really sounded good to me. Part of that was the vodka. I channeled it into sarcasm. I even mimicked his way of speaking. "I know one of 'em 'at's extinct in Kentucky 'bout right now."

I don't think he even heard that. He asked me, "Do you know what it's like to be a member of an endangered species?" He waited for me to speak, but when I didn't, he answered for me, "No. Not yet."

I tried to explain that I'd meant for none of this to happen, it was only natural creatures doing what they do naturally. He rocked without speaking for a long time. I thought this meant he understood my position, so eventually I asked for my due.

"Whazzat mean? Your *due?*"

"I know you're the connection between Angela Van Landingham and Twisting Creek. Tell me everything you know about it."

Again he gave me that look of fierce surprise. "I ain't tellin' you shit about shit!"

"Come on, Lonnie, we had a deal."

"We never had no deal where you pulled that shit today."

"I did absolutely everything I was supposed to do . . . at least until the lift it up and dance around part. Only because I didn't have the snake anymore."

"Because your stupid dog killed it. Just like you planned."

"That's bullshit."

"*You're* bullshit! You git off my property before I grab my gun and pump a magazine of nines up your skinny ass. Which is more'n what you deserve!"

So of course I did. I drove away and left him to his bottle and his insanity.

Now, in a traditional Hatfield-McCoy story, at this juncture I'd go get Charlene and her shotgun and her Ruger, and we'd drive straight back out there and see the thing was done right. But, as you've guessed, that's not what happens here. The reason for that is that when I got back to Big's, most members had finished eating. Everything in the kitchen was humming along, so I went out into the rear of the dining area, to my favorite table, which was unoccupied. Jezebel was up front with Charlene, who was just finishing off her introduction of a new act tonight, a young singer/songwriter from Buford County High. She's a senior, plays her guitar from a tall stool, wears jeans, has long straight brown hair parted down the middle. Everyone turned their attention to her while she sang a touching song about a boy she likes. I suspect he's a real boy somewhere in town. In the song she offers to do his homework for free.

That moment, with all the layers of this scene superimposed, washed away all the

disappointment and folly and humiliation. With that earnest young woman singing about early love as a commitment to team up for the good fight, and Ruby Akers resting her head on Leo's shoulder, and Charlene blowing me a kiss across the empty dance floor—it sticks in my mind as a poster for the human compulsion to pursue a dream, and to share it with others who do the same. One thing I've learned is that when you know you may be seeing something for the last time, it is much more like seeing it for the first time, than all the times in between. I sat there thinking, I love this place. I love everything about it. Even as it slips away, I will guard this moment forever in my heart.

Isn't it fascinating how one part of our brain can convince another part to stop thinking about something, and another part to pick up a completely different thread? I know it's called compartmentalization, and I've always been adept at it, but I've never had such a contrast between compartments. There I sat, at first spellbound, listening to our young folk singer's early heartaches; noticing that when Jezebel spotted me she came slinking over, as though I'd caught her being illicit; seeing all our guests and friends sitting here, composed and quiet for a while, following their own dreams of health and happiness. They build cathedrals to visions like this.

But then the brain decides to change thoughts. You've seen for yourself how quickly a feeling of joy can give way to visions of losing it all. You know what it made me remember? Boethius and Lady Philosophy: *Do you reckon such happiness to be prized, which is sure to pass away?*

I started pondering my grim future. I've already confessed that suicide isn't out of the question. You may recall the noose I was mentally creating from my prison bed sheets. That particular possible outcome stuck in my mind for a little while, and then for no conscious reason the switchgears in my head decided enough was enough, and the next thing I knew I was devising Monday's dinner special. Monday's special! Who the hell cares, right? Monday may be years away. But that's what I was thinking about. Something with salmon. And then literally from nowhere comes a brainwave shooting between those two areas and . . . have I solved the case? Have I?

No, maybe it's not that big, but let's just say it's a major fricking step. Here's how it happened.

It all started with *saumon en croûte de noix*, which of course is my pretentious gourmet way of saying walnut crusted salmon (310 calories, 4g carbs). It's odd that people around here, in a region with a lake, and a town named for a creek, an area with bait shops and boat shops, where men get together to trade fishing stories—a whole lot of people don't like eating fish. When these fishermen eat their own catch, it's after they fry it so hard it tastes like salted grease on a plank of balsa wood. So when I want to crank up their Omega-3s with cold water salmon, I have to try to make it not taste like salmon. My *saumon en croûte de noix* recipe uses Dijon mustard and a bit of sweetener mixed with crushed walnuts (also Omega-3 rich, of course) to disguise the fish flavor. And, if they truly must have it, we ourselves make a sugar-free ketchup they can dump on it. This is hillbillyville, after all. I figure, you know, I moved here, they didn't come to me in New York, so let them ruin my artistry with their ketchup, if that's what it takes. When in Rome . . . that's one of my mottos. Also, the more lycopene the better. That's another one. It's now well established that it lowers the risk of cardiovascular disease, and you may also be aware of a recent study in England showing lycopene to inhibit the growth of cancer cells in a test tube.

(Trust me. This is exactly what was going through my consciousness right then, but I keep forgetting that "recent" to me is about twenty years ago to you. I wonder how you'll look back on the state of science you're reading about here. Will it be, like, hey look! We've got this new thing called radio.)

Okay, let's complete the special. This was still me thinking. To fill out the Monday special, I'm going with potatoes. Folks here love new potatoes as much as they dislike fish, so to make up for the salmon I'll roast red potatoes in olive oil. (115 calories, 27g carbs) New red potatoes are becoming abundant in our farmers' market. Everything is becoming abundant—it's mid-August. (Can you pinpoint how my major breakthrough began? *Everything* is becoming abundant.)

If these folks love anything more than new potatoes, it's their prized white half runner bush beans. These, too, are flooding our markets. I'll cook these with onions in chicken broth. (85 calories). There's my special: 510 calories. That still leaves room for one square of dark chocolate (50 calories) with coffee.

Do you see it yet? Have you worked out my big breakthrough? In mid-August, bean vines are sagging under the weight of delicious and iconic white half runner beans. When did Mom and Pop Farley die? August 16. What killed them? Beans with botulism. *Canned* beans. Why the hell would an old farm couple eat canned beans in August?

You know what I think? I think they didn't prepare their own dinner. They died alone, at home. Two dirty plates in the sink. Who was it that served them a bowl of poisoned beans, and then left without a trace?

Advantage: Jake.

22

I HAD THE game on the truck radio and I was on my way out to Lonnie's when my phone rang. It was Charlene, so I answered. She said, "Hi Sweetcakes. Pretty big news. Are you driving?"

I told her to give me a second. I pulled over into that RV sales lot at the southern tip of town, not far from the turnoff to CR 7, where Lonnie lives. "OK," I said. "What happened?"

"I just got this straight from Victor. They found a body floating at the edge of the lake this morning."

"My God! Not Angela!"

"No, not Angela. It was Curtis McKeeler."

"Who? Do we know him?"

"What do you mean?"

"Why is this such big news? I don't think I know anybody by that name."

"He's Lacey Fouch's cousin's boyfriend. Late boyfriend."

"Holy crap! The earrings guy?"

"Yes, *that* guy!"

I know this is not crisp Thin Man and Nora repartee, but it's an accurate reflection of how blown away we were.

She said the body had been found not very far from a fully inflated inner tube, so speculation was he got drunk and went out tubing, maybe passed out and fell off, or was knocked off in the rapids following a rainy weekend. His body showed signs of a struggle, but they could just as easily be from collisions with the rocky cliff face where the creek makes its final twist before emptying into the lake. Anything before the coroner examines him is guesswork.

She added, "They didn't find the earrings on his person."

This made no sense to me. "Of course they didn't. He gave them to his girlfriend."

"No, he didn't."

"Yes, he did. Ask Lacey."

"I mean he gave them to her, but returned to take them back. He told her he messed up big time taking them and if he didn't return them real quick there would be hell to pay. The girl threw them at him and told him to go flea himself."

"I take it that's a rustic euphemism."

"Baby, you can take it any way you want it."

I asked her if she thought losing the earring evidence meant trouble for us. She said just the opposite, that a missing tourist and a rape and now a murder around the same lakeshore would surely take the spotlight off me.

It finally registered how important this was. I said, "Charlene, we need to figure this out and work out how to use it? Help me think it out, all right?"

She said she was on it. "Oh," she said, "one more news snippet. They found a red garter belt out there in the woods near where they found the panties. Does that tell us anything?"

It sure as hell does tell us something. It tells us Angela was dressed for sex. Not bare ground in a forest sex, but king size mattress with satin sheets sex. Torment them sex. Pout, feign reluctance, affect shyness sex. Fake virginal fear sex. The kind where she pulls fluffy red handcuffs from her purse and begs you not to make her wear them. How different for her now, wherever she is tied up, bound down, maybe gagged. No safe word. No quick-release mechanism. This time the terror is no game.

23

FUNNY—JUST LIKE THAT and I was back on the road again. I was forced to postpone serious consideration of who murdered Curtis McKeeler or who was waiting for Angie in what hotel room in what city, while . . . who . . . raped her in the woods near Lake Roosevelt. I had to postpone all that, because now my job was with Lonnie Farley. I turned the Reds game back on. This helped me focus, because I knew he'd have it on too, out on his big shady porch, which he did. He pretended not to notice my truck pulling up until the last instant. I admit I did a quick glance around for weapons before I walked straight over to his radio and turned it off. He looked up at me, more surprised than angry, and I asked him, "Do a lot of people still think you did it?"

"What the hell are you talking about?"

"Poisoning your parents."

He held my gaze. "I never poisoned nobody."

"That's not what I asked. The question is, do people still think you did?"

"Nobody never thought it. What are you . . . ?"

"That surprises me. You might think some overly suspicious people would follow the money."

"Then maybe you better ask your girlfriend about that."

"Do you think the good citizens of Twisting Creek will call it a toss-up between you and Charlene? Or even a conspiracy."

Then I laid it out for him, slapped him with it left and right. I said, imagine this scenario: some sort of expert in food poisoning comes to town, digs up old accounts of Mom & Pop Farley's deaths, and has a few thoughts on the matter. And what if this expert has the ear of a local journalist? And what if this journalist guarantees a front page story airing the food expert's observations? How many other news organizations throughout the Appalachians would line up to relay the story of a preacher suspected of killing his parents? I told him I had a two-part argument that when linked together would prove beyond any reasonable doubt that his parents had been murdered. I admitted it wouldn't hold up in court, but a regional media frenzy would make Lonnie Farley more hated in the South than Pontius Pilate.

Argument part one: I know precisely how many people die of various food borne diseases every year. It's part of my training to know things like that. I pummeled him with facts. For botulism last year, it was five. One-Two-Three-Four-Five, Lonnie. Across the whole country. In the case of Mr. and Mrs. Farley, canning without the weight got the blame. Okay—it's true that the extra pressure is necessary for total safety, but . . . botulism? Every time?

I assured him that I could have labs and test kitchens all over America cooking beans without the weight, then testing for botulism. I told him my guess would be, at the very most, one positive batch in a thousand.

See, Lonnie knows I am spinning this number out of thin air. But the thing is, it sounds about right. A clever gambler wouldn't bet against it.

Argument part two: Here's another thing. How many old farming families around here open year-old canned beans during white half-runner season? Much less farming people with a big bean patch out behind the house. I said for the sake of easy measurement let's say this number is also one household per thousand, which could still be an overestimation.

I taunted him. "Now combine these two statistics. Can

you work that out in your head?"

Lonnie's face sagged into a half-sneer, and he seemed to choke off a reply.

"Here's a hint," I said. "You have to multiply the big numbers."

He leaned forward with his elbows on his knees, and his necktie dangling in front of his belly. It seemed he was ready to say something, but changed his mind. He pressed hard on the chair arms, stood, and started for the screen door.

"Where do you think you're going?"

"For a bottle." He laughed. "You 'fraid I might be grabbin' a gun?"

"Promise you're not or I'll have to walk back to my truck and get my shotgun."

"Ha!" He walked toward the door. I could feel the floor boards give under the weight of his footsteps. Just inside the screen door he turned and spoke to me. "Old Crow this time, all right?"

I'm not as easily duped as I once was. I hurried off the porch and was waiting on the far side of the truck, watching for him through the windshield. He came out carrying a bottle of bourbon. I reappeared from behind the truck.

"You still don't trust me?" he asked. "You're going to hurt my feelin's if you're not right careful."

"Don't wait for me to apologize. I know I've got you by the balls. Killing me is your only other option. Did you figure out those odds?"

"About a million to one, I reckon."

"You went in there for a calculator, didn't you?"

For an answer, he held out the whisky bottle and two glasses. Then he asked, "Do you really have a shotgun in there?"

"I really do." I reached into the cab and pulled out Charlene's old double barreled twelve-gauge.

"Does 'at thang still work?"

"We've had it out practicing recently. She also carries a pistol in her purse, in case you're curious. We practice with that one too."

I guess he knew what I meant by that. I climbed the few steps back onto the porch. He sat down quietly, poured each of us a glass, and asked me, "Where did you get your boxes?"

"What boxes?"

"That you packed down here from New York. You left one in your trunk."

It took me a second to realize we were finally getting down to business. "Gosh, those boxes . . . from a neighborhood liquor store, if I remember correctly."

"That's it?"

"I think so. No, maybe one or two from the recycling bin in the basement of our building. Why?"

"Because I found a receipt or invoice or something in a plastic pouch taped to a box. On the paper was a phone number. I called it. Nobody answered. All I did was leave a message on the machine that does anybody want to talk to Jake Michaels, call me at this number. A week later, somebody did."

"Who did?"

"It was a woman. She never said her name. She read off her email address and I wrote it down."

"Her old email address isn't active any more."

"This one she gave me worked fine."

"So you emailed each other? How about texts?"

"Nope. Nothing but emails from then on. She always signed herself Angela Van Landingham. She asked a bunch of Bradley questions." He tried to talk prissy through his nose. "Where does Bradley work? Is Bradley a success? Where does Bradley live? Is Bradley married? Does Bradley still have a gorgeous collie? Easy ones. Then, can I recommend some quiet spot for a romantic getaway? I said to myself, if Charlene finds out about this, the fur will fly."

I don't know whose fur he foresaw in flight, but I'm guessing mine was in the mix.

"What else do you know?"

"Not much. I booked that room."

"Did you choose the dates?"

"Within some limits."

"That means you planned this whole religious conversion scam right from the start."

"Not like this. I thought maybe I'd catch you at adultery and threaten to inform Charlene. That's where my mind ran to."

I sort of believed that part. It was just petty enough to spark Lonnie's imagination. He couldn't have foreseen what really followed, unless Angela told him more than she ever would have. She'd have chosen her confidant more selectively than that. In fact, if she'd ever met Lonnie, she'd have sent him out to wash her car.

I asked, "What else did she want?"

"Did she have a pill problem when you knew her?"

"What do you mean, a 'pill problem'?"

"Did she take pills?"

The question sent a sharp shock wave through me. Did Lonnie somehow know about my fingerprints on her drinking glass? I offered, "She took a sleeping pill every night. Why?"

"Because she asked if I could get her some Oxy80's. Leave 'em at her cabin."

"Angela asked you to find OxyContin for her?" I stopped myself before I could say, *Oh, that was you!* "So now you're a drug dealer too?"

He tried to shrug it off, but I saw him knock back a good gulp of that Old Crow. "I 'on't see nothin' wrong with it. If a woman turns to me for help in her distress, I say the Good Lord wants me to do everything in my power to ease her pain.

So I passed her request on to a young man I know. Sometimes he helps people that way."

"You gave him her email?"

"I most certainly did. I'm not ashamed to say so."

"Who was this young man?"

Lonnie reached over to refill his glass. I saw him check mine, but it was still full. He said, "I wouldn't really like to name no names."

"Like it or not, I've got a million to one reasons why you will anyway." Still he hesitated. He was probably weighing his chances with me as an enemy versus a local drug gang. "Look, Lonnie, you know I'm not in this as a narc or drug lord either. I just want to find a missing woman, a woman who was once dear to me. And still a child of God."

He gave me his patented smirk, but said, "The grandson of one of my church members. Name's Curtis McKeeler."

Now *that*, as you can imagine, sent my head into a spin. I needed to wrap this up and call Victor. I said, "So give me her new email address and we're quits. No newspaper stories."

Lonnie said, "I have two reasons I can trust you on this one, Brother Jake."

This sort of spun me in the opposite direction. I didn't like the way he was puffing himself up so soon after his ignominious defeat. I asked him, "What are they?"

"One—you know I didn't really kill my mommy and daddy."

"If you say so."

"Two—I know what you did in New York City."

24

LET ME ASK one simple question: why isn't the whole world bipolar? In Florida last night about midnight, the earth opened and a man in bed asleep dropped into a dark sinkhole, and that was his end. I heard it on my truck radio after I left Lonnie's. This guy's final moment was the worst sort of nightmare we're ever likely to have, when with no warning we're falling and there's ear-splitting noise, not a hint of light, and we don't understand anything at all except terror and crushing pain. Only in this nightmare we don't wake up. This really happened. It happened to a human being. It happened to one of us.

Two hours later, I'm back in jail. Me, my prison books, a rotating fan, a swaybacked mattress and a bolted-down metal desk. Small, dingy window high on the wall. Black metal bars in front of me. The old kind, thick and round. That's where I am now. I know that sounds bleak, but something seems to have sent me on a gently manic swing—I think it was that ridiculous death in Florida—so I'm not yet ready to string bed sheets together. There are some positive developments to soften the impact, and I'm not reacting as though the earth had opened its jaws to swallow me whole. Not yet, anyway.

My first destination after leaving Lonnie's was Lake Roosevelt, that same picnic table. I looked across the water to cabin number twelve, where yellow crime scene tape shimmied in the breeze. I hoped that by sitting out there, alone, in the quiet, and within sight of Angie's last place of freedom, I could better digest the new facts, and decide how to make the best use of them. By now it was nearing the end of a sticky afternoon. The table was covered with sweat bees because somebody had spilled a Fanta and left it there, can and all. I wiped up the mess with a handkerchief dampened in the lake, and got stung once. This isn't important to the story, but it still pisses me off.

I laid my phone on the table and sat down for a long think. I didn't switch it off—too many things were happening too quickly—but I vowed not to use it until I'd reconstructed Angela's capture and come up with a plan. One of the day's revelations—finding that red garter belt—made one thing certain: she was meeting someone for premeditated sex. And, that someone was not a stranger. It sure as hell wasn't Curtis McKeeler. Whatever Angela's predilections, she isn't promiscuous. She doesn't go out cruising in sexy underwear. She was meeting someone she'd had sex with before, someone she knew well and trusted. The lack of any signs of a struggle at her cottage confirmed it. Angie is also not one to be taken without a fight.

The damn phone rang. It was Charlene. "There are two policemen here, one on the front porch and one on the back patio."

"What do they want?" The impact of this development didn't hit me all at once.

"They say they're here as a precaution."

"Precaution against what?"

"They claim not to know. They'll only say Victor sent them here."

"Have you talked to Victor?"

"I haven't been able to get a hold of him."

That's about where we left it, but almost immediately Victor phoned me. I asked about the cops at our house. He said he'd rather tell me in person, and he'd join me in ten minutes.

I didn't know it then, but they were to be my last ten minutes of freedom until ... until when? I have no idea. But I wish I'd paid more attention to them, to those last ten minutes. I thought I'd learned to look at everything as though for the last time, but as it happens I'm making no progress at all in that direction. I'm sure the dead guy in Florida put on his pajamas, brushed his teeth, flossed, turned off the bathroom light, and slopped off to bed without the slightest added awareness.

So what can I say about my ten minutes? It was hot and sticky, but at least the bees were gone now. I actively missed Jezebel, I remember that. She loves being outdoors so much, it was a pity I hadn't brought her along. But I left her at home this morning so Lonnie wouldn't have the chance to take a shot at her, and frankly I don't think she's all that crazy about Lonnie right now either.

Anyway, she wasn't with me, and I missed her. Oh, a little breeze would send the fragrance of sweet clover my way, then blow it on past. In high summer, the air in these woods is thick with the smell of sweet clover, honeysuckle, mountain thyme and wild onion.

Funny, isn't it, how relating those minutes to you reveal them more fully than when I lived them?

Some kids were swimming near the cottages across the lake. I heard them laughing and splashing. Life is there for relishing. But not at Cabin Twelve. Life isn't for relishing there anymore. It can happen in an instant. It started to sink in about here that Victor thinks even Charlene is in danger. Is our house to be the next one to have laughter stripped from it?

Victor came striding through the tall grass. He moved with authority, in his pressed khaki uniform, with his black duty boots laced up high, and his broad-brimmed sheriff's hat. He wore a black leather gun belt with the handle of his pistol pointed forward, and a set of handcuffs in a pouch. He had his half-smile ready, as though he'd prepared a joke for the occasion.

"You know, Jake, a criminal returns to the scene of the crime once, and that's enough. You've filled your quota. You don't have to live out here."

"I like it out here," I said. I guess I didn't feel like laughing. I got down to business, "Why are you guarding Charlene?"

"As a matter of fact," he said, his half-smile gone, "they're there for you."

"For me?"

He sat down and took off his hat. "Right now you're the star of this show."

I thought, fine. If you say so. Then I told him what I just told you, that Angela must have known the man she was meeting.

"So who was it?" he asked. "I've said all along she had an accomplice. We need to find out who she wore fishnet stockings for back home."

"Red ones, with silk roses sewn on at the top, where the garter fastens. And red patent leather spike heel shoes."

"Ouch," he said.

"I know."

A mental image like that deserved a moment of respect. When Victor next spoke, he asked, "Do you have any idea who her fancy man might be?"

"I don't know who it was, but it wasn't casual, it wasn't local, and it sure wasn't Oxy80's man Curtis McKeeler."

"You knew about that?"

"Lonnie told me. He hooked them up. How did you know?"

"We've had a couple of tips he was dealing. We're looking for the little posse he runs with. I didn't know about him and Lonnie."

"That's another thing I have to tell you. Lonnie was the initial link between Angela and me here in Twisting Creek.

He found my old car in a junkyard, and in the trunk there was a paper with the phone number of someone who lived in our building—mine and Angela's apartment building. Apparently it was someone who knew us—a neighbor, obviously—so when Lonnie left a phone message, this neighbor passed it on to Angela, who then called Lonnie. He booked that cabin for her." I pointed to it across the lake, but Victor's eyes stayed on me. He had a little squint that seemed to be seeing me for the first time.

He said, "Okay, we know she wasn't meeting Curtis McKeeler. So who was it? Likely it was her partner in crime. Let's start with a link between sex and conspiracy. You might do naughtier things for the one who's twiddling your button than you'd do for anybody else."

"But—at some point she really was with McKeeler. Or at least he had her earrings. I'm thinking her lover hired McKeeler to drive her to the big rendezvous."

"Where could that be? Let's work that angle. Does she know anyone at all in this region?"

"Not when I knew her."

"Lexington? Cincinnati? Huntington?"

"Nowhere even remotely near here. Definitely not."

"Then probably it was a rented room."

"An upmarket hotel. That's the most likely place. But then again I never would have guessed that cottage." I nodded in its direction and this time Victor turned to look at it.

"But," he said, "people usually revert to type." He made a note on the pad he carries in his shirt pocket. "Not that this helps us much with the real question: Who was she meeting?"

"Maybe the same person who contacted Lonnie for the pills."

"You think she didn't do that for herself?"

"Not her style. She's capable of many astonishing things, but not dealing with hillbilly pill peddlers."

"That would confirm the accomplice theory, but still doesn't tell us anything new."

"No, but I got the email address." Victor opened his eyes as far as they would go, as if to ask how the hell I'd done that. I said, "I got it from Lonnie."

He leaned back even more. "You're shitting me, right?"

"Not at all. Here it is." I handed him the scrap of paper where I'd written it down.

He read it aloud, "*avenger4sins@yahoo.com.* Is this for real?"

"I think so. Lonnie was extremely reluctant to give it to me."

Victor read and reread the address, as though some coded message within it could make all the difference. "I don't know, Jake. Lonnie Farley lies to people for a living."

"I have a little leverage over him."

He was skeptical. "You mean Charlene?"

Before responding, I waited long enough for him to know I wasn't going to tell him the truth. "Sure. He's practically family."

"I hope you know what you're doing."

"I think Lonnie's ready for a conversion."

His eyes said he was torn between cautioning me further and getting on with the investigation. Finally he reached into one of the pouches on his gun belt and took out a phone. "Can I send an email out here?"

"I guess so. Phones work okay."

He wrote a message, using quick thumb taps like a teenager, and sent it. "That should give somebody pause for thought."

I asked if I could see what he'd written. He showed me his screen.

I know who you are and where you are. If Angela is harmed in any way, I'm coming after you.

"But you don't know who or where he is."

"He doesn't know that, does he? We're playing for time. And I *will* find him. I promise you ... " His lips froze mid-sentence. "Or am I assuming too much when I say 'him'? Could she have been dressed that way to meet a woman?"

"Not a chance. Angela was a man's woman, and very particular at that."

He braced his chin on his thumbs while he weighed this new data, but he didn't seem to have eliminated his uncertainty. He was still worried about my Lonnie connection. He pressed me for details on how I'd obtained this address. I said, "Long story. Dead snakes. Statistics. Someday when this nightmare is over I'll fill you in over a beer."

"Over a few beers," he said. "In fact, gallons." He smiled way beyond a half-smile, and seemed to have a flash vision of a better world, one with beer, friends, and freedom, but then just as suddenly his face lost its animation, and his smile was gone. "Right at the moment, though, I have to explain why I need to take you back inside."

To show you how far my thoughts were from what Victor had in mind, I thought "inside" meant indoors. I actually looked up at the sky for rainclouds.

He saw my confusion, and continued, "I think I've worked out what's going on here. At least it's the most probable explanation I can come up with, and if I'm right, your Angela's life is in serious peril as long as you're free."

That didn't clear me up a whole lot. I now understood that "inside" meant jail, but I had no idea why. "Surely you don't think I ... "

He put his hands up, as though to ward off a blow. "No, no. Not that. I'll lay out my theory for you. But first, I need to know something very important. This is crucial, Jake, and I'm not asking as a friend, or officer of the law, either one. This is life and death for a woman you once loved. Am I right? You did love her, didn't you?"

"A long time ago."

"So tell me the truth—does she have some serious reason to hold a grudge against you for this long? Because if she does, I think I understand what's going on. Some of it. A lot of it."

I had to tell him. It was almost like a confession, but not in a police interrogation, more like to a priest. I felt pinpricks around my eyelids. I said, "I've been concealing one thing from you, but I swear it was not only to protect myself. Once you learn what it is, you'll have to make a painful decision, and I wanted to spare you that. Do you still want to know?"

"No, if you put it like that, I don't *want* to know. I *have* to know. It's my job."

"Do you need every detail?"

He tried to smile at me, this fine man. "You can leave out the red spike heels, and the, uh, whips, or whatever."

"I stole from her. She broke up with me and fired me from her restaurant—a restaurant I made popular—so I took my revenge and stole several thousand dollars' worth of equipment. And I got away with it, as you can see." I cast him a rueful, ironic look.

"What kind of equipment?"

"Cookware and so on. You know that beautiful copperware you can see hanging in Big's kitchen?"

"You stole all that stuff?"

"Carried it all off before dawn the same day I came to Twisting Creek. Third degree larceny, when I get caught." I tried to say it as though I wasn't already caught.

"You stole it and hung it where I could see it every time I came into Big's?"

"Hide in plain sight, so they say."

"You know what you are?" He hesitated, trying to decide what I was.

"I'm a thief."

"You're a godsend! Can't you see? I was trying to make

all this work within the context of a lover's quarrel, but that seemed like too little foundation for such deadly dealings. Look how this ties in with my theory. I figure there are at least five crimes at work here, all at the same time. Six, if we include your burglary." He started enumerating them on his fingers. "One, you carry off the store. Van Landingham wants to get back at you somehow, but doesn't know where you are. We believe she has a conspirator, a man, a sexual partner. By my analysis, she discusses with him her unfulfilled desire for revenge. When they locate you by some means— which I now know was Lonnie Farley—they decide to fake her disappearance, and frame you for it. Nothing too serious. There will be no dead body, so no murder charge. Eventually we'll find her safe back in New York, with some dopey excuse why she ran out and left her stuff here. Medical emergency, or whatever. So that's crime number two: falsifying evidence.

"Then, crime number three. Think about it—this case has been nothing but static for a week. It might not seem like it, because this and that has come to light, but the real case hasn't budged an inch. I say that because until the GoMart message, we still didn't even know if she was dead or alive. How do you explain that? Normally lack of progress points to a corpse. Yet now we learn—assuming the lipstick message to be genuine—she's alive. She's been kidnapped. What's a kidnapping without ransom demands? It could be a sick sex abduction, but according to what Curtis McKeeler's girlfriend says, he had to eat his pride and ask her to return those earrings. And we know that Curtis was afraid. That points to him being outnumbered, and he'd been caught pinching off more than his share. That means this isn't only about sex, it's mostly money. So that's number three: kidnapping. Number four: rape. Of course McKeeler's murder makes five. The tricky part is number six, which has to make sense of the one great kink in my investigation: why doesn't someone respond to the ransom demands?"

"How do you know they're not?"

"If somebody wants money to free your loved one, you have only two possible avenues. You can contact authorities, or you can try to work it on your own, which really means you pay up. But something very unusual is going on here. No police involvement, and no ransom paid either."

"Do you know that?"

"We know she's alive and hasn't been released. If somebody paid, why is she still captive? And if no ransom has been paid, why not? That leads me to Crime number six. Somebody convinced her to frame you for her murder, because they want her dead. They planned to kill her as soon as she was a safe distance from here, and you would be the one convicted. The intended murderer didn't want to leave clues anywhere near Buford County, so he hired a slime ball Oxy dealer to chauffeur her somewhere distant, where the actual murder would take place. Her body would be found out in the open somewhere, and you'd be arrested, thanks to the airtight case against you that she herself had set up."

"But that means McKeeler knew our *avenger4sins*."

Victor didn't need time to think this one out. "Not at all. McKeeler could have been hired by email. He could have dropped her off at a street corner somewhere. Or coffee shop. Anywhere. Maybe she even paid her own fare. Our perp would be nowhere in the picture. He'd simply meet her after McKeeler dropped her off, then take her away and kill her."

I couldn't see any flaw in the theory, and told him so.

"It's speculative, but it provides direction," he said. "Here's another thing. Now that I think on it, there's no doubt in my mind that at the time of your arraignment, your New York larceny would have come to light. If it became known there was bad blood between you and the deceased, that you had taken prior criminal action against her, even Leo Akers couldn't get you off."

"Holy shit. Could that still happen?"

"Yes, it could. Of course it could. But not if we find Angela alive. If I'm right, it's a pure fluke she's not dead already." This conclusion was a punch in the stomach, the kind where you have to remember to breathe. Victor saw that and added, "But we'll take it, right?"

"So what kind of fluke interfered with their plan? Not me or you, that's for sure."

"Curtis McKeeler did. He didn't know that the guy who hired him to transport Angela wanted her dead. Instead of driving her to the appointed spot, he calculated he and his pals could rape her, rob her, and extort big money for her."

"But why would anybody want to kill her in the first place?"

"Beats me. Love, power, money. Those are the three big ones. Why did you want to steal her stuff?"

"That was nowhere near this level of crime."

"You're nowhere near as nasty as some people."

"But still . . . "

"You say she has plenty of money. Who gets it in case of her death?"

I had no idea. She was something of a loner. She almost never mentioned family. I got the idea she was happy to live the solitary life. Solitary except for me, then later solitary, period. I told him that, then said, "I follow your logic, but why do you want me back in jail when you know I didn't do it?" I knew it couldn't be for the New York thing, because he genuinely didn't know about it until I told him.

"Because you're the linchpin of this whole thing. Whoever it is wants her dead, they're counting on you to take the blame. If she dies while you're in custody, they have no fall guy."

"So you're saying she'll be safer if they know I'm on ice?"

My little joke surprised him, and his laughter surprised

me. "You know that expression? You should write a prison diary yourself. Chef on Ice."

I could only laugh with him. He doesn't know about these memoirs, or about you. You see why I'm in a pretty good mood, in spite of being in jail?

Also, even though I haven't quite figured out who set Angela up, I may have figured out how to figure it out. The only problem is, to pull it off I have to return to New York City.

25

A PHOTOGRAPHER FROM the Guardian was waiting with Yolanda in front of the courthouse for my official off-to-jail news item and photo-op. I flashed a big smile and waved. Charlene was beside me, also smiling, with her arm linked in mine. Jezebel was with us in the photo. In fact, they both went inside with me, up to my cell, and Jezebel stayed the night.

In Yolanda's printed account of my re-incarceration, she made it clear I was being taken into "protective custody" because I am "a person important to the investigation." I insisted on that. Charlene did too. We want everybody in town to know I'm not under arrest. As long as I'm "inside," I've got an airtight alibi against a frame-up, and we want to be as certain as possible that *avenger4sins* knows about it, so Victor emailed him the link to the story and the photo on the Guardian's website. He believes that if *avenger4sins* doesn't ransom Angela outright, at least my confinement will cause him to open negotiations with the kidnappers. This will buy us time to locate and rescue her.

Victor also enlisted the assistance of Vicki Yapita-Crosby. She has been sworn to secrecy since finding the HELP FIND JEZEBEL message. She returned to the GoMart station and, under the pretense that she needed to hire someone to help her with housecleaning, located the man who signs himself "Humberto" on the restroom sanitation logs. His name, it seems, really is Humberto, but at work he goes by the nickname "Jose" because apparently it's easier for gringos to remember.

I don't mean to be uncharitable, but I suspect there's some kind of undocumented worker obfuscation going on here, but I can tell you right now that if this man's tip proves valuable, Humberto/Jose may soon be a legal green card holder, because what he explained to Victor—or rather to Vicki, who was acting as translator—is that when heavy rains fall in the area of Buffalo Run, the sewage systems of houses by the creek tend to cease functioning. At least that's what we infer. What he really said, according to Vicki, was, "Every time it rains these local *nacos* come in and make a mess in my restrooms." *Nacos*, Vicki says, means something like *trailer trash*.

Humberto/Jose's insight has no bearing on what I now see as my main contribution to solving this case—for that I need to get to New York asap—but for Victor it means everything. Do you remember how he fretted over the near impossibility of locating a suspect, in an era when anyone can be transported anywhere in no time flat? He even used my escape from New York (inadvertently, as it turned out) to illustrate how easily a criminal can lose himself in the big wide world. But here comes Humberto/Jose to narrow the big wide world down to the low-lying plain where Buffalo Run flows into Twisting Creek Valley. It's still not a simple matter—it's a long stretch of converted coal camps, pre-fab houses, trailers, obsolete barns, homemade sheds, old smoke houses, hunting shelters, not to mention garbage dumps, out-of-commission RVs, junk cars and abandoned backwoods farmland—but still it's better than searching the entire globe. How to remain undercover and still conduct the search is Victor's problem, not mine. Mine is getting out of jail and on a flight to New York.

It's not like I don't understand the risk I'm running. Victor laid it out clearly: if Angela is killed while I'm outside, my New York revenge burglary will come to light, and even Leo Akers won't get me off. This prison cell is my safe house, a literally iron-clad alibi against life without parole at Eddyville. Smart money says stay put. However, some voice inside my head urges me not to play safe. I see that I'm repeating past behavior. It's almost the same argument I used when I attempted to justify my burglary to you: what I'm doing is stupid, but look at the alternative. If Angela is killed while I'm on ice, I'll be fine. I may not be fine in NYC, but I'll be fine here. Yet, how can I live out a long and happy life, knowing I could have tracked down the man responsible for her death—but I did nothing? My unanswerable and eternal question would be, *Could I have saved her?*

It's really one hell of a choice, when you think about it. It's an altogether fucked up choice. But never mind, I've made my decision. My stupid, correct, decision. This is why, when Charlene and I were alone in my cell, my second question (your well-being was my first) was, "How can I get out of here?"

26

I COULDN'T BELIEVE it either, but after Charlene left, well after dark, I heard the whine of the elevator and here came a guard leading Lonnie down the corridor. Jezebel heard it too, and came over to stand beside me. She didn't appear agitated. She was showing interest, nothing more.

The guard said, "He's asking to see you. He's clean. Orders are I can't let him inside with you, but he can sit out here in the hall. It's your call."

I searched Lonnie's sagging, bloodshot face, those pale jowls streaked with red, like forks of lightening through white sky. I asked, "Have you come to make sure I'm really in here?"

"Naw," he said. "I come to explain some things."

I turned to the guard. "Can you find him a chair?" I heard metal dragging in another cell, and then the guard scooted a chair to a spot in front of me. It was a straight-back desk chair identical to the one in my cell. Lonnie sat down in it. Jezebel moved forward an inch or two. I sat down in front of Lonnie, angling my chair enough to situate his face between two cell bars. I asked the guard, "Can we talk in private?"

He looked up and down the empty corridor. "I'll move to the far end. Long as I can keep an eye on him."

Lonnie's eyes followed the guard's slow walk to the far wall, and then he spoke to me in a near whisper. "I ain't never killed nobody. I swear before the Living God."

"Fine. Swear all you want. It doesn't mean you did or you didn't. It may mean only that you're a liar. Given your track record, that wouldn't surprise many people. Least of all the Living God."

My snide remark was rewarded with a look of pain all across his face.

"But I want you to believe me. That's the main thing."

"Then you're in for a major disappointment."

His whole, lard-like head tilted forward as in prayer, but a forlorn one.

"Listen, Jake. You and I are going to be brother-in-laws."

"Brothers-in-law. Get something right for a change, why don't you?"

"Huh?"

"That's how you make the plural. The *s* goes on brother, not law."

He looked up and damned if his whole outlook didn't have a kind of glow surrounding it. "Really?" he asked. "Is that true?"

"Jesus, Lonnie."

"This is great. Tell me more stuff like that. Tell me when you catch me in mistakes, okay?"

"I'd be correcting every third fucking word, wouldn't I? Now why the hell are you here? Brother-in-law."

"No, seriously. It's a good thing to know, since we're going to be them. I like knowing it. I can learn more."

"I never said you were stupid. Not like that, anyway. Not like dumb. Pretty much every choice you ever made that's right now part of who you are—they were all stupid. But I don't doubt you could have memorized a few rules of grammar."

"Okay." He seemed to be seeking a compromise point on this. "But feel free to jump in and help me out whenever you want to."

That sounded fine to me, so I dropped the subject.

Then it slowly dawned on me that the topic of self-improvement was what Lonnie's visit was all about. He wanted to unburden and better himself. Or else, he wanted me to think that's what this was all about, when in fact it was about him trying to manipulate someone who, with one word to a reporter, could raise bloody hell all around him. This is not a fifty-fifty choice, by the way. With Lonnie, always go with the phony possibility.

I wanted to say, Look, I've got quite a busy day ahead of me, so get on with it. In fact, I think I did say that.

"Honest Jake, if I'da knowed I had a chance at college I would have studied better in high school, paid it more mind. But it came too late for me. By that time I tried to tell myself that it was Charlene had it wrong. I was the lucky one. I didn't have to waste my time with degrees and qualifications. I could take my half of the inheritance and show them how a man could live. And we saw how all that turned out. Do you know how many plans and schemes I failed in?"

"I remember something about an extremely late racing car."

"A dead last race car, is more like it."

"So you're saying you killed your parents because they got rich at the wrong time? Lonnie, you can't blame the timing on your parents. That's where you prove Charlene right. You really are criminally insane. You talk like you're not—occasionally—and you've got a peculiar charm that lets you pass for sane. But you're not. You've jumped the gap over into crazy. The timing wasn't your parents fault."

"It wasn't mine, either."

He was lasering me with those eyes again. If there's one thing you have to admit about Lonnie, he never hesitates to look you square in the eye. I thought about how he'd sentenced himself to the state he was in. As had I—let's not forget that. Mine is seven years. His is life. My statute of limitations will expire, two years and three months from this date. His never ends. He's stuck in the tattered remnants of his own past. He took his parents' lives, so he had to take *on* their lives. He had to become them. In terms of world view, he's stuck as a member of a primitive tribe, uneducated, unenlightened, and unquestioning. The statutes of limitations on murdering your parents: eternal.

"Spoken like a true lunatic, Lonnie. It's divine punishment on earth. Maybe karma. It's a rare and beautiful thing to watch."

"What is?"

"Life sticking you up the ass."

He leaned forward and grabbed the bars in his hands. "I never killed nobody, Jake. Get that straight." Jez stuck her nose between the bars, touching both his hands with her nose. He took a moment to settle himself. He tried to sneak a peek at the guard, then, in a softer voice, he said, "If I did kill anybody, it was myself."

"Not killed. Nobody's dug your grave yet. And when they do, don't expect me to clear the weeds off."

He smiled sadly. If this was an act, I didn't know how to read this Lonnie. I'd never seen him off stage, so to speak, because he was always on stage. I'd never dreamed I would see him off stage, and defeated, too. In a way, I hesitate to admit this—but it was truly enjoyable. With all the zillions of thoroughly nasty people who don't get the torment they deserve, Lonnie was a shining example of the human condition occasionally getting it right.

I gave him time to rebound. I could tell he was grateful for that, because in a short time I saw mischief grow in his eyes, and he said, "They's going to be a timbler rattler makes its home on my grave, and don't you mess with it. Keep your damn dog away too." He opened one hand and Jezebel lifted her nose into the palm. "I just noticed for the first time, she don't lick."

"She doesn't think it's appropriate for superheroes to lick."

"She can sure take a snake in her mouth and give it a good shake."

I watched him stroke her down her nose, causing her to squint. He repeated this two or three times, smiling at something. I said, "You're not dead yet. You're insane. Not dead. And it's she doesn't, not she don't."

"Thanks." He gave Jezebel's head a final pat, and said, "I may not be dead, but I'm not insane, either. What I am is trapped. I turned myself into a little boy that watches his sister get lucky and go off on a different road, one I can't travel. It's the hell I deserve. It's all the proof I want of God's justice."

That's where I remember the conversation stopping. There was probably more. It seems an awkward way to part company, but it's the last thing I remember.

27

I LAY AWAKE in my cell most of the night, going over and over in my mind every piece of information I could recall about Angela's life outside our relationship. I hadn't dwelled on her this much since the day I left New York. I tried to dredge up even the tiniest bits of data, from the return addresses on the few Christmas cards she received (I remember New Hampshire was in there, as was Boston, and somewhere in Germany) and the rare comments she made about her childhood, like the bunny slope skiing accident that still occasionally caused her left shoulder to act up. I tried to recall the names of her friends. Maybe I mentioned to you a woman named Delia, who was supposedly in some book club with Angela. Their friendship pre-dated our meeting. Other than Delia, I suppose I was the oldest friend she had.

Mostly I recall big blank areas. Once when I asked her why she didn't visit her parents, she said they were divorced and she didn't want to upset one by visiting the other. Supposedly one was in Arizona and one in Central America. She was unclear about where—Belize and Costa Rica got a mention—or even which parent it was. She was fuzzy about where she'd grown up. "God—all over," she'd say. I know where she went to college—UMass—only because I noticed a lacrosse sweatshirt in a box of clothing bound for St. Vincent de Paul, and asked about it.

Even this paltry background information dates from the first few months after I met her. Soon we were so involved with starting and developing *Le Plat Nourrissant* that it became the central venue for our lives. Every acquaintance we had was in some way connected with the restaurant, either as staff, customer, supplier, or media. The advantage of that, from my current standpoint, is that I knew almost everybody she knew. Therefore, if the mysterious *avenger4sins* isn't a new acquaintance, if he goes back three years or more, it's likely I know him. Or I know someone who does. If it's someone she met recently, then my only hope is that one of the friends we shared has continued to be in contact with her, and will know about Angela's more recent lovers.

Mixed in with my specific and methodical recollections, there were long moments when my thoughts turned to grand strategic reflections. I knew I needed to use every clue at my disposal, which for the moment meant the few clues already in my head. It somehow occurred to me that this very paucity of clues might in itself be a clue. In other words, I asked myself the simple question that can overturn entire systems of philosophy: Why? Why did I know so little about the woman I'd loved and lived with for so long? Why had she kept me at arm's length, and for years, at that? Had there been a plan in process all along? Was the sincerity I saw in her attitude toward me nothing more than a clever business tactic, seasoned with a healthy dollop of sexual passion? In essence this was the reasoning that led me to burglary in the first place, but at that time I was responding more to my brutalized emotions than to a careful investigation of cause and effect. And quite honestly, after a very short time in Twisting Creek, once my heart shifted to Charlene and my ambitions became concentrated on Big's, I stopped dwelling on Angela. In an odd way, I forgot about her. In my mind, all the goods I'd stolen, along with all my restaurant experience, became neither more nor less than my contribution to the fulfillment of Charlene's grand vision. Was this how Angela saw me all those years? As a path to a goal?

And now, if she was so single-minded as to run roughshod over all laws and morality (which is basically what I did, to a lesser degree) then who was the man she plotted with? Who, in fact, would have leapfrogged her in terms of ambition and offense? Who wanted her to take my part of the restaurant from me, then wanted her dead so he could have it all?

Lying there on my sagging cot, wide awake in the darkness of my cell, I tried to work out a step-by-step search list. One thing that made this a nearly impossible task was a precaution I'd made when planning my burglary and escape: I destroyed my past. By that I mean I burned my old address book, tossed my phone into the Hudson River, deactivated Facebook, and I never, not even once, logged onto my old email. I was afraid police could track me down that way. By now all my contact lists would be long since closed down. Even worse, I usually only remember people by their first name. Or occasionally only a last name. That's absolutely standard with me. I never dreamed it would become so important to locate my old NYC names. In some cases I remember buildings where they lived, but not apartment numbers. My god! I am such a schlemiel!

Still, we're now playing by the rules of reality, and that means I need to get out of here, get to New York, and track down some people. First stop: our old apartment building. Someone there had passed Lonnie's message on to Angela. That means that, at least as of a few weeks ago, someone in that building knew where to find her. The most logical candidate was our across-the-hall neighbor, old Mrs. Wannegger. She was often coming or going when we were. There would be a short conversation while waiting for the elevator, or on the way down to the mailboxes and trash disposal. She was retired, and didn't like to go out in bad weather, which meant she had a lot of things delivered in boxes—one of which may well have made its way to the trunk of my car and on to Twisting Creek.

That's where I would start. With that small plan in place, I suppose I felt free to doze off.

What a funny thing sleep is. I don't know if I slept for thirty seconds or three hours, but during that time something magical was happening inside my brain. When I woke up I knew the name of the man I was looking for. The answer seemed to be resting on my forehead, waiting for me to come by and pick it up. I knew the man who called himself *avenger4sins*, knew it as a dead solid revelation. Also prepared and waiting for me was the warning that my intuition has often been completely wrong. Remember the crowd creating a commotion outside the jail the first time I was in here? I thought it was Lonnie's evangelicals, but it turned out to be Big's customers? But even beyond that note of caution, also waiting was a method to confirm my suspicions: find the fiery young Jamaican waitress named Fiona something. Mini-skirted Fiona with the runner's legs, the eager server who flashed seduction signals like a beacon, flashed them to me and to nearly every other male who'd ever stepped through the door of *Le Plat Nourissant*. I may not remember her last name, but I remember exactly where she lives—or at least where she lived then. I can still close my eyes and see the front of her building—a drab red brick walk-up in Hell's Kitchen, with a side entrance just off W 51st St. You don't need to know just how I know that, but I've been there before, and, with a little luck, before the day is out, I'll be there again. Poor old Mrs. Wannegger can enjoy her retirement in peace, while I pay a surprise visit to a Jamaican temptress.

28

Since I wasn't really a prisoner, it wasn't hard to break out of jail. Late yesterday evening I asked Charlene, Victor and Leo Akers to meet with me in the cozy interrogation room located two floors underground at the court building, where I explained to them what I've already explained to you—that my conscience won't allow me to play it safe, not when I'm convinced I can uncover the identity of Angela's would-be murderer. Leo chimed in that I was legally free to go where I chose, Victor said his main concern was that my removal from the jail might become known outside our small circle, and Charlene, although no doubt her mind was racing with catastrophic scenarios, simply nodded her understanding of my moral dilemma. It should be easy to see why I love her so much.

Our little group broke up at about nine o'clock. Victor said he'd arrange the "escape" while Charlene booked my flight and hotel. At two o'clock this morning, I was already awake and ready to get out of there. I heard the hum of the elevator, followed by Victor's footsteps down the corridor. My cell door wasn't even locked, so he pushed in and sat down. "You fly out of Cincinnati in four hours. United, non-stop, arriving Newark at eight o'clock. But first I need to tell you a couple of things. A couple of really serious things."

"Fire away!" I said. I was feeling a touch manic before my flight.

"One, I had a quiet word with the operations manager

out at Mountain Utilities and at nine o'clock this morning they're going to close the water flow to those lower houses at Buffalo Run. Officially, it'll be a pump breakdown. We hope the kidnappers will come back to the gas station, where we'll have eyes watching for them."

"Great idea," I said. "Let's hope it works."

"Two, I have to emphasize for about the hundredth time, when you leave this building you are sacrificing your one unbreakable alibi in case of Angela's death."

"I know all that. And you know why I have to do it."

"I understand, but I don't necessarily agree with your reasoning. If news of your burglary comes out, it will be easy for a prosecutor to hang a murder rap on you. With a plea bargain, maybe manslaughter first degree. Ten to twenty years. Your life will essentially be finished."

"Okay, Victor, stop. Stop right there. You've made yourself clear and I appreciate it, but if I stay here and do nothing, my life is essentially finished anyway. And now, I need to get going." My heels were bouncing up and down. I was ready to move.

"One more thing." Whatever he was going to say, he wanted to look at his shoes when he said it, but he forced himself to look me in the eye. "I'll give you two days, then I'm calling in the FBI."

This was a shock. I said, "The FBI? Are you required to bring them in after so many days?"

"No, not required, but it's a good idea. They have more resources . . . "

"Victor, this case is extremely delicate. I think I can crack it. The FBI will move in and trample all over the fragile plans we've got in place."

His face was solemn. "Maybe they will, I don't know. But I need their help."

I remembered what Leo had told me, about the parade

of local fast food franchisers who paid friendly visits to the mayor to demand my arrest. I said, "You mean you need political cover?" I wasn't even angry when I said this. I meant it more as a sincere request for information.

He sighed sadly, and said, "I need to keep this job, Jake. For more reasons than anybody will ever know, I need to win the November election."

His face went slack. I looked away. I didn't want to say, *But Victor, I do know. The whole town knows.* This was a man—like a million other men, I suppose—who needed to keep his job in order to keep his wife, and needed to keep his wife to keep his kid. I tried to imagine the terrible pressure of a political battle that could cost you your child. I wasn't going to begrudge him a little political ass-covering when his family was at risk.

I said, "Two days it is, then. Now, let's get this thing started." In fact, I had plenty of time before my flight. Mainly I wanted this conversation to end.

"One more thing," he said. "I need to know where you are at all times."

"You need to keep me on a short leash?"

"It's for your own safety." He seemed to try to leave it at that, but his innate honesty won out, and he added, "For the most part."

I didn't press him on it. I knew that by releasing me last week he risked running afoul of authority, and by allowing me to leave the state he was courting serious trouble. I said, "I can tell you now where I'll be staying. There's a little hotel not far from where my old restaurant was, in the part of the city called Hell's Kitchen. Charlene's making the booking, so she'll have the contact details. It's called Rotterdam House."

We walked down the long flights of gray, fungus-smelling stairs, to the ground floor, which had a direct exit to a small loading dock. A van was waiting there. Victor peered out into the darkness and motioned me into the back of a van. I found myself surrounded by boxes of candy bars and crates of soft drinks. Since I was alone back there, I saw no reason not to grab a Snickers and a couple of packets of what people around here call "nabs," or peanut butter on crackers. We pulled over at a dark spot on a county road, where I left the van and got into Charlene's truck. This time she drove.

Everybody knows that false love ends in heartache, but until our ride through the dark night toward the Cincinnati airport, I'd never understood how much more painful it is to sacrifice true love. You know that I have felt hopeless before, and have had dark thoughts of running away to avoid arrest and its excruciating consequences, but I now believe those episodes were only warm-ups for that ride to the airport. At first I tried, once again, to explain my reasons for taking this drastic step. She repeated that she understood, and confirmed it by pointing out that if she didn't, she wouldn't be driving me "to my doom." Those were her exact words, although she chuckled as she spoke them.

I knew that soon I would leave Kentucky and the last hope of any intervention by Victor or Leo, or anybody else. That's what's going through my mind as I sit here now, in a wi-fi café in the Cincinnati airport. I'll finish this note to you, send it off to Fumiko, and then board my flight. The airport, as you may know, is in Kentucky, just across the Ohio River from Cincinnati. Somehow that calms me, as does the knowledge that Charlene can still crack jokes, but it's clearly a temporary calm—sultry, heavy with the threat of an approaching storm. Sometimes when that happens you just want to be done with the calm and let the storm do its worst.

29

MY PLANE LEFT late, arrived late; airport taxis appeared sporadically. The Jersey turnpike was congested, the Lincoln Tunnel was jammed. We moved down 8th Avenue inches at a time. I spent so much time with my talkative Senegalese driver that I almost began to understand a few words. I'm not even sure whether it was English, or whatever language they speak in Senegal, but one more slowdown and I would have been fluent. The delay didn't really bother me, because I remembered that Fiona and the women she shared an apartment with didn't stir much before noon.

I checked into the Rotterdam House, a much seedier hotel than I had anticipated. The lobby was busy with college-aged Europeans with their hair in dyed, dusty dreadlocks, men and women alike. They carried old-fashioned canvas rucksacks, and wore baggy, enveloping bits of apparel that didn't seem to fit into any standard category of clothing. Not really my kind of hotel, but it was near both *Le Plat Nourrissant* (or, as I was soon to find out, where it used to be) and to Fiona's apartment.

I dropped my bag in my room and headed straight back out. All those young Europeans were filing out of the lobby and onto a minibus just as two large American men in dark sport coats were trying to enter. I could see in an instant that they were policemen. If their appearance didn't give them away (and why would anyone wear a jacket in mid-August, and in this hotel, except to conceal a shoulder holster?) then the glare one cop laid on the boisterous students blocking the door told it all. That's when I realized that Victor had notified the NYPD of my whereabouts.

Indeed, when I joined the line of pot-smelling young people, the sport coats turned to exit behind me. My instinct was to sprint away from them, but I tried to calm myself and focus on getting to Fiona's without forcing their hand. I passed my old restaurant, now a Peruvian place called *Lima Fresca*. I had to control the urge to go inside. I felt like a car whose steering wheel pulls to the right by default. I knew— no, I intuited—that such a maneuver would somehow incite the beefy gentlemen behind me, so I held my course until I reached the side street entrance of Fiona's building.

Before I entered, I looked behind me. I tried to be casual. Have you ever thought about how unnatural it is to turn around and look behind you? It's hard to do so without appearing fearful or suspicious. I pretended to be checking out the sky for rain, but I'm afraid it was a transparent ruse. The cops were many steps behind me, but they were there.

I skipped the entrance bell and walked directly up the two flights of stairs to the floor I remembered as Fiona's. On the second landing I waited a long time, at least long enough for those two cops to reach the main entrance. I didn't know how they might go about following me from there, but I knew I could wait at least long enough to hear them enter the foyer. They had no way of knowing where I was going—I only vaguely remembered it myself. I remembered the positioning of Fiona's door down a connecting corridor, but I wasn't positive about which floor it was on. That means the policemen would need to check each floor. As long as I could hear them, either by footstep or the sound of the lift, I could avoid them. Then I realized they could split up. In fact, they probably would. That would be the smart way to track me, presuming I wasn't armed. Given that I'd just arrived in town by air, I could hardly be expected to have a weapon on me. Wouldn't Victor have told them I posed no threat? Yes, he would have. Not so much to make me an easier prey, but to avoid an overreaction on their part that could end in my death.

Here, listening in the silence of the stairwell, I had to fight back the hurt of Victor's betrayal. If I started to grapple with that, I'd never get down to the task at hand. I tried to reconcile my two immediate needs: find out what Fiona knows about Angela's recent lovers, and avoid arrest. Only then could I consider Guadalajara or Tokyo or wherever. I remembered I'd left my passport in my bag at the hotel. *Shit!* I was at the mercy of fortune. If the two men trailing me split up, one on the stairs and one in the lift, I was trapped. It was all over.

In any case, I stood there for a very long time and heard no one at all. I decided it was safe to move on. At the end of the corridor I found the flat I recalled as Fiona's. If she had moved, then I was in trouble. Plan B would be to go to my old building and start with our old neighbor Mrs. Wannegger, but I knew in my heart this was the more certain way. Fiona was the sort of person who makes it her business to know other people's business. A few questions with her would either confirm or quell my suspicions. I rang the bell. I heard the scuff of plastic sandals, and then a woman's Jamaican-accented voice called through the closed door, "Who is it?"

Surely she had seen me through the peephole. Didn't she recognize me?

"It's Bradley Michaels. I'm a friend of Fiona's."

I waited for a response. If it was "Fiona who?" then I was out of luck. Instead I heard the woman retreat from the door and call out "Fiona! Somebody named Michael to see you."

Soon a different Jamaican voice was at the door. "Michael who?"

"Bradley," I corrected her. "Bradley Michaels. From *Le Plat Nourrissant.*"

"My, my, my!" The door opened. "Miracles do still happen

after all." She checked out my belly—first thing, I swear it. "How you have changed, boss man."

I'd completely forgotten that some of our waitresses called me that, even though I had nothing to do with their positions, beyond reporting the odd complaint from customers. I suppose it was because I was living with the real boss. Boss woman, I suppose, although I never heard anyone refer to Angela that way.

Fiona stepped back to get a better look at me—or possibly to allow me to get a full look at her. She was wearing a short pink blouse tied in a bow just under her breasts, high enough to showcase the ribbed muscles of her abdomen, with a line of sinews cutting in a wedge all the way down to where her low-riding jogging shorts covered the convergence. And those legs! Muscled seduction implements, long and slightly bowed, as though already in position for spreading. Fiona had always exuded sex appeal. She could walk to a table of businessmen and have all of them slavering before she whipped out her order pad. Hell, she'd had me slavering at one time, but, as I said, it was long after Angela had gone cold towards me.

"You haven't changed much," I said.

"Thanks, I guess."

"Can I take you out for coffee?"

"I'll make you some here."

"I need to talk in private."

She stepped into a pair of sandals—she didn't put on any more clothes, which was fine by me—and we took the stairs down to the street, where I tried to sneak a look for those police officers, but they weren't in evidence. Fiona turned a corner and we took seats in a sidewalk café that I don't think had been there when I left town. Sometime while we were sitting there it occurred to me that this scene—a mixed race couple drinking coffee—was one that Victor and Shelley lived every day. In New York we drew not a look. I made up my

mind to ask Victor if it was the same in Twisting Creek—
provided I ever returned there again.

"Where've you been keeping yourself?" Fiona asked.

I made up something off the cuff. "I have my own
restaurant in Seattle."

"Need some help?" She laughed.

Did the idea run through my mind that in fact I could do
exactly that: take Fiona to Seattle and open a restaurant, or is
that only me rethinking it now? I was going to have to start a
new life somewhere, with somebody.

But no. Not without you and Charlene. It might not be in
Seattle, or anywhere in the USA, but it would be with you two,
if I could manage it in any conceivable way.

"You'd hate Seattle," I told her. "It rains all the time."

"Does it really?" she asked.

"No. Not Really," I said, because in fact I had no idea.

"So what brings you back here?"

"I was wondering about Angela."

"Don't tell me you're still in love with that bitch."

"Did you really dislike her that much?"

"We all did. You did too, near the end, if you recall."

"Maybe I'm getting sentimental in my old age."

"Or maybe you've come back for revenge. Or should I say
more revenge?"

"What do you know about that?"

She turned her face away and looked at me askance. "Only
what people say."

"And what might that be?"

"Only that she done you dirty out of a load of coil."

"A load of what?"

"Coil. Dosh. Money, dear man."

"Do they say anything else?"

"Only she treat you like a magga dog and you get your
own back. I know a bunch of restaurant stuff went walkies,

about the same time you did."

"Of course I have no idea what you're talking about."

"Idle susu, I don't doubt it."

"Susu means . . . "

She laid on her accent thick as lard. "Wot you tink it mean, mon?"

"I'll guess . . . bullshit?"

"Up to you. I was thinking gossip."

"Did anybody believe this outlandish susu?"

She laughed, whether at my use of her idiom or at the idea that it was outlandish, I'll probably never know. She said, "What does it matter? You're not at Rikers Island. You're drinking coffee with me here, on a fine day, free as a bird."

"I wonder if Angie believed it?"

Fiona shrugged. "Wot do I care wot she tink?"

I smiled at that. "What happened to *Le Plat Nourrissant*?"

"She sold up here and opened a shishi place on Columbus Circle. Only the best for her ladyship."

"Do you know who her next lover was after me?"

Her eyes opened as though somebody had slapped the back of her head. "Do I know him? I *should* know him. He did me just as dirty as her ladyship did you."

"Tell me more."

"Well, he said we had an agreement. He would leave his wife and then walk me down the aisle, you know. He kept half of it." She laughed through her nose.

"You mean he left his wife?"

"But then your old lady moved in and I was swept into the gutter."

"Who was it?"

"Only Mr. Fat Wallet Eric Woodruff himself!"

Angela's so-called financial advisor. This was all I needed. Total confirmation. Why had it taken me so long to figure it out? Who besides the man who helped her do me out of my share of the business, would do her out of hers? I even remembered—vaguely—where his office was. Once Angela and I had shared a taxi downtown. She needed some "financial consultation" (perhaps involving Agent Provocateur garter belts) and exited the taxi somewhere near Battery Park. My still-unsuspecting eyes followed her as she entered a building with a magnificent Art Deco door. I know that brings to mind the Chrysler Building, but it wasn't there. This was a more modern building with a mixed décor, including a beautiful, eclectic door. I can still see it, with its graceful iron filigree, and wide gold-and-stained-glass fan light above it.

"Do you know if he still works in that same building?"

"Susu was he hit hard times after the crash, but by then I didn't give a shit." She laughed at herself. "No, I take that back. I did give a shit. I was thrilled."

"Do you think you can find it?"

"I think it was on Fulton Street."

"Care to ride downtown with me?"

She looked at the clock on her phone. "No can do, boss man. Work in less than two hours."

"In that case we both need to get moving. First, look behind me and tell me if two men in dark sport jackets are lurking about."

She gazed around, surreptitiously at first, then craned her neck all around. "Not a sign of anyone. Somebody on your tail?"

"I guess I was being paranoid."

I walked her to her door and then grabbed a taxi downtown. I asked the driver to cruise Fulton Street. I scanned buildings on both sides, looking for the obvious landmark of an ostentatious entrance into a building constructed on false assumptions and the backs of over-mortgaged families. When I finally spotted it I almost leapt out of the cab without paying.

I entered grandly through those magnificent doors, with

my sights set on accomplishing the impossible. At least it seemed that way to me. This was the single most amazing thing I was ever likely to do, and there was my goal, engraved in the brass of Frederick Lowe's Office Directory: *Eric Woodruff, Financial Advisor.*

In the lobby a young Asian woman was on the phone at the reception desk. Across the shining marble foyer, two men in dark brown uniforms manned a metal-detecting gate. The sight gave me pause. I hadn't seen a security gate in an office building for three years. When I walked toward it, one guard, without speaking, pointed to the receptionist. I walked up to her desk and inquired about the office number of Eric Woodruff.

"Is he expecting you?"

I laughed. Probably I was the last person he expected, but I said, "Yes, he is."

She picked up the phone. "Your name, please"

Then I had an idea. I took out my phone and sent a two word message to *avenger4sins.* It said, *Hi Eric.* "Just tell him to check his email. Not the normal ones. The avenger one. He'll know what I mean."

She smiled up at me while she placed the call. She thought this was some guy-game between Eric and me. She was right, in a way. In a very deadly way. There was still a trace of fun in her voice when she delivered my message to Eric. Whatever she heard as a response transformed her face in an instant. She moved the handset away from her ear and looked at it as though it had malfunctioned. I stood there looking at her. She didn't want to deliver Eric's message to me, but she knew she had to do something. Finally she said, "He may be too busy to see you."

"Call him back. Tell him I have a message from Angela."

She punched his number and was still holding the phone when the elevator doors opened and we all turned as a loud voice called out, "Security! Grab that man!" The surprised guards looked back and forth between Eric and me. "Him!" Eric said, pointing frantically at me. "I recognize him! He's a thief and a fugitive!"

The guards moved for me. I think they expected me to flee. When they saw I was standing my ground, it scared them. One man reached for a weapon and the other grabbed my arm. I tried to jerk loose. With my free hand I gestured toward Eric, who stood by the elevator, unsure of his next move. The other guard spun me around and attempted to pin my other arm behind me. They were dragging me to the floor.

Just then two broad-shouldered men wearing sport coats came through those great art deco doors. One flashed his police badge at the security guards and the other clambered around the guards' desk toward the elevator, where Eric stood, dumbfounded.

No more dumbfounded than I was when one of the policemen told Eric, "If you'll just come with me, sir. We'd like to ask you a few questions."

The other turned to me and said, "And you, Mr. Michaels— you should return to Kentucky asap. They need your help down there."

The guy seemed to know what he was talking about. In the taxi to the airport I got a text from Charlene: *Victor needs to borrow Jezebel.* I texted back: *Not without me. I'm coming home.*

30

I MANAGED TO get on the eight o'clock flight to Cincinnati, non-stop, which cost a bundle, by the way, but it got me to Cincinnati by half past ten. Charlene, Victor and Jezebel were all three there to meet me, along with another woman, a stranger to me. I had no idea what that was all about, but Victor introduced her as deputy somebody, a name I instantly forgot. (It's Esta Runyon.) I really only wanted to be with Charlene, yet here I was with two surplus passengers. I almost wished Victor and the other woman would sit up front and let Charlene and me have the back seat. Not for what you're thinking, you low-minded brat. Only to hold her and to decompress.

As it was, Charlene's attempt to give me the romantic lover's welcome was tempered by Victor's kudos for a job well done, leaving me feeling short-changed on both sides, with this other woman standing off to the side, looking embarrassed.

I just realized what a carping little complainer that makes me! Of course it was satisfying. It was doubly satisfying. The returning hero, home from the hunt, lauded by his soon-to-be wife and his by-now best friend. What sort of crybaby would ask for more?

On the ride home Victor said that his contacts in the NYPD now had the *avenger4sins* password and had emailed the kidnappers that he was getting their ransom together as quickly as he could. "This will buy us some time," Victor said. He then explained the plan for the following morning. He wanted to search the bottom land along Buffalo Run, house by house, out-building by out-building. This extraneous woman riding along with us, Deputy Runyon, wasn't extraneous at all. She was key to the planned operation. She was on loan from Clark County because Victor wanted a trained law officer that Angela's kidnappers wouldn't recognize on sight, as they would local deputies. Also, Victor wanted a woman, on the theory that a woman knocking on doors of strangers was less threatening than a man, therefore more likely to cause the occupants to let down their guard, and less likely to start gunplay.

Wearing the standard olive green Mountain Utilities uniform, she would travel door to door along the stretch of houses affected by the water stoppage, apologize to everybody for the interruption of service, and explain that it came from a break or blockage in the water mains. She would indicate a leather pouch she carried (which in fact held a pressure gauge and a handgun) and ask if she could measure the current pressure in their kitchen taps. If residents protested that there was no water flow whatsoever (which they would, since the water was completely shut off) Deputy Runyon would say that even a measure of the air pressure in the pipes could help pinpoint the source of the problem.

Jezebel would accompany her.

"I admit this is risky," Victor said. "Somebody might recognize her. But if we're going to locate the Van Landingham woman without getting her killed, this dog is our only hope." He patted her on the head, and she squinted her willingness to be part of whatever it was we were talking about.

Charlene said, "People aren't going to let some strange dog come prancing into their house."

"I've thought of that. What if we say she's been trained to sniff out gas leaks? We say that's a worry because the underground gas pipeline runs through the same culvert as the water pipes. Make it sound like any cross leakage would be an unlikely event, but we want to put public safety first." He looked at Esta Runyon. "Think you can sell that one?"

"I don't see why not," she said. "With all the explosions in the news lately, people are sensitive to this kind of threat."

"Good point. This will explain why we've sent a dog sniffing all over their property."

Runyon looked around sharply at Victor. "Hey, how likely is it there's a woman accomplice?"

"Highly unlikely."

"Because if a woman answers the door—which is what usually happens on a weekday—there's probably no use spending much time on that house."

"Yeah. Don't rule anything out. Keep your mind as open as your eyes, but, as you say, if there's a woman present, it's probably not the right place. In fact, if she seems reliable, you might engage her in friendly conversation. Ask her about the neighborhood. Ask if any local yay-hoos are causing trouble. You never know where good clues might come from."

We would start at nine o'clock, about as early as any cold caller is likely to get any kind of welcome. Runyon would drive a Mountain Utilities van, with Victor, a couple of deputies, and me hidden away in the back. Victor, in his heart of hearts, didn't want me along, but he didn't get Jez without getting me in the bargain, so he agreed, on condition that, in the event of gunfire, I stayed put in the van.

I agree to his condition. Of course I had no intention of following through, or of mentioning Charlene's little Ruger .38 that I would conceal under my shirttail.

At home, Charlene gave me the royal treatment. She told me to go stretch out on the back porch while she made for me a panini of corned beef and swiss on rye. She brought it on a tray with homemade bread-and-butter pickles, a nice handful of sweet potato chips, and a tall glass of sweet ice tea. Truly, I was becoming a southerner. I don't usually eat like this in front of her, because she's still limiting her own carbs—this is the main reason I started having breakfast at Fifi's—but in this instance I probably deserved a splurge.

The three of us (four, counting you—lest I forget) sat in near total silence for a long time on the back porch glider. Charlene held my head in her lap, while Jez tried to maneuver herself into some sort of comfortable position at my feet. It was unusual for Jez to put herself to that much trouble to maintain physical contact. Normally if both Charlene and I are together, Jezebel is content to lie on the floor somewhere nearby. It seems the atmosphere last night, though, was so rent between great relief on my return, and the great weight of responsibility waiting for us in the morning, that even Jez felt the old puppy urge to cuddle.

Charlene stroked my hair. She said, "I have my ultrasound appointment next week. If it's conclusive about gender, do you still want to do that pink or blue cupcake thing?"

"Yes, absolutely."

"Your idea is to keep it a secret even from ourselves, right? Then unveil it for us and the whole crowd at Big's?"

"It'll be fun. What do you think?"

"I'm in."

"We'll have the ultrasound guy write down male or female on note paper and seal it in an envelope. I'll give that to Rusty, swear him to secrecy, and let him bake pink or blue colored cupcakes, completely covered with frosting. On signal we, and all the guests, take a bite, and then we'll know whether we've got ourselves a boy or a girl. What kind of frosting do you want?"

"Chocolate, I guess. What do you think?"

"Sure."

"No, wait—salted caramel. Now *that's* icing."

"Fine with me. How many should Rusty prepare?"

"As many as we have guests."

"And how many will that be?"

"Lots."

"Don't you dare get used to this dessert thing. It's a one off."

"I reckon if a girl can't have a cupcake on her wedding day, what's the point of getting married?"

"To have lots and lots of sex without going to hell for it. I thought that was the point."

"No. It's mostly about cupcakes."

What I love so much about this conversation, which I didn't think of at the time, is how casual it was, how normal and inconsequential. After the drama I'd been through only hours earlier, and with Angela still held captive out there, somewhere, probably only miles away, possibly being raped or tortured, and with a potentially deadly search for her looming the next day, Charlene and I could discuss cupcakes on a quiet Dogwood Street back porch.

She thought about it a while, then asked, "Do you think we should have the wedding at the same time? Just sorta let the whole gender-cupcake thing be part of the reception?"

"At Big's?"

"Of course at Big's. I'd never even consider anywhere else."

"Sure. We could ask Rusty to do a wedding cake, also blue or pink."

"Along with the cupcakes?"

"Sure. When?"

"Oh, I don't know. Soon after my ultrasound, I guess. In a week or two?"

"Charlene, I want to ask you a question, okay?"

"Ask away, big guy." She gave the top of my head a hard squeeze.

"The night I proposed to you, up on the hill, under the Perseid shower . . . "

"You romantic young fool . . . "

"You said something I still don't get. You said if we were married we wouldn't have to testify against each other. Remember?"

"I sure do."

"But why? Did you really think I'd killed Angela? Or did you want me to think you had?"

"No, idiot! I didn't want to have to testify about all that restaurant loot you transported down here in the trunk of your car."

"You *knew?*"

"Of course I knew."

"But how?"

"Look, even sweet little hillbilly women know that's not the normal way to transport expensive restaurant gear."

"You knew I'd stolen it?"

"Let's say I assumed it was hot."

"Then how did you know to trust me enough to hire me?"

"You forget I'm a mind reader."

"But not a real one."

"I read you like some cheap-assed paperback, didn't I?"

I couldn't argue with that. "Then back to my original question: when do you want to have the wedding? Or can we really decide on the date, with this Angela drama still hanging over our heads?"

She didn't answer, which served as an answer, and that's where we left it, with the Angela drama still hanging over our heads. I further ruined the romance by mentioning that in the morning I would need to borrow a handgun.

31

AT PRECISELY NINE o'clock in the morning we piled into the back of the van. A local deputy drove, Esta Runyon sat in the passenger seat, and Jezebel stayed in back with Victor, another deputy and me. They were all wearing Mountain Utility uniforms. I only wore summer clothes, sports shoes, loose shorts and a billowy Hawaiian shirt to hide the pistol I'd tucked into a suede waistband holster.

We sat around a pile of tools. In a questionable situation the officers could exit the van and fake a normal water main assignment by removing wrenches and so on, while at the same time putting themselves in readiness for a capture.

One problem was that we couldn't see outside. The Mountain Utilities van had no windows at all, much less one-way windows. It was a problem that Victor acknowledged, admitting he couldn't solve it. We had to trust our driver, and our ears, to alert us at the first sign of trouble.

Victor had brought along Angela's pajamas in a sealed plastic bag. Before our first stop, I opened it for Jezebel and let her sniff. She placed her nose to the opening and immediately jerked her head back. She looked at me with the same pained eyes I'd seen back at the lake cabin.

My expression was equally pained, though for a different reason. I knew she was walking into danger. My stomach burned at the thought of asking her to enter what could become an instant firefight, but I understood Victor's logic. Without her nose, and her intimate knowledge of Angela's distinct aroma, this search would never end. If it became an open manhunt, the kidnappers would kill Angela. First thing. Simple as that.

I looked into Jezebel's sad brown eyes and stroked the little knot at the top of her head. Of course you know exactly what horror that brought to mind—the day I'd rubbed her head as I raced her to the vet's, with a rattlesnake head dangling from her neck. The day I thought she was dying. I recalled the glorious relief that lifted my heart that day. It seemed years ago. In fact it was only last Sunday. Part of the relief involved an unspoken promise never to put her in such a position again, yet here I was, sending her into a den of very evil men. Drug dealers, rapists, kidnappers, murderers. But there I sat, trying to smile bravely. "Don't you worry, sweet puppy. It's going to be fine. Go find Angela, girl. Find Angie." And every time Deputy Runyon opened those rear doors, Jezebel bounced out, prancing, nose to the ground, tail high and flicking, as though in hot pursuit of nothing more lethal than a rabbit in the vegetable garden.

That day I learned that police work is like what people say about being a soldier in a war zone. It's incredibly boring—until it isn't.

It stopped being boring just before lunch.

We stopped at an old farmhouse set back from the road far enough that our driver, who called out events as they happened, said he couldn't be sure who opened the door, a man or a woman. "Damn!" He said. "I wish I could use binoculars." Victor had ruled them out as an obvious give-away. Water line repairmen don't watch customers through binoculars.

"Where's Runyon?" Victor asked.

"Officer inside. Dog still on the porch. Some discussion about her, seems like." His eyes seemed to focus harder on the porch scene. "Ho! She's turning away."

"She *who*?" Victor expected more precise play-by-play.

"Jezebel. She's coming back towards here."

"Where's Runyon?"

"Inside. They closed the door on her. Uh-oh, sir! Dog's tracking out towards an old shed or smokehouse."

I asked him, "How's she moving?"

"Straight line, in a hurry."

"Let's get out," Victor said to his men. "Act nonchalant. Pull out some tools."

Victor himself was too well-known and visible, so the white deputy left the van first. He dragged out a tool chest while looking over his shoulder for Jez. "She's heading straight for that shed."

"Where's her nose?" I asked.

"Directly on the ground."

I couldn't see a thing. I was starting to get frantic. Victor tried peering out through the gap between the door and the side of the van.

"What the hell is happening?" I asked.

"She's circling that shed."

"How?"

"Real excited."

I couldn't take it anymore. I stepped out of the van. I did try to conceal myself behind an open rear door, but I sure as hell wasn't going back into the van.

Victor didn't even see me. The driver stepped out too, and we all watched spellbound as Jezebel sniffed at the side of the shed. She started digging wildly, just as she had done for bones at the graveyard. I thought to myself, *If you've trapped a skunk in there . . .* but before I could specify retribution she whirled, looked straight back at me, and barked.

"This is it," I told Victor.

"Move easy, men," he said. "Don't rush the building."

But then something happened to overrule his instructions. Jezebel dipped her head to the ground and wriggled her way beneath the wall of that shed. In a flash, she was out of sight. "She's inside!" I said. I think everybody said it. We all ran toward the shed.

Jezebel raised a frenzied cry. Fierce barking bled into vicious growls. We could hear a man's voice inside scream, "What the FUCK!" There were more shouts from inside the shed, then, confusingly, gunfire from the farmhouse. Victor dispatched one deputy to the aid of Deputy Runyon, while the rest of us moved on the shed. I took out my little Ruger. I only had five shots to work with.

Victor ran as hard as he could and laid a shoulder into the wooden shed door. Its rusty hinges burst loose, all nails and splinters. In the darkened space the first thing I saw was Angela, tied, gagged and blindfolded in a corner. A man was moving a gun toward her head. I said, "Hey fuckhead!" He spun toward me and I shot him twice. After that, bullets were flying everywhere. I don't know who shot who. Jezebel had her jaws clamped on the back of one man's arm, on the tricep. Her hind legs were nearly off the ground. He was trying to shake her loose, and when he turned toward us, I saw one side of his head fly away. Blood rushed down what was left of his face.

Now everything was so quiet in the shed that I could hear Angela sobbing through her gag. Victor called one officer by name and said, "The house." They ran out, leaving one officer with me, Jezebel, and two bleeding bodies that either were, or soon would be, corpses. I ran toward Angela, fell to my knees, peeled back the blindfold and rolled the gag down her chin. She was trying to speak, but what came out sounded more like primitive howls of agony. I drew her head to my chest and held it there. "You're okay now, Angie," I said. "It's all over. It's all over now."

She cried in wracking sobs that sent shock waves through my body. I was shuddering along with her. I kissed the top her head and kept saying, "You're safe now. You're safe."

Jezebel, the calmest presence in the room, nuzzled her ear, and licked her face. Apparently even superheroes do lick, sometimes, in an emergency.

Now I realized that the gunfire in the house had stopped. Deputy Runyon came into the shed. "One perp killed, one in custody." She addressed her fellow officer, "The sheriff wants you inside. I'll attend to the victim." She knelt in front of us. "Don't worry, ma'am. You're safe now, and an ambulance is on its way."

Angela put her hand to the side of my face, pulled me in tight. I felt her tears on my cheek. Jezebel, seeing evidence of affection she wanted in on, put her nose to Angie's ear, and whined. Angie pulled her close and rubbed her tears into Jezebel's absorbing ruff.

Jezebel lifted her muzzle and sang a quiet tune.

32

EVEN MY WEDDING morning found me sitting at my usual work table at Big's, preparing menus for the following two weeks. That's because Charlene and I will be honeymooning—in Mexico. Yes, I knew you'd get a laugh out of that. Now that I finally have no need to flee across the border, I'm on my way there.

The place was a beehive. The whole staff and lots of additional workers came in early to prepare for Big's biggest day ever. Fumiko brought me an espresso. I said, *Arigato*. She smiled, and said, *No*. She backed away a step or two, but no further. I looked up at her and noticed she was beaming. I thanked her again and returned my attention to my menus.

There was the great hubbub of enterprise throughout the restaurant. Workers were moving tables and carrying trays and placing flowers and hanging decorations; the Big Boned Boys were setting up, clanging some guitar-tuning notes; I heard angry shouts from the kitchen, but I'd let Rusty deal with that. I was in no mood to put myself out.

Workmen hauled in two big signs and placed them face-first against the wall behind the stage. Although the words were hidden from view, I knew what they said. One said Amanda Mae Michaels and the other Emerson Lee Michaels. Charlene and I decided on these names late last night, after considering hundreds. Even once we'd officially decided, it was with the proviso that we could change our minds this morning, but I suppose the sign painter has settled it. That means that later this evening I can address you by name. The other name we'll . . . I don't know . . . save for later?

In the quiet center of this whirlpool, Fumiko still stood there, waiting for something, apparently from me. I looked back up at her. "What's up?"

"I hope it's good," she said.

I've noticed that she often begins with what I think of as a follow up comment. "I'm sure it is. What are we talking about?"

"I wrote a *haiku* to honor your baby girl or boy. It's name *Sakura*, because your baby is due during time of *sakura*. Do you know what means *sakura*?"

Since my knowledge of Japanese culture is minimal, and most of that is culinary, I was pleased she'd picked something I knew. "Cherry blossoms, right?"

"Do you know why *sakura* is a symbol in my country?"

"Because they're so lovely?"

"Yes!" she said, encouragingly, a born schoolmarm. "But not all."

"Not all are lovely?"

"Yes. Yes, all are lovely, but there's more. Do you know?"

"Maybe you should just tell me."

"Their beauty is perfect, then gone. Beautiful and make me cry. Same as us. Can you read it?"

She handed me a paper and I read:

> *Change in springtime will*
> *Jezebel ear look left right,*
> *Cherry Blossom days*

"That's lovely, Fumi-chan," I said, although in all honesty I didn't quite get it. I read it over to myself, and then asked, "But *Change in springtime will* . . . ?"

She's cute when she's puzzled, but still, I think she'd rather be clear than cute, so I helped with a hint. "*Change in springtime will . . .* what?" I turned the paper toward her. She read it again, looked up at me sheepishly, rapped her knuckles into her forehead, borrowed my pen, and added a period after "will."

She returned the paper to me. "Better?" she asked.

"It's perfect," I said.

Do you remember when I told you how your mom, when given a compliment, looks away and touches something? Not Fumiko. She locks onto your face and glows, I mean bright red. She held that look a little while. I had the feeling that the fire on her face had jumped the gap between us. My own face felt warm. She released abruptly, with a formal bow, lower and more pensive than her normal everyday bow, and then she skipped away, clutching the notepad to her heart as though it had become spirit, a paper prayer flying from a temple wall.

Those shouts from the kitchen escalated, and now the voice leading the charge belonged to Charlene. It seemed I would need to involve myself after all. I walked over and leaned my head through the serving window, and what I heard is what might be called in more polite circles a wedding crasher. I heard the dulcet tones of none other than Brother Lonnie. Now, I've told you—and in the main I stick by this— your mom is far more even-tempered than I am. A line graph of her moods would show a seascape of calm waves, whereas mine would be at least a squall. However, when the subject— or far worse yet, the person—is Brother Lonnie, our mood lines are reversed. I knew I needed to get into that kitchen double-quick, or else Twisting Creek would soon have another murder to gossip about.

When I pushed through the doors, I saw Charlene right up in Lonnie's face. I heard her shout, "You ever set foot in Big's again and I'll unload two barrels of buckshot up your fat ass. I swear I will. I hope you think I'm bluffing, and I hope to *god* you try to test me on it. I'll bury you in the wettest corner of that graveyard and threaten to sue anybody who so much as pulls a weed off your grave."

I didn't say a word to her. I simply took Lonnie by the shoulders, turned him around, and marched him out the back door. He offered little resistance, but once on the street he turned toward me to plead his case.

"All I want is to go to my little sister's wedding! Is that too much to ask?"

"Yes, it is. Way too much. Light years too much."

"But why?"

I remembered how he'd told me he was stuck in his own childhood. Right now he was whining in character.

"Don't even ask. If you don't know, it's not for me to tell you."

"You didn't mention those stupid beans to her, did you?"

"Nope. She hates you this much without even suspecting you murdered her parents. That would seriously up the ante."

"But I never done it!"

Does Charlene suspect him? If so, reconciliation will be impossible. I decided it was better to proceed as though she didn't.

"Lonnie, at this stage it hardly matters whether you did or not. Charlene hates you for what you've done with your life. There's enough guilt there already that you need a complete character makeover."

"Then help me, Jake! I'm lost in this . . . " He tried to find a word to describe where he was lost. I waited for him. I thought he might say web of lies or maze of deception. Or something Biblical, though I had no clue what it might be. Eventually his shoulders slumped and he repeated, simply, "I'm lost."

"Okay," I said, "here's a start. First of all, don't turn up here again today. After the wedding we'll be gone for two weeks. During that time I'll work on her. I'll have more sway as her husband. Not to say her lord and master."

Lonnie gave me his smirk. One thing's for sure, he does have a sense of humor. I don't know if that helps or hurts his chances of rehabilitation, but I have to think it's a start.

I smiled and continued. "During that time, you need to do something to show good faith. First thing—lose some weight. Give up carbs for two weeks and you'll lose ten pounds. If you're successful, we'll talk. Maybe by then I can get you past the rope line."

"You want me to become a member?"

"Lonnie, listen to me: this advice is strictly for your benefit. For my part, I don't much give a shit what happens to you."

He did something rare—he looked away. It was as though a painful facial palsy had taken away his fine motor control. Maybe I'm going soft on my brother-in-law—I don't know— but to me the pain looked real.

He finally said, "Then if you don't give a shit, nobody don't."

"How about the people at your church? They care about you, right?"

He shrugged and smiled sadly, like a man who'd surrounded himself with fools, only to learn that a person can be defined by the company he keeps. He still didn't look at me, but said, "I wish you and Charlene all the happiness in the world. I truly do."

He started walking to his truck. I called, "Lonnie." He turned. "It's *nobody does.*"

"Huh?"

"If you don't give a shit, *nobody does.* Not *nobody don't.*"

He seemed to consider the implications of this. Some vitality returned to his face. "But that don't make no sense. They really *don't* give a shit. Not they *does* give a shit."

"That's just the way it works. I can't change it. *But that doesn't make any sense.*"

"No, it shore don't."

"No, I mean the correct sentence is, *That doesn't make any sense.*"

"You're not messing with me?"

"I'm afraid not. So that makes two things. Lose ten pounds, and learn some fucking grammar."

"Whew!" he said, and turned again towards his truck.

When he opened his door I said, "If you do . . . "

Once again he looked me in the eye. "Okay. If I do, then what?"

I said, "How about this for your third assignment. I think I can put together a delicious two hundred calorie version of *serpent à sonnettes au curry*. Can you guess what that means?"

"Curried serpent?"

"You got it. Curried rattlesnake. And some grilled vegetables with olive oil and zatar. Watermelon sherbet. All for under five hundred calories."

"Seriously?"

"The Friday after we get back from Mexico. Friday is always karaoke night, too. You have a nice voice. Do you sing?"

He ignored that question completely. "How're you fixed for rattler meat?"

"Could use some more. In fact, I don't have any."

"And you can get me right with Charlene?"

"No. You can change and get yourself right with her. Maybe. I can't promise anything."

He lifted his right hand to wave goodbye, and called out, "I'll see if I can't come up with a few rattler steaks." He got into his cab, but turned toward me and rolled down a window. "I had a little eastern massasauga that coulda made some mighty tender eatin', only some damn dog got to it first."

The rest of the day—what can I say? I married your mother that day. What better day could any man ever have? You'll be subjected to hours of professional video of it, and even more handhelds. It'll seem like everybody you meet from birth through high school has an hour-long presentation of our wedding day on their mobiles. And the social media postings. They'll breed like rabbits. I really do pity you. Seriously.

It was the only day in Big's history when people could burst the six-hundred-calorie limit. And burst it we did. To smithereens. We announced in advance that we were all going to eat like wild hogs, and we got an event-permit to serve alcohol. I have no idea how much all the festivities cost. As you may have noticed, I pay no attention whatsoever to financial affairs. You will have also realized that I played it the same way at *Le Plat Nourrissant*. I think we've spotted a pattern, don't you?

Angela was there! I danced with her! Doesn't that just make you want to stand up and cheer? Over these two weeks, she's been living as a house guest of Vicki Yapita-Crosby. Vicki says any sane person would get PTSD from an ordeal like Angie's, so she's helping her through the stages of overcoming that. Of course I visit her every day. With Charlene. And yes, Angela has patted you on the head, via Charlene's amniotic fluid. She's rebounding at an amazing rate. Partly that's due to counseling, no doubt. Partly because she's stubborn as a mule.

And get this: the entire town has thrown its support her way. The rescue story is still live. It's been detailed in the Guardian, from the first report that she might be missing, right through to the death or capture of all parties involved in Victor's six crimes. No, wait—five. I'm off the hook—obviously. Only yesterday Angela told me that at her rescue, at the moment the bag came off her head, and she could finally see for the first time in days, and what she saw with that first glimpse was my face—from that instant we became family, unlike we'd ever been before. She didn't cry or anything when she said it. She was sort of perky about it. There was a trace of consternation in her eyes that I would react like *You cleaned me out of ten years of my life, and now we're bloody family? Well,*

I think not, missy . . . But of course I didn't even consider that. Not for one second. (Maybe for five minutes, but definitely not for one second.)

What I really did when she walked in, confident, sophisticated, dressed for a wedding, was give her a big hug. I said to her, "That photo of me playing tennis . . . you kept that by your bed because . . . "

"Great legs," she said.

"That's what I thought." I laughed. You probably laughed, too. If you did, you get a hint of why I loved her for all those years, all those years ago.

So as I say, we danced. The first one was a boisterous one. I remember it was our Big Boned Boys doing an early Rolling Stones tune deemed suitable for a wedding: *Satisfaction*. The next one, a slow dance, was sung by that local teenage girl I told you about, the one who plays a guitar and writes her own songs. I invited her myself, because for some reason I'm touched by those high school ballads of hers. I don't know why. I didn't enjoy high school all that much. Or maybe that's the explanation. She sang a sad one about a boyfriend and girlfriend opening their SAT results, and staring at the gap between their numbers. In her song, those numbers act as a signpost with arrows pointing down two diverging paths. The idea was that I'll never forget you, but you realize this means we have to be friends now. You might well think I requested this song, but I didn't. Surely the singer—Lisa Venable is her name—chose it purposely.

THEN! The Big Boned Boys joined Lisa on stage and she starting wailing *Rescue Me!* I couldn't believe it. They had the whole place jumping. Angie and I hurried into rhythm, arms waving and legs flailing. Angela laughed like a child on a playground. As well she should. I later learned that the song was her suggestion.

As I say, community support has helped her heal. People

have sent her lots of cards and flowers. She hasn't been reclusive. She stayed tucked away for a couple of days, but people know where she is and sometimes they stop by to ask about her. Often she sits on Vicki's front porch and greets people out there. That's usually where Charlene and I meet with her. One day I asked her why, when she wrote that HELP FIND JEZEBEL message, she didn't say HELP FIND JAKE MICHAELS.

She said, "I knew you had a new name, but I was so tense I couldn't think what it was. Plus, I didn't know how many people knew you, but I knew everyone would know Jezebel."

The story of my New York burglary hasn't come out yet. I suppose it will, eventually, when Eric Woodruff goes on trial, but that won't bother me. By now everybody knows that even Charlene considers Angie a friend, and the past is past.

Of course Jezebel visits Angie every time we do. She trots over to her chair and lays her head on Angela's lap. It's the same gesture of empathy she shows crying children, but with Angie she uses it even without the tears. I suppose she thinks they're buried deep in Angie's heart, so she combats them as though they'd already broken free. For her part, Angie puts her cheek directly against Jezebel's face, and makes a quiet humming sound.

Who else attended the wedding? Just about everybody you've read about in these memoirs.

Yolanda was there, mixing business with pleasure—because you can believe we will dominate the front page of tomorrow's Guardian. What Charlene noticed about her that maybe other people missed—I know I did—was that our Asian Mafia seemed to act as a model for her, because she was the first non-member woman to go straight up and ask a fat man to dance.

The trouble with describing an event like this is the same as hosting it: everybody gets a handshake or a hug and a few minutes of conversation, but it's not a day for depth. Instead, each person, individually so important to my own personal narrative, gets a mention, and it's on to someone else.

The value in a day like this, though, is in the power of a crowd of happy people pooling their happiness for huge returns. It's in watching Leo and Fumiko set the pace at jitterbug, and watching the whole Asian Mafia, dressed like sophisticates, dancing like kids. It's sneaking a look at Victor just in time to see Shelley and him share a private laugh, possibly about the upcoming election, which by now is a foregone conclusion.

More than anything, of course, it's about Charlene. Did I detect a hint of the nervous bride? I think maybe for a little while earlier in the day, but then she threatened to shoot Lonnie's ass off for him, and that perked her right up. She didn't even thank me for getting rid of him. She only said, "You shouldn't have come in that kitchen. You weren't supposed to see me before the ceremony."

I told her I'd take a day and make it up to her, when she was eighty-five or ninety, and not look at her the whole day. But on this day there was no hiding from me.

Toward the end of the evening came the moment you've been waiting for. Are you Amanda or Emerson? Two men made their way up front to hoist the two panels bearing the names Amanda Mae and Emerson Lee. Charlene took the stage, and when everybody had noticed her and got quiet, she explained what would happen next. She motioned to the kitchen doors, and our whole staff of servers marched out carrying trays of cupcakes.

Charlene addressed the guests. "Each one of you is about to get a cupcake, but nobody can take a bite or peel down the paper until we all count down from ten. It's just like midnight on New Year's Eve, only this time when you get down to number one, you bite through the icing and check the color of the cake inside. If it's pink, you shout out *Amanda Mae*. If it's blue, you shout *Emerson Lee*. Okay? Those are the two names Jake and I have chosen for this kid," she patted her belly. "We don't know its sex yet either. This is how we'll find out."

While the cupcakes were being distributed, Fumiko came out of the kitchen carrying a big sheet cake covered in the same caramel frosting as the cupcakes, and with something written on it in vanilla frosting. She bowed formally, said something to both of us in Japanese, and handed over the cake. She bowed once more, and skipped away. We read:

> *Change in springtime will.*
> *Jezebel ear look left right,*
> *Cherry Blossom days*

A ten-second countdown timer was projected on a screen behind the stage. Charlene started the countdown, calling out *ten, nine, eight*. About there, other guests started to join in. By *five, four, three* the hall echoed with one voice, and at *two, one* it was deafening. There followed an odd two or three seconds of relative silence that I hadn't expected—I suppose people were busy peeling away cupcake wrappers—and then we heard enthusiastic shouts of *Amanda Mae! Amanda Mae!*

And that's how we learned we were going to have a daughter. Amanda Mae Michaels. Nice to meet you at long last.

Keeping to the ritual, I fed Charlene a big bite of cake. For the sake of a comic photo-op, I smashed it into her face a little bit. Well, a lot, really.

"Mmmmmm!" she said. "That is soooo yummy!"

"Do *not* get used to this," I warned her. "This is a one-off pig-out." I said it into the microphone, and the crowd laughed.

"Hmmm, I'm not so sure about that. Now that I've got this ring on my finger," she raised her left hand for all to see, "I can get as fat as I want to. And anyway," she rubbed her hand across her still-flat belly, leaned into the microphone, and said,

"I think maybe I could stand to gain a few pounds. What do y'all think?" She started doing a little belly dance. The whole room whooped and cheered.

Jezebel had been keeping a keen eye on that cake, so I fed her a big bite of it, smearing it on her face just as I had done Charlene. There's a funny photograph of that, too. You'll see it a thousand times.

I led Charlene onto the dance floor. The Big Boned Boys struck up with "Whole Lotta Love" (my idea) and she laughed so hard she could barely move her feet. Couples were dancing all around us, but we hardly moved. You were in my arms, you and your mom. Jezebel saw evidence of affection and she wanted in on it. She stood for a graceful twirl, one of her best ever, and Charlene invited her into the circle. Now that I had all three of you in my arms, I held on as tight as tight could be, held on for dear life. Cherry blossom days.

www.ingramcontent.com/pod-product-compliance
Lightning Source LLC
Chambersburg PA
CBHW070815180626
46818CB00001B/277